The
CURIOUS
SECRETS
OF
YESTERDAY

OTHER TITLES BY NAMRATA PATEL

Scent of a Garden

The Candid Life of Meena Dave

The CURIOUS SECRETS OF YESTERDAY

NAMRATA PATEL

LAKE UNION
PUBLISHING

Text copyright © 2024 by Namrata Patel
All rights reserved.

Published by Lake Union Publishing, Seattle

www.apub.com

Amazon, the Amazon logo, and Lake Union Publishing are trademarks of Amazon.com, Inc., or its affiliates.

ISBN-13: 9781662515071 (paperback)
ISBN-13: 9781662515064 (digital)

Cover design and illustration by Kimberly Glyder
Cover image: © Anna Sovina / Shutterstock

Printed in the United States of America

For my ancestors

AUTHOR'S NOTE

How do hyphenated identities define the in-between? For my character Tulsi Gupta, her Indian-American hyphen has been defined for her. As a spice healer, she has a duty to preserve the ancient traditions of Ayurveda. Tulsi's family trade traces back thousands of years, passing down from mother to daughter, each carrying on their responsibilities—but Tulsi has spent her life in Massachusetts.

The hyphenated identity is something I've wrestled with myself. How do I define my hyphen, the small dash between Indian and American? For me the line between one culture and the other blurs. Early on, I tried to balance my life in an Indian family and my life as an American teenager. Oftentimes, the two were hard to merge. I wore a lot of denim and Cure T-shirts, and I was ashamed to bring Gujarati food for lunch, afraid the other kids would say it smelled funny. In my twenties, I fully embraced being Gujarati by competing in garba dance competitions through FOGANA, a national Gujarati association. I learned how to make undhiyu and roll a perfectly round rotli. When I moved to Boston, I became a lobster-eating Red Sox fan. From Spokane to London, I assimilated as I thought necessary. A pendulum that swung depending on where I was—not who I was.

This back-and-forth led me to a question that will take a lifetime to answer. What I do know is that I get to define that hyphen. There will never be an equal balance, but I have a better idea of the person I see in the mirror. And I'm glad that it's not solely about geography.

In *The Curious Secrets of Yesterday*, Tulsi takes her own journey as she learns how to untangle the knotted roots of her ancestry and takes the first steps toward something all her own. It's not easy, but for her, it's necessary to understand who she is and who she will become . . . for now.

CHAPTER ONE

It was the tattoo of a Buddha wrapped in barbed wire that caused Tulsi Gupta to have an identity crisis right in the middle of the pedestrian-only cobblestoned street in the sea-adjacent town of Salem, Massachusetts. The black ink on the brown-skinned forearm of a stranger caught her notice, and in less than a minute her whole existence distilled down to one fact: she didn't live a life with pieces that could be permanently etched on her body. No great adventures, no fantastical experiences, no traditional milestones. No outsize success or devastating loss. Her life was as unadorned as her ordinary brown skin. Her time wasted in a mundane routine of living the same day, week, month. For the whole of her thirty years.

The brush of a passerby prodded Tulsi to move. Her feet knew the way, the route memorized from decades of taking the same path. There was privilege in having an average life, she rationalized. Not needing to process extreme highs or lows meant security. She stopped and leaned one hand against the brick wall of a familiar shop to steady herself. She'd done what was required of her, prescribed. Tulsi had ceded to the responsibility of a path passed down to her by three-thousand-year-old ancestors.

Tulsi turned the corner and went down a narrow lane dotted with dumpsters. The alley was reserved for the various shops' staff, so they could enter through the back of their storefronts. The muggy early-morning air heightened the odor of discarded garbage as she turned the key in the big metal door. As soon as she entered, the smell changed. Familiar aromas of coriander, asafetida, and cloves punched her, as if to say, "This is your world." She scrunched her nose against its pungency. She'd lived with it for so long that most days she never noticed. Now it overwhelmed her, heavy with the knowledge that today would be the same as yesterday.

The back office of Rasa, her family's spice shop, held odors from its opening day, on Tulsi's second birthday. Wedged between a café that had gone out of business and a trinket store for tourists, this was a place her grandmother built. Not to sell their wares, but to serve as spice healers for their small community.

The shop was her second home, the first being the house she shared with her mother and grandmother. With these homes ten minutes apart, her geographical footprint was contained within a few miles. From Cambridge Street to Hawthorne Boulevard, from Church Street to Peabody Street. Her whole life was here in the smallness of this large town less than an hour's drive from Boston, in the northeast corner of America. It was rare to venture out, her friends too spread apart to meet up for dinner. Not that she had time or healthy disposable income for such luxuries. Saving for dreams she'd never attempted to make real was the only way for her to believe in someday.

Tulsi scanned the scuffed beige walls of the back office, the weathered furniture, and the tiled floor with thin cracks. She was as frayed as the building. The years had taken a toll, the ups and downs of retail, the cycles, and seasons. Somehow she'd given in to the permanence of existing solely in this space even as the earth moved, shifted, and evolved.

It was barely eight in the morning, but like a programmed robot, she performed her routine to get Rasa ready for the day. The lights on, the register ready for their first customer, the water feature whirring to life for a calm client experience. Rasa was designed as an invitation to discover, learn, and share what ailed people and offer a recipe for relief. Her mother and grandmother were well regarded in their community for their abilities. Locals and tourists appreciated their skills derived from ancient Vedic history—there was lore around them. And it constricted Tulsi's life. She was the future, the one who would carry on, produce the next generation. It was all to ensure that the Guptas would not be the last of their line of spice healers.

"Good morning."

Tulsi glanced up as her mother came through the back door. "Hi." The mere presence of Devi centered her. Her mother was peace and serenity. Of the three Gupta women, Devi served as the primary spice healer, while her grandmother, Aruna, had shifted to adviser. Tulsi had yet to take that final step to replace Devi. One more test. The one she'd put off for the last five years.

Devi placed a travel mug on the metal desk behind which Tulsi sat in a dilapidated swivel chair, sorting through invoices. Tulsi eyed the blue mug. It would have cha, with ginger and black pepper, and one teaspoon of sugar. Made specifically for Tulsi's *dosha*, or composition of energies. She didn't have to sip it to know the taste. As with everything else in her life, the routine was imprinted. Six days per week. On Mondays they rested.

"I'll go check the health of kokum," Devi said. "I picked out a few weak flowers yesterday, and I'm worried it's the whole batch. Ma has a feeling that it's going to be a big day."

"Ba and her sixth sense."

"I know you don't believe in it, but she's tuned to the energy of her chakras. You have to acknowledge that she is often right in her interpretations." Devi pulled her long, thick black hair up in a knot at the nape of her neck.

The gray was more obvious now, and Tulsi noticed the faint lines on her mother's forehead. Devi was strikingly beautiful, and not because Tulsi was biased by love. It was an objective truth, and one of the many things that Tulsi hadn't genetically inherited. They had a resemblance in that people could see their relationship, but where Devi was soft, Tulsi was angular. Her mom had curves and natural grace, while Tulsi could stand behind a light pole and no one would notice her. It was Aruna ba who had passed down Tulsi's bony fingers, raspy voice, and frizzy hair.

Tulsi, to establish some semblance of control, wore hers in a pixie cut. It was a small way to stand apart from Aruna and Devi.

"Betty is coming in this morning," Devi said. "She's doing well after three rounds of internal purification, and I finished her recovery blend last night. It's in the bin below the workstation in case I'm not here or we're busy."

Tulsi nodded. "Do you have any more client orders to work on today? I can handle the front." Anything to avoid the never-ending and dreaded paperwork.

Devi shook her head. "I'm hopeful. I agree with Ba—it will be a good day."

"Always the optimist," Tulsi said.

"Just like you." Devi gave a small wave and went into the shop.

Tulsi smiled to appease her mom, but she wasn't feeling very positive.

She recalled the Buddha-in-barbed-wire tattoo, wondered what made that person choose that specific visual. The incongruity of it stayed with her. She imagined he was likely an interesting person with an eventful life. Tulsi glanced at her bare arms, then grabbed a black pen from the drawer. She placed the tip of it on the inside wrist of her left hand. Her mind was blank. There was nothing. At least not unique or specific to her.

She dropped the pen on the desk and stood. It was time to open. If she was lucky, an interesting stranger would come in and tell her all about themselves. That was the only thing that diverted her these days. If someone looked to be a chatty type, Tulsi would pepper them with questions. Anything to live through someone else's life.

In the front of the shop, Tulsi unlocked the door and flipped the sign to OPEN, then waited and watched the street. A few people passed, but it wasn't very crowded. Across the cobblestoned path, the chalk-board was out at Missy's Miscellaneous. Today's riddle was "What is not alive but grows, does not breathe but needs air?"

Fire. Tulsi knew the answer because the riddles were always reused from a book Missy sold in her shop. "There seem to be more people out today. Hope they make their way in here."

"Is that why you're in a mood? It's not good to worry. Stress is dangerous." Devi came out from behind the counter. "We're fine. You know we've had slow periods before, and we always get through them. Besides, we do not do this for money. This is our work, in service of all those that need us."

"Bare necessities and humble lives," Tulsi said, repeating their philosophy on materialism.

"We're comfortable," Devi added. "We don't need more."

You don't. Tulsi regretted her inner voice. She did want more. Not shoes or handbags. But . . . that was the problem. She didn't know. It was the most irritating kind of discontent, one without aim or goal. She'd lived to passively oppose what she'd been given. Most people had interests, ambitions, motivations. Tulsi pursued nothing, merely went in whatever direction she was pointed toward. She had interests. What she lacked was passion. That desire she saw in others around their careers and pursuits. Instead, Tulsi was rooted to the spot where she'd been born. Growing but not living.

"Tulsi, why are you blocking the entrance?" Mrs. Bishop barged in and went around her.

There was no bell that twinkled to indicate her passing through. Noise was reserved for the outside.

"Sorry." Tulsi moved aside.

Mrs. Bishop gave her a look. "What's wrong?"

Tulsi clearly needed to fix her face today.

Mrs. Bishop looked her over. "Usually you have a little quip."

"She didn't sleep well," Devi said.

"This humidity, I swear. I can't even sleep with my wife. She's like a furnace that gets hotter as the night goes on. Thank God for two bedrooms." Mrs. Bishop was in her usual garishly patterned caftan that she paired with her orange slide-on Crocs. Her face was round and tight from Botox injections, even though she talked a great deal about living a natural lifestyle.

"How are you feeling this morning, Betty?"

Mrs. Bishop clutched Devi's hands. "My stomach is almost back to its natural state. More importantly, Sarah and I are back in good spirits, thanks to you and fenugreek."

"Couples are my mom's specialty." There. She quipped.

"And that is why she is my favorite." Mrs. Bishop let go of Devi's hands and leaned one sturdy elbow on the wood-and-glass counter to face Tulsi.

"Mine too." Tulsi gave her mom's arm a squeeze before moving to the area by the register.

"And when are you finally going to step in, become *the* spice healer, take over so your mom can become adviser and your grandmother can retire?" Mrs. Bishop asked.

Never. Instead, she took a fortifying breath. "Still need to pass that last test." Her grandmother would be the one to administer it. An oral and practical exam to gauge how capable Tulsi was so she could work without direct supervision.

Most of her friends had graduated from high school, then gone off to college and beyond. Not her. She'd been enrolled in what Tulsi silently called Aruna Gupta's School for Spice Healers. She was the only student. After decades of weekly lessons, Tulsi had yet to graduate and didn't particularly care to.

"She's close," Devi said. "I predict it will only be a few more lessons."

"Mm-hmm," Mrs. Bishop said. "It's been that way for every year for the last I don't know how many. Isn't there a blend you can give her to remove whatever is blocking her?"

"This isn't an ailment. She doesn't feel ready, and that's okay. Spices are complex," Devi said. "It takes time and patience to get a feel for them. Getting even one part of it wrong can cause harm."

"How much damage can a pinch of this, a dash of that do?" Mrs. Bishop asked.

"Three teaspoons of nutmeg can put you in a psychotic state," Tulsi offered.

"Tulsi," Devi reprimanded.

"What? It's true. You didn't add any to Mrs. Bishop's blend, did you?" Tulsi said.

Mrs. Bishop let out a bold, full laugh. "Now that's more like the Tulsi I know and love."

"Don't encourage her, Betty," Devi said.

"Take it from me, Tulsi, passion is the greatest motivation. Tap into yours," Mrs. Bishop said. "And I'll take a bottle of nutmeg powder. Next time David hassles me for the gavel at our HSBA meeting, I'll make him a big batch of cookies and dump half a bottle of it in the batter."

"I will not sell any to you," Devi said. "Not if you're going to use it as poison."

"You're amazing, Devi, but you really need to understand humor," Mrs. Bishop said.

Devi adjusted the pleat of her baby-pink dupatta she'd paired with her white cotton salwar. "Your jokes are dark."

"As Sarah would say, 'Just like my heart.'"

"She would not," Devi said. "Also, poisoning is not a laughing matter."

Tulsi left them to their conversation to check that their stock was organized. She shifted a jar of ajwan to show the label as it sat in a row along the wall. Each jar had seeds, powders, or dried herbs. Another row was for seasoning blends for quick recipes or generic use. There was so much online now that customers came in with all sorts of random questions, like what was the best turmeric for lattes made from matcha? Or could the salt from the Himalayan lamps be used in cooking? She'd taken critical thinking in high school and wondered if they'd stopped teaching it.

Tulsi checked the tabletops with larger jars organized by category, where customers could pick out dried chilies, neem leaves, and peppercorns. Others had a variety of kokum along with rare herbs and spices.

The front window area was lined with small tables and soft chairs where patrons could sit and chat with Aruna or Devi, and confide in them their ails.

Tulsi's family's lineage was believed to trace back to Dharti, the Vedic Hindu goddess of Earth. Those powder-blue padded chairs where her mother and grandmother sat were meant for her too.

But Tulsi did not want to take her seat.

CHAPTER TWO

A week later, not much had changed, though Tulsi *had* worked on her attitude. She'd forced herself to brush off her restlessness. If she'd drawn out the tattoo of Buddha wrapped in barbed wire and hid it in her drawer, well, that was her business. She didn't know why, but the image meant something. As if the universe had put a sign in her path.

"What's making you smile?" Devi asked.

Tulsi glanced at her mom, who was stacking satchels of personalized blends in a small ceramic container. "I was thinking that maybe some of Ba's sixth sense might be rubbing off on me."

"Oh, do you feel something? What is it? Good, I hope." Devi clasped her hands, a wide smile stretched across her beautiful face.

Sometimes she forgot how literal her mom could be. "No, it was a silly thought."

"Don't dismiss the things that are surfacing," Devi said. "If your subconscious is trying to tell you something, pay attention."

Before Tulsi could reply, the front door opened.

"I need a little more of that special fenugreek and maybe another recipe to use it with," Mrs. Bishop said. "Sarah and I are back to enjoying each other, if you know what I mean."

"More like you're having a good time and don't want it to end," Tulsi said.

"Tulsi, we don't discuss private things in the open," Devi said. "It's not for us to comment."

"Oh bull," Mrs. Bishop said. "The girl is right. Who knew fenugreek was good for not just the stomach but also the loins. You know your stuff, Tulsi. Take the test already."

Tulsi shrugged.

"It's not school," Devi said. "Ours is an oral tradition. Of course, there are ancient texts to study, but a majority of our work requires fluency in the proper usage of spices and herbs. From there, it's years of practice to develop an intuition. I am still learning what works for you, and we've known each other for over twenty years."

"That's why I run a cheese shop. It's all done by taste." Mrs. Bishop laughed. "Did your mother tell you about the latest news from the HSBA meeting last night?" Mrs. Bishop was one of the founding members of the Historic Salem Business Association.

"No, she didn't. Mom thinks gossip invites bad energy."

"Only if it's negative," Devi said. "In this case, I believe it's good news."

"Well, don't keep me in suspense." Tulsi leaned both elbows on the counter.

"You're going to have a new neighbor soon." Mrs. Bishop grinned. "A handsome young man. He's scruffy and on the quiet side, but well mannered."

"Someone bought the deli?" Change perked her up. The idea of a new person in their community was the exact diversion she needed to get out of her funk.

"His name is Lucas," Devi said. "He plans to convert the space into a café and restaurant. The deli counter will become a coffee and tea bar."

"Baked goods and sandwiches during the day and sit-down dinner service in the evenings," Mrs. Bishop added. "He even got a coveted liquor license."

"That's going to be so good for all of us," Tulsi said. "When does he plan to open?"

"In a month. He has some renovations to do and got the final approvals at last night's meeting," Mrs. Bishop said. "Lucas officially has all the right permits and is using a local crew, which makes me happy."

She wanted to know more, everything about this stranger and his plans. This was the most excitement they'd had in their little historic district area since Gemma and Mr. Rhodes called off their truce and started their chalkboard-sign war. "Where is he from? Local?"

"No. He doesn't have any regional accent, so maybe from the Midwest," Mrs. Bishop replied. "He didn't say much about himself, barely got enough words out to get the business done. I'm thinking loner. Ex-military. Though Missy thinks he's a hit man, and all of this is cover for a mob bust. I keep telling her not to listen to all those crime podcasts. Henry, of course, thinks your new neighbor is in witness protection."

"I don't get that read of Lucas," Devi said. "My senses say he's shy, possibly lonely. Let's give him time. Get to know him at his pace."

"Who?" Aruna came in from the back office. "Tulsi, you left the *Charaka Samhita* on the counter again. I told you to keep it with you so you can study whenever you have time."

Tulsi took the small book from her grandmother. Still the first volume, only ten more to go. But it was the formative and original text that documented Ayurveda and was required reading.

"The deli is going to open as a restaurant," Devi said. "We met Lucas Sharma last night."

"Indian."

Tulsi grinned. Aruna ba put people in two buckets. Indian and non. The Indians were judged more harshly.

"I didn't ask," Devi said.

"Sharma is usually a Punjabi name." Aruna turned to Mrs. Bishop. "Alone or family?"

"Not sure," Mrs. Bishop replied.

"Young?"

"I'd put him in his midthirties."

Oh no. Tulsi needed to get out of her grandmother's line of sight. She opened the book in her hand and pretended to concentrate.

"That's not too old."

She ignored the comment from her grandmother.

"That is an interesting idea, Aruna," Mrs. Bishop said. "He is very good looking, Tulsi."

"Sorry, can't hear you." Tulsi held up the book. "Studying."

"You haven't dated since, well, I can't even remember. Who was that last boyfriend of yours? Doesn't matter, time to build a bridge and get over it," Mrs. Bishop said. "Isn't that a saying on one of your T-shirts?"

"It's not about him." Not in the way Mrs. Bishop implied. Kal was when she'd become aware of the curse. She could never put anyone in its path, especially when it meant continuity. One that she was haphazardly trying to permanently sever.

CHAPTER THREE

Later that afternoon, Tulsi glanced up as a woman came in, camera held up to her face and talking to her phone. Most of her commentary was a play-by-play of what she'd seen and where she'd come from. As she spoke, she used words like *cute, cozy,* and *delightful.* Tulsi was glad her grandmother wasn't behind the counter, because Aruna ba detested people on their phones as they wandered and browsed. Rasa offered a soothing atmosphere, a place to quiet the mind and spirit. They didn't even play music in the shop. The only sound came from small water features in discreet corners, offering a sensory respite from the external world.

The woman panned the camera around as she stroked her perfectly french-manicured fingernails along the wall of small spice jars and sifted her fingers through the large container of dried ginger, ignoring the sign that asked customers to use the tongs to keep their stock sanitary. The woman's face was fully made up in the way of a news anchor. Red lips, pale skin, thick eyelashes, and sharp brows. It all complemented long blonde hair that fell in waves over her white sheath dress. Self-conscious, Tulsi tugged at the hem of the green T-shirt she'd paired with jeans and smoothed down her pixie cut that often spiked in random directions as the day went on. Finally, she touched her cheeks and couldn't remember if she'd only moisturized her face that morning or if she'd put on any makeup.

"OMG, I love it in here. It is so serene, and the cool tones are so soothing. Your interior designer is very talented." The woman put her phone on the glass counter along with her giant pink-and-white designer tote. She smelled like she'd just soaked in a bath of rose petals.

The compliment made Tulsi stand straighter and puff out her chest. "It was me." Tulsi gave her a cheerful smile and deepened her voice. That, along with slowing her speech, conveyed an enchanting environment, which tourists seemed to expect of a shop in historic Salem. Playing into it often meant more sales.

"You have an eye." The woman pointed to Tulsi's T-shirt. "Easy as pie. Adorbs."

"Uh, thank you. I like clichés." Tulsi had started her collection of shirts with puns and overused phrases a long time ago, and now it had become her almost-daily uniform. While her mother usually wore maxi dresses and Aruna wore loose pants and blouses, Tulsi had a dresser filled with T-shirts, slouchy cotton pants, shorts, and a few pairs of jeans. "Your dress is really pretty. I could never pull it off."

"Don't be silly. You just need a different fit to make up for your lack of curves. I bought it from a little boutique in the Berkshires," she said. "I posted about it last week. All part of my *Explore Massachusetts* series."

"For television?"

The woman laughed. "No one watches that anymore, though I am hoping for a streaming deal at some point. I have so many ideas. Right now I'm on YouTube, Instagram, and TikTok. I'm still building my brand and following, which means I'm always in search of something new, and I want to be the first to blow it up. I'm Savasana Skye on socials, but IRL you can call me Skye."

Tulsi nodded. "I'm just Tulsi." She bit the inside of her lip at the moniker Skye had adopted. If Aruna ba came out from the back, it would become a painful interaction for Skye. Her grandmother did not like anyone to freely use Vedic terms by people who did not have full experiences or deep understanding. A Sanskrit word, *savasana*'s English translation would be "corpse pose," and having it as part of a person's name was nonsensical. But thanks to yoga classes at local gyms, the word had morphed to mean "serenity" or "peace."

"Nice to meet you," Skye said. "What are your social handles? I'd love to follow you."

"We're not on there." Tulsi was barely online. Of course she was aware of the channels and had accounts, but living an uneventful life didn't give her much to talk about to her twenty followers, who were mostly friends from high school. Rasa didn't do any promotion or advertising, so being active on there didn't make sense. Besides, Aruna ba preferred their business to be in person and customer service oriented. It was only a few years ago that Tulsi had won a small battle with her grandmother to put up a website for their store. There wasn't much on there, only a page with a large image of their storefront, their name, and location. Aruna ba wanted no mention of their client work, so Rasa was simply presented as a boutique spice shop.

"It's a shame," Skye said. "You should really put yourself out there. You never know where you'll end up, and it could be good for you and this shop. I wouldn't have found you if it wasn't for the cheese shop I popped into. The woman who runs it was amazing, such a character, so much personality. She's the one who pointed me here."

Tulsi laughed. "Mrs. Bishop is one of a kind and our biggest fan."

"She let me take some footage and gave a little dissertation on the history of cheese, which I'll have to edit down, of course, but did you know that it goes all the way back to 5500 BC? In Poland." The woman made a head-exploding gesture with one hand.

"She knows a lot," Tulsi said. "Like casu marzu is an illegal cheese because it's full of maggots and can kill you."

"Eww." Skye made a face.

"Exactly." Tulsi liked her. Skye was very different from anyone Tulsi knew. There was a confidence, bubbliness, and style about her. Tulsi made a mental note to check out her videos.

Skye scanned Tulsi from head to toe. "Has anyone ever told you that you would look great on camera? With your sharp features, button nose, and spiky lashes, you could transform from sweet to evil with a mere expression. And thick eyebrows are all the rage right now. If you want, we can do a little interview here for my channels."

Tulsi aggressively shook her head. She had no makeup on, and who knew what her hair looked like—besides, what would she even say? Uncomfortable with the intense focus, Tulsi redirected her. "I'm not really as outgoing as Mrs. Bishop."

Skye waved off Tulsi's concerns. "Don't be silly. I think you'd be great. I've been doing this for a few years, and I can see it in you. You need to own it, shoulders back, hip cocked, and let that sexy Selena Gomez voice do the rest."

"Thanks, but I'd rather be behind the scenes," Tulsi said. "Is there anything specific you're looking for? If not, feel free to browse."

"That's too bad," she said. "I'd still like to feature your shop, if that's okay with you. Like I said, I'm looking for something new and interesting."

Tulsi glanced behind her to the back room. She didn't think Aruna ba would be okay with it, especially from someone who didn't appear to be of Indian descent and went by "Savasana." "I don't think so. We like to keep a low profile."

"Oh, I get it," Skye said. "You're going for mysterious and magical. Which is super interesting, like an old-timey place that's a throwback to days before the internet. You know, there's a huge audience for that. People in our generation like quirky and unknown. You should totally lean into that."

Tulsi wished it were all intentional. Mostly, though, they stayed low-key because Aruna ba and her mother preferred it that way. When Tulsi pushed to do more, they would ignore her. "This isn't for marketing or publicity. As my mom likes to say, we're practitioners of one of the oldest approaches to medicinal healing. Our spices are sourced from around the world and are as close to their natural state as possible to help people."

"Amazing. See, people need to know this. There is so much potential here," she said. "I mean, it's all the rage right now, health and holistic remedies. You're not even busy. Like, at all. OMG, idea! I can help you. My brand is wellness travel and hidden finds. This could be an awesome partnership."

For a few minutes, Tulsi was tempted. To imagine doing something more, to have the world know about them. She wanted to tell Skye about special clients and personalization. Then she heard her grandmother puttering behind the curtain that divided the shop from the back room. Aruna ba avoided any sort of spotlight or publicity. She always said spice healers didn't draw attention to themselves—it was about remedies. They led quiet lives. "I'm sorry. It's not what we would do."

"What a shame," Skye said. "But I get it. It's scary to put yourself out there. Do you mind if I take a few pictures, at least? It's not like I can tag you anyway, since you don't have any accounts online."

"Sure. That's fine." It was better this way. There was no point in drawing attention to Rasa when her goal was to have the shop end with Tulsi.

Skye wandered off with camera in hand, and Tulsi kept one eye on her as she strolled around the shop, taking photos of everything, including herself in front of the wall of petite spice bottles.

"These are so cute. Baby spices." The woman grabbed a few small jars with Rasa labels, then took more photos before coming up to the counter. "What do I do with these?"

Back in her comfort zone, Tulsi happily explained. "Well, dried neem leaves are great to calm ulcers. Chewing them also helps with teeth or gum issues. The fennel seeds help digest fiber or grain-heavy meals. And triphala is a powder made up of three dried fruits. If you take a spoonful each day, it helps prevent constipation."

"Wait, these little things can do all that?"

Tulsi nodded.

Aruna came in from the back with an armful of freshly dried herbs. She glanced at the young woman and then at Tulsi. "Problem?"

Skye gave Aruna a wide smile. "I was offering a promotional opportunity, a feature on my YouTube channel."

"Not interested," Aruna said.

"Yup. I've been told." Skye dug into her tote as Tulsi rang up the bottles. "Can I pay with my phone?"

"Sorry, only cash or credit card," Tulsi said.

"Wow, très old school." Skye handed over her card, then leaned closer to Tulsi. "But seriously, if you ever change your mind, just DM me. You'd be surprised how much even a single post can help turn things around."

Tulsi nodded and handed over the receipt.

"Thank you. I didn't notice these. What pretty satchels." Skye poked at a box Aruna placed on the counter.

"These are for some of our regular customers. It's a special blend for their needs and includes a recipe to help them heal," Tulsi said.

"How interesting," Skye said. "So if I wanted something like that for me?"

"It's a long process," Tulsi said. "It could take a week or more to create."

"Alas, I leave this evening for Bar Harbor," Skye said.

Tulsi kept the smile pasted on her face as Skye left. Maine was a little more than a half-hour drive, but she'd only been as far north as Portland for a day trip with her mom a long time ago. The idea of Skye wandering from place to place was appealing. Jealousy was an ugly emotion. She knew that. Instead, she had to find a way to channel it into something. Nothing too dramatic or tattoo worthy. Maybe if she didn't have the anchor of Rasa keeping Tulsi in place, she could actually live a different life. She glanced at her grandmother. For sixty-eight years, this was her focus, her dream. Her mom had followed the same path. Tulsi didn't want to be on it, not anymore. She had to find a way to—how did Skye say it?—put herself out there. Tulsi clutched the edge of the glass display counter. She couldn't wait. The idea of getting to her mom's age, Ba's, and still sitting here wishing for a different life wasn't going to cut it. She needed to act. Now.

CHAPTER FOUR

The three-story Victorian house on a green, leafy street was the only home Tulsi had ever known. Apparently they'd lived in an attic apartment for the first two years of Tulsi's life, but she had no recollection. While tourists flocked to the nearby black-painted Witch House, she liked hers with its cotton-candy-pink-and-deep-purple exterior. The whimsy on the outside didn't necessarily match the decor inside. Less cheerful, their home showed its wear with uneven floorboards, rooms made of inconvenient angles, and the general shabbiness of a house that had been lived in for close to three decades by the same family.

The couches and chairs were covered with Aruna's crocheted blankets, with pilled wool from hundreds of washes. Devi's experimental abstract watercolors crowded the walls, all variations of land and seascapes. Tulsi's puzzles, from crosswords to jigsaws, were strewn around tabletops. It all felt cramped, though not cluttered. While in school, her home had been a place that she'd come to for rest from her busy life of friends, study groups, theater rehearsals, soccer practice. Now it had become her only variation from her days at Rasa. Everywhere she looked, she noticed age—the splintered wood on the window trim, the streaks on what used to be a shiny coffee table, the lumps in the beige sofa, the faded paint on the walls.

"Focus." Aruna ba pointed to the gold platter on the wide granite kitchen island.

"I am." She pretended to scrutinize the powders and herbs in front of her as her grandmother explained each spice and its various properties and uses. On the tray, each pile was divided into six rasa quadrants—sweet, sour, astringent, pungent, salty, and bitter. Each person's dosha dictated what blends were needed for treatment. Anything from fatigue to indigestion was an indicator of imbalance, and adjusting life to doshas was a way to stay healthy.

Tulsi believed in the work. She just didn't want to commit her whole life to serving others. Her grandmother and mom had done nothing else, and they'd impressed on Tulsi that it was the calling all the women who came before them had answered. Tulsi often wondered if any of them had been restless, reluctant. Wished for something more.

"Let's talk about the mix you made for Elizabeth Howe." Her grandmother spoke exclusively in Gujarati when at home.

"I got it wrong." Tulsi, who understood fluently, responded in English, not only because it was easier, but as a tiny rebellion. She could speak Gujarati if she had to, but beyond her mother and Aruna ba, there was no one else she could converse with in their home language.

Her grandmother waited.

"I lost focus, became distracted." Ayurveda was a medicinal science, and there was an order to it that Tulsi typically bypassed in an effort to just get the task done.

"Everything in nature is a combination of five elements—earth, water, air, fire, and space. You must start there first, before the rasa."

Tulsi heard the exasperation in Aruna ba's voice, and a twinge of guilt surfaced at her deliberate sabotage. These lessons had started on Tulsi's tenth birthday. At first it had been exciting to be just like her mom. Tulsi had been a diligent student, followed precise instructions and strutted around, steadied by the knowledge of who she was and what she'd been chosen to do. Somewhere around the time her high school friends began to apply for college, share their dreams of what they'd hoped to become, got to live away from home, study abroad, things shifted for Tulsi. Everyone else got to do things, but she was tied to the *Charaka Samhita*.

That was when her senses turned against the spices. The heady smell of toasted cumin that had once been a comfort became a sign of changelessness. The yellow stains of turmeric were forever embedded in the granite countertop, the bitter taste of asafetida in khadi became anathema. She lost the joy.

"There is a difference between memorizing and understanding. If you don't know it deeply, instinctually, you can't practice as an Ayurvedic healer. Now tell me what you did wrong." Aruna pointed her bony finger to the small mounds of spices on the platter and swung her long thick braid of gray hair off her shoulder.

"I added tamarind powder." Tulsi heard the exasperation in her grandmother's voice. Once they'd had a gentle relationship where they would spend early mornings picking herbs together in the garden. Now they circled around each other, a silent conflict neither would face head-on. "Sour and bitter shouldn't be combined without balance, because it impedes digestion, and Ms. Howe wanted something to help calm her nerves as she waited for the test results from her biopsy. My blend would cause stomach upset."

There. She'd appropriately regurgitated what she'd been taught. Just enough so Aruna ba didn't think she was completely inept. But she also knew she needed to step up her incompetency if her plan was to work.

When it came to their profession, Devi was a natural—intuitive and well versed. Tulsi's mom could hold a delicate saffron stamen and know its potency. Ba was passionate and determined. Her grandmother didn't need to measure. She could eyeball the amounts to create the right mixture. The two people she loved most had deep respect for the ancient art of Ayurveda.

But it wasn't for Tulsi. Their line of spice healers would end with her, gradually, naturally. As long as she showed that she couldn't grasp the knowledge, she could delay taking over. Eventually her mom and ba would accept that Tulsi was never going to be ready, and she could finally build a life on her own terms. They would be saddened at Tulsi's inability. At least they would know it wasn't their fault. It was solely Tulsi's lack. Until now she'd been playing the long game.

The Buddha in barbed wire had poked her out of complacency. She didn't want to wait another ten years, twenty. It had to happen soon. She needed to figure out a way to escape. To do what or go where, that was still unknown. And the how eluded her.

In middle school, Tulsi would occasionally have dinner at the house of her best friend, Cassie. Her parents would ask, "What was one thing that interested you and one thing that bored you during the day?" Everyone around the table would take a turn. They would talk to each other about their feelings and tell each other what they wanted, needed. Tulsi could add only things like "asafetida made you fart less." Since then she'd widened her knowledge by reading novels, watching YouTube travel videos, and taking free online courses, from astronomy to philosophy. She dabbled. Yet nothing inspired her. Cassie's passion was to record history, and she now worked at the Library of Congress. Mercy wanted to make art accessible, and she started a nonprofit. Her friends did things. Tulsi let things happen to her.

Now Tulsi knew that she'd been passive for so long that it had become a part of her. Doing just enough to make herself feel like she was doing something, when in fact she'd been stalling.

"If you cannot get even the basic recipes correct, what hope is there?" Her grandmother grasped the edge of the counter.

"I know. Maybe with a little more time." She wasn't brave enough to give an honest answer and reverted to the oft-repeated phrase.

"Twenty years, that's how long I've been working with you. How much more patience am I expected to have?" Aruna ba clenched and released her fingers.

It was a trait Tulsi had inherited, a way to control emotions that were never to be exposed. Moderation and release. That was the Gupta way.

"Be calm, Ma." Devi entered the kitchen. "Tulsi is making progress, however slow. Remember last week? She made a lovely paste of chili and wild garlic for Rebecca Martin. It helped her with the metabolism boost she'd asked for."

Tulsi's chest constricted. Her mom always showed unwavering faith in her. While Ba would be angry when Tulsi turned her back on their legacy, Devi would be devastated. Her mother was fragile.

Aruna ba looked directly at Tulsi. "One step forward. One step back. That's standing in the same place." Aruna took the platter away and added the spices back into their jars, then stored them on the counter next to the stove. "I was a master by the time I reached eighteen. Your mother passed me with her abilities when she was barely twenty. I honestly don't know what is happening with you."

"Your circumstances were different, Ma." Devi filled three mugs with hot water. "Your mother was sick, and she needed to pass everything on to you as quickly as possible. It's different with Tulsi. She has both of us, so there isn't a sense of urgency. But, beta, you do have to apply yourself and practice. I know you say you're busy with the business part of Rasa, but you can't ignore your studies. Ba is right. You have to start taking on clients. For our future and yours." Devi went to the herb garden by the wide kitchen windows and plucked a few mint leaves, rinsed them, patted them dry, and rubbed them in her hands to release their natural oil before adding them to their mugs.

"At least find a man." Aruna reached for the mug Devi held out. "Give me a great-granddaughter I can train while I'm still able. Go meet that new neighbor. I got a look at him, and he seems worthy."

"Because he's Indian? Since when has that mattered to you?" An easy out. One she'd refused to take. She'd broken one heart, wouldn't do it again.

"If you had Devi's talents, I wouldn't care," Aruna said. "But a little more Indian in the genes couldn't hurt. His line likely has Vedic practitioners."

Tulsi swallowed a sip to repress the gurgle of bile in her stomach. She wouldn't let another person become a victim of the curse. And she wouldn't pass this predestined life on to another generation. "So he can die just like my grandfather, just like my father." The room stilled. It was the first time she'd spoken her thoughts aloud. Her grandmother's expression reset to neutral. Her mom's eyes filled with tears. Tulsi turned away, stared down, noticed a mysterious yellowing bruise on her thigh.

She could hear her own heartbeat in the silence. Theirs wasn't a family that talked about the weight of the past, merely stingy details when it came to their personal history. All the conversations they'd never had filled the kitchen and suffocated her. She'd been twelve when she'd first asked about her father. Devi had told her he'd never had the chance to know about her. She'd asked why, and her mother had broken down.

"Like your grandfather, the fates took him from you, us . . ." She hadn't known what that meant. Once her mother had finished crying, Tulsi had asked what *fate* meant. Devi had tried to explain with words like *destiny*, the *will of gods*, and still Tulsi hadn't understood. Then she'd asked outright, *Was my father dead?* It was then that both Devi and Aruna ba confirmed it. "An accident. While he was at college." Their words faltered, and they offered no further details. Tulsi had asked for a name, the tiniest of knowledge of him. Her mom had devolved into tears. It was when she saw Aruna ba's damp eyes that she finally stopped asking. That was when Tulsi had learned an important lesson— her mom wasn't strong enough to deal with the hard parts of life. Her grandmother avoided them. Tulsi had let it go. Stopped being persistent and began her slow walk over emotional eggshells.

"I didn't mean to say that. I'm sorry." Tulsi tried to comfort herself. That her mom still felt deeply about a love from over thirty years ago was truly awe inspiring. Tulsi should be glad that she'd come from such devotion.

"That's enough for today," Aruna murmured. "Go study. I'm heading to the bank to take care of some errands. A long walk will cleanse this energy."

Tulsi needed to ease the pain she'd caused. "Mom, let's go to the beach or have lunch along the water. Maybe drive up to Newburyport for ice cream."

Aruna gave Tulsi a disappointed headshake, then left the room.

"How about we have a quiet day by ourselves?" Devi said. "You can take time to read. How are you doing with the *Charaka Samhita* translation?"

An escape and a change of subject. The reset was already in motion. Yet she wasn't ready to face the book that had become a steady weight in her tote bag, simply there to be carried to and from here and Rasa. "It's our only day off. Can't we do something? Maybe go down to Boston?"

"I'm tired," Devi said. "I think it's best if we took the day to relax and rejuvenate. And the light is good. I should spend some time with my paints."

The disappointment sat heavy in her chest. It meant her mom hadn't forgiven her. She craved a "Tulsi's day out." As a child, those had been her rare indulgence. Once every few months, Devi would wake up Tulsi very early and they'd sneak out in their used Toyota Camry. For the whole day the two of them would do whatever Tulsi chose. They'd watched runners cross the finish line at the Boston Marathon, were sprayed by whales splashing in the Atlantic Ocean, toured the Ben & Jerry's ice-cream factory, and kayaked along the Charles River. Tulsi hugged those memories close. Once she'd reached high school, those days were replaced with Aruna ba's lessons. Only one luxury remained—an annual trip over Thanksgiving, just her and Devi.

Alone in the kitchen, Tulsi sat with her lukewarm mint water. The silence in the house wrapped around her like a boa that would slowly squeeze the life out of her. She had to free herself.

CHAPTER FIVE

Instead of studying, Tulsi left the house in her "Ants in Pants" T-shirt and a pair of shorts. She thought about not telling anyone, but ten minutes in, she texted Devi to let her know that she'd gone out and would be back later. The day was hot, and Tulsi regretted forgetting her cap as the sun stung her skin. But she didn't turn around, only moved farther away from the pink-and-purple house. The sea air, though warm, offered a bit of respite as she strolled along the harbor walk. The streets were so familiar Tulsi didn't need to look around. Some breweries and restaurants had recently opened, but they were different versions of what had been there before. Turnover didn't change the monotony.

Uninspired, she crossed over Congress Street and made her way toward Rasa. There was always paperwork and her pastimes—puzzles, paint by numbers, e-books, and daydreaming. She imagined being someone else, different names, different backgrounds, and always free to go and do anything she wanted. Those people in her head did things, climbed Mount Everest, won the World Cup, invented, created, built. It was never her. She knew she wasn't as brave as the fictional women in her head. Living vicariously sustained her heart enough to manage the monotony of her days.

Rasa's office was dim and overcrowded with boxes, notebooks, a computer, a small sink and microwave, and a mini fridge. As she entered, a waft of nutmeg, cinnamon, rose, and clove assaulted her nostrils. Before she could get to her desk, a loud noise from the alley startled her. Then she heard a gravelly voice yell out orders. "Set the crates down. We'll unload them later."

What must have been a large vehicle let out a series of beeps and backing-up alarms. Her least favorite noise, high pitched and constant. She rubbed her temples. Their new neighbor. She'd yet to reach out and introduce herself to Lucas Sharma, had avoided him. Mostly because any sort of interaction would expose both of them to matchmaking. But she'd have to meet him sometime. Over the weekend, Devi had gone next door with a welcome basket full of essentials for a new business, including stationery cards with markers to handwrite the names of display items. Her mother had reported back that their neighbor was a lovely person with a good aura. Nothing beyond that.

A loud clang, then a roar of power tools cutting through something, made it impossible for her to hear her computer sound. She ducked out into the alleyway. A giant delivery truck blocked most of it, but luckily there was enough room against the brick wall to go a few steps to the open door of the old deli.

"Hello?" she called out, as there was no one around.

She went farther and saw the condition of the kitchen. The old appliances had been ripped out and replaced with fancy stainless-steel ovens, freezers, and a massive stove with a grill. What seemed like it would become a prep station of sorts was only half-complete. Tulsi navigated the empty boxes, torn-up plastic, and paint cans as she swept through to the front of the store.

Then she saw a man, his back to her. His massive, wide back. Through his long-sleeved T-shirt, Tulsi could see his well-defined biceps and triceps. They weren't the kind that were built in a gym but maybe on a football field. She also appreciated his firm round denim-covered butt, because while she wasn't interested, she still had eyes. Tulsi called out again, over the sound of the power drill, but he didn't turn around. She moved closer, waited for the drill to stop, then tapped his shoulder.

He turned but wasn't merely jarred. Before she knew what had happened, she was spun around and pinned against the display glass, her arm bent behind her back. His arm was like steel banded around her shoulders. His grip was like a vise around her elbow. Her neck was turned so that her cheek was plastered to the side of the cool glass display case. There wasn't pressure. He wasn't hurting her, just held her completely immobilized. It had all been so fast that she was shocked, but now she tried to relax into his hold. That was what she remembered from the self-defense classes she'd taken at the YWCA with her mom, grandmother, and Mrs. Bishop. As she went slack, so did his arms, just enough for her to move her cheek off the glass and closer to his face. His breath smelled like coffee.

"I come in peace." Tulsi managed to speak. "I'm your neighbor. Next door. If you're Lucas Sharma, you met my mom, Devi. She brought you a frilly basket full of office supplies."

After a few beats, he released her, and Tulsi turned slowly so as not to jar him. Just to be on the safe side, she raised her hands. He had a stern look on his face even though his jaw was no longer rigid. Attractive. If you liked conventional, and she didn't. Or so she told herself. She appreciated it, but she couldn't act on it, never again. Besides, Tulsi preferred a soft face, not such a broad build, closer to her height at around five eight. She didn't like being towered over like she was now. Lucas was too barrel-chested. His dark-brown hair was mussed with waves that curled in different directions. He didn't inspire fear in her, more like curiosity.

"Never sneak up on a person with power tools."

His voice was thick and deep. She tried to put him at ease with a friendly smile, which he didn't return, and she wondered what he looked like when he laughed. "Sorry. I, um . . . came by to say hello. I'm Tulsi Gupta. Your shop neighbor and Devi's daughter."

He relaxed and wiped his hand on a nearby towel before shaking hers.

There was warmth as their palms touched. Instead of leaning into it, knowing she could like this contact, become dependent on it, want more, she pulled away. "Do you usually attack your visitors?"

"Not an attack, more like defuse a threat."

She laughed. "Because I'm so intimidating. My grandmother used to tell me not to go outside on a windy day because I'd be carried away like Dorothy."

He furrowed his forehead.

"*Wizard of Oz*? Kansas?"

"No, I got the reference," he said. "Just don't see you as weak."

She repressed how much she liked the compliment. Though she would wallow in it later. She was rarely seen as a strong person. "Thanks."

He nodded. Then turned back to the table he was in the middle of putting together.

"You're Lucas, right?"

He gave another nod as he focused on his work.

"Not exactly the chatty type, are you?" Tulsi moved to the other side so she could face him as he finished joining the table legs. "That's okay. I can carry the conversation for both of us. So where are you from?" She should have just done as she'd intended, ask him how much longer they'd be working, then go back to her side of the shared wall. Instead, she wanted to stay, show him that his read of her as a strong person was true. Even if she was only trying to prove it to herself.

"Are you in the Witness Protection Program?"

He looked up, frowned. "What?"

"We're a small community," Tulsi said. "No one knows much about you except that you're quiet and keep to yourself. And some people watch a lot of TV."

His laugh echoed in the mostly empty room. "Nothing like that."

She moved around the space. The front window needed a good scrubbing, and the walls could use a few coats of paint, but she could see how much work had already been done. "My mom, who assesses people very well, says you're shy. Is that true?"

He pulled out his earbuds. "No, just not a people person."

"I never understood that phrase," Tulsi said. "You are a person, and we are people."

"Is that a joke?"

Tulsi crossed her arms. "Guess not since it didn't land."

"Listen," he said. "I have a lot to get done."

Yet she wasn't quite ready to leave and go back to her dark office, with only videos for company. "I won't stop you. Go ahead. I'm sort of at loose ends because it's my day off, and while I have things to do, they're the kind that I want to put off for as long as possible. You know? There is inventory and invoices, my least favorite part of running a business. And taxes make my eyes cross. Do you plan to do all that yourself or hire someone?" She meandered through the small dusty area. Against one wall a workbench was cluttered with woodworking tools.

He didn't respond, and she saw that he was focused on making sure the wooden legs were level. She wondered if he was generally not talkative or just a "one thing at a time"–type person. It didn't matter. She was used to being in her own thoughts. She liked to talk, but unless there were chatty customers, it was usually one-sided or in her head.

"You're lucky with this location," Tulsi continued. "It's a very busy area and designed for people to walk around. Though the cobblestones do get slippery when it rains or snows. We all put out little signs to make sure people are careful. Most of the shop owners are friendly and supportive. Sometimes there are little squabbles, like Gemma and Mr. Rhodes's silent feud over the placement of their chalkboard signs. For the most part, though, it's usually something that gets resolved fairly quick."

She came close and inspected the almost-finished table. It looked nicer and heftier than IKEA. "You have good taste in furniture."

Lucas looked up. "Thanks."

She took it as a sign that he wasn't bothered by her chatter. "The deli that was here before had plastic tables and chairs. They were cute in a kitschy way but definitely not comfortable. This looks sturdy. If you want to test the weight, I can sit on it for you. Because I'm strong."

Finally, he rose and put the drill down on a nearby counter. "It's good. The wood glue needs to settle a bit."

"Are you going to be ready to open by the end of the month?"

"Hope so." He glanced around.

"If you need help, I'm happy to lend a hand." What was she doing? This was supposed to be a perfunctory meeting after which she would keep her distance. She couldn't be seen with him, at least not by Ba or her mom. Yet she didn't want to leave. "I'm not good at putting stuff together, but I can paint."

"I have someone coming by to take care of it," Lucas said.

He wasn't a people person. "I'm sorry. I tend to ramble. I can talk to anyone. It's part of my job." She shrugged. "Customer service."

"I'm better in the back, yelling out orders," he said.

"Yes, Chef." She uttered the phrase from a popular television show.

He smiled, and Tulsi almost lost herself staring at his beautiful face. It was the first time since the Buddha tattoo that she felt slightly content, less restless.

"What about getting the word out?" Tulsi asked. "The HSBA has a communication person—Gemma is the current one. She does promotions for all of our shops. They put ads in local newspapers, and once a year there's a coupon book, which is now digital, but you can put in offers or discounts. I'm happy to brainstorm some ideas with you. I took an online marketing class from Salem State University a few years ago."

Not that Rasa ever participated in the HSBA advertising sales. Aruna ba had a strong point of view that they were a place for healing, not a store that offered a two-for-one deal.

Lucas set the table against the wall, then faced Tulsi. "I have someone doing publicity."

She nodded. "For a person who keeps to himself, you have a lot of 'someones.'"

"Marine," he said. "Enlisted at eighteen. I get referrals for ex-military who have their own businesses."

"You must have seen a lot of the world," she said.

"Some."

"What was your favorite place?"

"Hard to say."

She got the sense that she'd worn out her welcome. "Okay, I'll leave you to it. If you need anything, I'm . . . um, we're next door."

"Thanks." He turned away from her.

Tulsi headed toward the back exit.

"Listen," he said. "It's chaotic in here, and I can't afford you getting hurt. The deductible on my insurance is pretty high."

She accepted his peace offering of sorts, the way he tried to soften his dismissal of her. "Next time I'll bring a hard hat."

He had the deepest dimples she'd ever seen. They were incongruous to the sharpness of his features. "You have your own?"

She gave him a wide smile. "I'm sure I can find one."

"I meant what I said earlier," he added. "I'm not really the let's-be-friends kind."

"Then what type are you?"

"The let-people-be sort."

That statement marked her. It was honest and unapologetic. Mostly, though, it was so simple in the way he saw himself. She wished she knew how to define herself so succinctly. Tulsi waved. "Good luck with everything."

She left him to his work and was glad for his lack of friendliness. It was better to keep her distance from Lucas. It would be too easy to like him, and he'd stirred that part of her she'd shut down since Kal. It wasn't only that she didn't want to indulge Ba's hope for the next generation. It was also that she knew that Lucas could be the easy path away from doing the hard thing, which was to escape.

CHAPTER SIX

Each year the Viking costume became heavier and smellier. Tulsi took off the large blond horned helmet head to get some air. It was a humid, gray day, and the nearby ocean gave the air a thickness that made it difficult to take a full breath. Luckily the weather hadn't deterred people from coming out to Summer in the Park, an annual outdoor festival near the historic district. Local shops set up tables under tents to make their wares available to all. The HSBA had done monthslong advertising to get the crowd out, and judging by the amount of people around, their efforts had paid off.

Visitors strolled from booth to booth with an iced something or other in their hands. Some stopped for samples from Mrs. Bishop's cheese shop, others waited in line for a tarot reading. Several were gathered around a booth that sold candles with literary quotes. It was for the younger kids that she'd donned the Viking costume, which had become an expected part of the festival. The HSBA put on an event each season. Halloween was next, which meant decorating contests along with the costume parade. She shook her sweaty head to pull herself out of this weird mood and forced herself to play with the kids who ran around her with ice-cream-streaked faces.

"Beta, why don't you sit and have some water?" Devi called her over.

Grateful for the break, she went behind the Rasa booth and flopped her costumed body into an armless metal chair. The big, padded bottoms of the Viking costume poured over the sides of the seat. Lucas was set up next to them. Since his entry was late, Devi had made room for his samples alongside theirs. And since his signs weren't ready, Lucas had written *The Pearl* on a sheet of paper and put it in a frame, which sat upon a little stand. A few locals wondered if he'd chosen the name because of the Steinbeck novel, but Tulsi hadn't heard his explanation.

She sent quick glances but mostly avoided him. Normally she would have tried to become his new best friend, especially to hear his stories of travel. Her natural nosiness would help her get to know everything about a person. But not with Lucas. He reminded her too much of the way she'd been initially wrapped up in Kal, her certainty that he was her salvation. It was better to avoid temptation. Still, she didn't want him to see her dressed as a Nordic warrior with a sweaty face. It was her own vanity and nothing more, she reasoned.

Tulsi did salivate over the treats he doled out, particularly the small bowls of caramel-coated, chilled gulab jamun. She'd tried one from servings he'd handed Devi and Aruna ba earlier and had to walk away before she ate all of them from his large cooler under the Pearl's table. Sweet and sinful, each dense brown ball had an airy texture inside from the milk powder and flour mixture. Instead of sugar and rose syrup, he'd made a sauce of caramel and cardamom in which the jamun was soaked. Slivers of almonds and crumbled pistachios were sprinkled on top. All other gulab jamuns would forever pale in comparison.

She saw that it wasn't only his dessert that brought people over. So many of the Pearl's visitors seemed to take a minute to flirt or at least check him out in appreciation. Apparently scruffy-looking chefs were popular, and not only for the free samples. Tulsi spied Vivian, coming over for the third time while taking a break from her tarot readings. Tulsi wondered what the cards would say about her own reaction to Lucas. But the last time she'd had her cards read, they indicated she would go on a grand adventure. Apparently that had meant that she'd once again be a Viking mascot.

"Is it the food or the man who made it that has you so captivated?" Aruna pointed her handheld electric fan at Tulsi's sweaty face.

She sat up. "What? No, neither. I mean, well, the gulab jamun are really good, but I was staring into space."

"Mm-hmm," Aruna said. "Though I wouldn't blame you for being interested."

"Stop." Tulsi rose. Even though they weren't aggressive about it, she smarted at even the slightest innuendo. She reminded herself that they nudged, not pressured. She needed to take a beat and not snap. "I'm going to go back to the kids."

"Tulsi." Devi turned toward her. "Can you run to the shop? We're out of black salt. We usually can't move the stuff, and today we ran out in half an hour, and more people have come by to ask for it. Bring everything we have in stock."

Tulsi took a big chug of water, then recapped the metal bottle. "I have another hour before I'm done, and then I can help here."

"Go first." Aruna handed her a Post-it. "Here are a few more things to bring back with you. I'm surprised at the interest, but if a few more understand the benefits of our spices, then it will be worth it."

"There are a lot more tourists than usual this year," Devi said. "I'll have to send Gemma a thank-you. She's done such a great job with marketing."

"Whatever it is, I'll take it." Aruna reorganized the jars. "We can't afford to miss out on the good days. I worry that it has been too slow, and we still aren't maintaining a steadiness like we used to."

"Ma, don't stress. We're fine." Devi smiled as two women approached. "Hello, welcome. Would you like to try this chili, lime, and pink salt mix? A pinch on these apple slices will give you a refreshing pick-me-up."

Tulsi recognized one of them. "Skye?"

"OMG, it's you. Why are you dressed like that?" Skye pointed at her.

Skye looked like a magazine ad in her yellow sunflower print dress and loose blonde hair. Tulsi looked down at her muscular padded suit, the pink flesh tone faded and pilled with age. She held the head under her arm, the horns wilted thanks to the many years of wear. "It's the Salem State University mascot."

"Did you go there or something?" Skye's friend asked.

"Part time." More like a class here and there.

"What does that costume have to do with this?" Skye swept her arm over the small jars of spices.

"My daughter is involved in the community." Devi patted Tulsi's shoulder. "It's a nice way to keep the kids occupied."

"That's so sweet," Skye said.

"How do you know Tulsi?" Devi asked.

"We met when I came into the shop on my way up to Maine. Thought I would stop by as I head back to New York City. These look so yummy." Skye reached for a treat.

Tulsi watched as they dipped, bit into the Granny Smith slice, then oohed over the flavor combination. After their samples, they requested black salt. Aruna glanced at Tulsi.

"We have more at the shop," Devi said. "If you come back in twenty or so minutes, we can hold one for you. My daughter is heading there now to get more."

"Twenty minutes? If you can hold one bottle each for us, that would be great."

"Why all the black salt?" Aruna asked.

"Magic," the friend said. "But then again, you know."

Aruna frowned. "Is one of the Wiccan places using it for a spell of some kind?"

"The magic of black salt. Everyone is talking about it," Skye's friend said. "It's supposed to attract wealth."

Before Aruna could speak, Devi cut her off. "The biggest benefit of black salt is that it helps with acidity and indigestion. I recommend a pinch in warm water first thing in the morning, then waiting at least thirty minutes before eating."

"And if you sprinkle it in the soil of your indoor plants," Skye said, "you can expect your bank account to flourish as well."

"Well, no—"

"Oh, how cute," the friend interrupted, stepping toward Lucas's table. "These look so adorable. Wait, are you both the same business? Like, did you make these with these spices?"

"No," Lucas said.

"Too bad." The young woman pouted. "It would be cool to have magical desserts."

"Don't mind my friend," Skye said. "Junie found your Instagram. Tulsi, I'm so glad you finally decided to take my advice."

Tulsi stopped, Viking head in hand. "What did you say?"

"Your account," Junie repeated. "I love it."

Both Aruna and Devi looked at Tulsi.

"I don't know what they're talking about," Tulsi said. "Honest. But I'll find out."

"If it's bringing in customers," Devi said, "I don't see why that would be a bad thing."

"That's what I told her," Skye interjected.

"We are not hawking our goods," Aruna said. "Putting ourselves out there devalues what we do. I have told you time and again, Tulsi."

"I didn't do it, but I'll see what I can find out." Frustrated, she put the Viking head back on and walked off.

"Bye." Skye waved to her. "Good to see you again."

Tulsi headed to the shop, confused and worried. Why would anyone create an account for Rasa? She ran through a list of people who might do it as a way to help them. She would ask Gemma. Maybe it was part of her marketing plan. By the time she got into the office, Tulsi was thankful for the AC and once again removed the head and left it on the desk before reaching for her bag.

The first thing she did was grab her phone. She found the account after a few tries. It wasn't just on Instagram but also Facebook. There were comments from people who were excited to check out Rasa, with a few going back and forth, validating uses of spices to heal. None of it seemed bad, considering she didn't know who was behind the account.

It looked as though it had been active for a few days, and the follower count was up to a few thousand, which didn't seem like a lot. She made a fist, then relaxed her fingers before she sent off a message through the app to ask who was behind the account. Tulsi didn't want to make it a public thing, because social media conversations could get out of hand. She wasn't wired to be confrontational, even behind a screen name.

Out of curiosity, she found the Pearl's account. It featured pictures of what Lucas was serving at the festival. She read closer, and there were a few hashtags that were similar to the fake Rasa account. It could be a coincidence—they were mostly generic, with the name of the festival, the city. Except one was not random. On fake Rasa it was #Rasabythesea and on Pearl's it was #Pearlbythesea. It felt too similar to discount. Could it have been Lucas? Maybe this was his way of helping them? Or thanking Devi for the welcome basket.

She would have to ask him, which meant talking to him. She ignored the little flutters in her belly at the idea of it. It was business, she reminded herself, her responsibility to figure out if he was involved in any way. Nothing more.

She scratched her sweaty head with an oversize padded finger as she waddled her way through the shop to grab things from Aruna's list. She rummaged around for a box to carry the stock, and as she rose to make her way to the shelf wall to load everything, she spied a man knocking on the front door.

Tulsi shook her head and pointed to the CLOSED sign, but he knocked again. The box under one arm, Tulsi unlocked the door. "We're not open today, but you can go to the park and get what you need from our booth."

"No, I mean, I'm not here for," he stammered as he stared. "I mean, you're . . . sorry, what is it that you're wearing?"

She sighed. "Festival. I'm a mascot. Go down this street to the right, and there's a big park on the other side. All of the shops are set up there."

"It's just . . ." He stared again. "It's really astounding."

"I'm a Viking," Tulsi responded. "The head is in the back."

"No," he said. "I'm sorry. I'm just a little in shock."

"It's a costume," Tulsi said. "Not a big deal."

He paused, took a deep breath, then let it out. "Okay, let me start again. It's not your costume. I'm stunned because you look like someone I used to know."

Tulsi hesitated when he asked if he could come in. Her instinct told her he seemed safe, so she let him in but stayed by the door in case she had to make a run for it. The street was crowded, so she wasn't too worried about not getting help. "Who? Who do I look like?"

He ignored her question. "Rasa. It's an Ayurvedic term, isn't it?"

Tulsi nodded. "It means the six original tastes."

"I know."

There was kindness in his eyes that went along with a distinguished, handsome face.

"I learned that from Devi. That's who you remind me of," he said.

Startled, Tulsi stammered, "You know my mom?"

His mouth opened as if he were the one dealing with shock. "She's your mother. I hadn't realized. I can't believe this, after all these years."

She'd never seen him before. He was taller than her, though not as tall as Lucas. He had features that appeared Indian, with thick black hair cropped short. He was lean but not skinny or toned. Lanky. The wrinkles on his forehead and around his eyes gave him a well-lived look, one that put him in his late forties or early fifties. "How do you know her? Are you a client?" Though she doubted it.

"No. I'm . . . I knew her from . . . it was ages ago," he said. "I suppose it's been long enough that she likely doesn't remember me. I'm in Boston for a few days and learned about this shop, so I came by to check it out. I was curious if there was a connection."

"Just on the off chance?" Tulsi said. "That's a lot of effort."

"Your mom," he said. "She was special."

Tulsi was wary. Devi was a beautiful woman, and if this guy was a stalker, she'd already confirmed too much. "Through Instagram? Is that how you came across our store?"

He laughed. "No. I leave all that to my daughters. I was doing some research around local suppliers of boutique spices and found your website. I thought I would come check it out. I guess a part of me was drawn to the name too. This is all such a remarkable coincidence."

Tulsi said nothing. If he was shady, there was no way he'd get to her mom.

"I didn't get your name," he said.

"And I don't know yours."

"I'm Ashish." He held out his hand. "Most people call me Ash."

Tulsi raised her arm and gave him her puffy, large, pink-fleshed hand. Amused, he took a thumb and shook it. "Do you work here too?"

"Yes," Tulsi said. "Minus the costume."

"Is it a family business?" Ash glanced around.

"In a way." Tulsi put the box still under one arm on the counter and began filling it with bottles of cardamom, mint leaves, and, of course, black salt.

"Your parents have done a wonderful job here."

She paused slightly with a bottle in hand but didn't mention that she had only one parent. Not plural. But it was best not to correct him. She'd once read an academic paper on psychology that mentioned that most people filled in the blanks based on their own biases.

He wandered around the tables and looked at the labels on the jars. "Your stock is unique and very curated. Less processed."

"We take pride in that," Tulsi said.

"I'm in the retail business too," he explained.

Then it clicked. "I get it now. You're here claiming a long-lost friendship with my mom just so you can buy us out." She'd been looking for an exit strategy, and maybe this was it. Not that Aruna ba would ever entertain the mere idea of it. It couldn't hurt to see an offer.

"Not exactly." He cleared his throat. "Are you selling?"

Put on the spot, she couldn't lie. "No. It's that this has happened a few times. Someone will pop in and offer cash. You said you're in retail, and I know that the building is worth a lot of money, and it's a prime location. What do you want to put in here? Novelty store? Souvenirs?"

"It's nothing like that," he said. "I honestly came by to browse. I didn't expect to find you or Devi, for that matter. It's all happenstance." He tucked his hands into the pockets of his slacks. His white button-down shirt was open at the collar. "I would at least like to say hello if she's available. We were once . . . close."

This was news to her. Tulsi knew all Devi's friends. Though she didn't know anything about her mom before Tulsi had been born. "When did you know her?"

He gave a wry smile. "Childhood. We met when we were in elementary school."

Immediately she wanted to know everything. Here was a link to a past her mom and grandmother never spoke about. "I can't imagine her being so little."

"We all are at one time," Ash said. "I know you're busy. I can come back."

"Or you could give me your contact information." Tulsi held herself back from saying she would pass it on to Devi.

"I can AirDrop my number to your phone." He held up his cell when Tulsi nodded.

"Let your mother know," Ash said. "Maybe she'll remember me."

She gave him another curious look.

"I'm going to be in Boston for a few more days." He tucked his phone into the pocket of his dark slacks. "I hope to hear from her."

She gave him a nod and watched as he left. Instead of rushing out, she leaned against the counter. Ash seemed genuinely interested in seeing Devi. What if . . . then she laughed. The idea of her mom and Ash was too silly to even consider. Devi had never gone on a date, not once, during the whole of Tulsi's life. Devi's heart had permanently shattered after the death of Tulsi's father. Though maybe . . . Tulsi picked up the box and let things roll over in her mind. What if she found her mom a match? Turned the tables, so to speak. If her mom had someone else, a partner that she could lean on, someone who would be gentle with her and support her . . . her heart raced. This could be a way, a faster path toward something else. If Devi was busy with someone else, then maybe it wouldn't shatter her mother when Tulsi announced her decision to leave their sacred profession. The more she thought about it, the larger the idea became. By the time she headed back to the booth, Tulsi was smiling. She was finally going to take action.

CHAPTER SEVEN

That evening, once everyone had escaped to their rooms to bask in their window AC, Tulsi quietly came out of her bedroom and glanced around as she approached the attic door. She hadn't told her mom about Ash, not yet. First, she needed to do a little recon. There had to be a yearbook or class photo, anything that might help her learn a little more about the man who wanted to see her mom again.

She couldn't remember the last time she'd gone up to the attic. Hopefully she wouldn't step on any critters who might have made it their home. It was usually Aruna ba who climbed the rickety steps herself to store things she refused to throw away. Devi had once explained that it was because Ba had grown up poor, the not-having-enough-food-to-eat level, that it made it difficult for her to throw anything away. So up in the attic it all went, from old teakettles to broken fans.

With determination, Tulsi turned the knob, pushed the door open, and quickly shut it behind her. Immediately she sneezed. She felt her way around in the darkness and found a light switch that luckily still worked. She climbed up the short flight of steps, using her hand against the wall to guide her. At the top step, she scanned the room. It was grim and dusty and smelled like the inside of an antiques shop that was going out of business. Tulsi looked for another light because the staircase bulb wasn't bright enough for her to see, then saw a long string hanging from the slanted ceiling and tugged it. The bulb was weak but offered enough light for Tulsi to take in her surroundings. Old furniture, worn and splintered, was shoved haphazardly against the walls. One corner had stacks of cardboard boxes. There were chests and a random hat rack that looked like a tall candelabra.

As she made her way around the space, Tulsi stubbed her toe on an ancient typewriter left randomly on the floor. She lifted her leg to rub the pain, then made a mental note to give herself a pedicure, because the current blue polish was chipped and peeling. Her fingernails weren't in great shape, either, and she needed to fix that before she went around to talk to Lucas about Instagram. Not that it was for him. More that if her nails were done, her life was under control.

Tulsi surveyed the room. There had to be something in here that might help her learn more about her mom in grade school. Maybe there were pictures she'd drawn that Ba had kept. She knelt and sifted through a few plastic bins. Mostly there were papers with recipes of blends, notes on potency and effectiveness, uses. She scanned them before shoving them back. Her grandmother would say that one cannot memorize a recipe—tradition held that each Ayurvedic healer had to create their own methods and ways to use spices. The *haath*, which literally translated to "hand," was very important. Effectiveness, potency, and the curative properties of blends relied on the healer's haath, and no two were the same. Tulsi hadn't even attempted to see if she had one.

She began to sift through boxes she'd found stacked in the corner. There were old books, journals, more scribbles of notes. Box after box, but nothing useful. She sighed in frustration. Sweat made her blue tank sticky, and her bare legs were sooty with dust beneath her pajama shorts. The back of her hair stuck to the nape of her neck. The last box was squished and had long lost its shape. The red Staples logo had faded so much that all the vowels had rubbed off. The lid was stuck and took some effort to pull off. She sighed. Old magazines. *Woman's Day. Good Housekeeping. Vogue.* All dated from the early nineties. She sifted through them just for laughs and then realized she had the same pixie haircut as Winona Ryder. She dropped the magazines back in the box.

It was then she spotted a long metal case under the stack. She pulled it out. It was black, rusted, and the edges sharp enough that a corner grazed her knuckle and left a crease of red. This had to be something important, because it had a flimsy lock in the middle. Tulsi grabbed a bobby pin that kept her bangs away from her face and jimmied it into the tiny keyhole. After a minute or so, she felt it give and removed the lock to flip the lid open.

A letter. She gingerly picked up a timeworn envelope, thick, stuffed, and sealed. She held it up, tried to see through the paper for any words or letters. Nothing. Only that it was addressed, ready to be mailed, missing postage and a return address. Tulsi recognized Aruna ba's ragged handwriting because her grandmother dealt with hand tremors for most of her life. But the name, the person the letter was addressed to, was unfamiliar.

Hema Patel, 8 Walnut Avenue, Chicago, IL 60646.

She searched her memory but had nothing. They didn't have a big community of Desis around them. Aruna ba refused to socialize, even though Tulsi knew there were mandir events in Ashland, and sometimes she came across websites advertising garba dance during Navaratri.

"They're gossips and users. We are better by ourselves." It was Aruna ba's response when Tulsi would ask why they didn't participate in these traditional gatherings. It was Rasa or nothing.

Who was Hema Patel? As far as Tulsi knew, they'd never gone to Chicago. Maybe it was a relative. Except, just like Devi and Tulsi, Aruna had been an only child. No siblings. Not even cousins.

Tulsi wanted to tear into it, read what was inside. She hesitated. This didn't belong to her. Plus, she'd come to find out the connection between Ash and her mom. This wasn't her business.

She should put it back. Lock it up. Except. She stared at the envelope. This was information about the past that was never discussed. She rose and restored everything back to the way she found it, then turned off the lights and headed back to her bedroom. The letter was still in her hand.

CHAPTER EIGHT

Tulsi spent the whole next day on autopilot. Business had picked up a little, and a few more customers had mentioned Instagram, but Tulsi's mind had been too preoccupied with the letter that remained sealed. She'd hid it in the box of sweaters in her closet. The fact that she'd done that instead of sharing her find with her mom and ba meant that it was wrong to have it. But she knew they would take it from her, and she would never know who Hema was or what was written to her.

That evening Tulsi found her mom in the small sunroom that faced their backyard. Devi had repurposed it as her studio over a decade ago. The floor was covered in old sheets to catch any paint splatters, finished artwork leaned against the walls, and a few unfinished paintings rested on the floor. The evening sun streamed through the screened porch as Devi worked.

She was perched on her stool, a brush in her hand, dabbing at the mostly blank canvas.

"You're starting something new." Tulsi went in and stood behind her.

"Trying." Devi put the brush down. "I'm waiting for inspiration."

"Blue sky is a good start, even if it's just in one corner."

"I'm blocked," Devi said.

Tulsi put a hand on Devi's shoulder. "Creativity needs a clear mind. Isn't that what you always told me when I tried a new hobby?"

Devi stood and stretched. "I never realized I was so eloquent."

"You have your moments." She gave Devi a quick side squeeze, then wandered the porch to look out to the yard. "It's a nice night. I love that it still stays light this late. Remember how much I hated my nine p.m. bedtimes in the summers?" Tulsi had once met a customer who was on her way to Utqiaġvik, Alaska, for a year to do a dental rotation for the small community up there. She wanted to know what it would be like to live six months in darkness and another six in light.

"And now you crash by ten." Devi rose and moved to stand next to Tulsi. "Beta, are you feeling ill?"

"I'm fine," Tulsi said. "I just came to see how it was going in here."

Devi tucked a stray hair behind Tulsi's ear. "You've been distracted lately. Quieter than usual. If your stomach is off, I can help."

If only this was all tied to something physical, that would be easy to treat. But she knew her mom wouldn't be able to have a conversation about feelings, wishes, or dreams. Those would make Devi uncomfortable. Tulsi wished she could share her restlessness but didn't think her mom could help except to say it would pass. That was their family motto. Every problem, challenge, or conflict would resolve itself as long as they didn't give it any air. Most of the time fights didn't require any reconciliation. Everyone would go to their corners and, a few hours later, pretend it never happened. "Just the weather. It's been so hot that it makes me lethargic."

"Beta, your kapha is out of balance," Devi advised. "A few days of mainly warm food and drink will help. How about I make you saffron milk?"

"I'm still full," Tulsi said. "Your veggie lasagna was great."

Devi laughed. "Now I know you're sick. I'm a barely passing cook. You and Aruna ba are much better. Since it was my turn, I'm happy it was edible."

"Ba and I are alike, aren't we?" Tulsi wanted to be more like her mother. Serene. Happy. Never bothered by anything. Unless it was conflict, then her mom could be easily reduced to tears, which would shut it down. It was an incredible superpower that frustrated Tulsi to no end. "I always wonder why I'm not more like you." She pointed to her black-and-white T-shirt that said WITHOUT A CARE IN THE WORLD in block script before an orange flame.

"You are. In so many ways," Devi said. "We have similar features, our eyes, our height, cheekbones. How many times have people commented that the three of us resemble each other so closely? You are a part of me and Ba."

"I don't mean in the looks department."

"I think you are as lovely on the inside as out," Devi said.

She had that printed on a white T-shirt with pink script. "Maybe I'm like someone else, in the other branch of my family."

Her mom stilled. It was on the tip of Tulsi's tongue to change the subject, give Devi an out, but she stayed silent. Waited for a response. She'd often broached the subject of her father's side of the family and had been met with silence or tears. Eventually it had stopped mattering. Her mom and ba were enough.

"It's a good thing you and Ba share similarities," Devi said. "Both of you are driven and determined. Without the two of you, Rasa wouldn't exist."

Disappointment sat heavy in her heart. If only her mother were able to face the past head-on, a question like who Hema Patel was could be easily answered. Tulsi used to believe she and her mom were like Princess Merida and her mother, the queen, from the Disney story *Brave*. They loved each other so fiercely. They met each other halfway. And eventually it was the queen who supported Merida in pursuing her dream. It was unconditional love, nurturing at its best. And also a fictional movie.

Tulsi tried a different approach. "So Cass, Mercy, and I have been texting about Lucas. They heard about the café from their parents and are excited to check it out when they come for a visit over Christmas. They asked me to sneak a picture of him to send to them."

Devi put her brush down. "He is handsome."

Tulsi gave a head bobble that could mean yes or no.

"He's not too old," Devi said. "I would say about six or so years older than you. That's not a problem, as you're thirty. He's very sweet. I can see the two of you working out well together."

"There's been a lot of talk about me dating, between you and Ba," Tulsi said.

Devi faced Tulsi. "It's been well past time for you to consider it, don't you think? Your only serious relationship was eight years ago."

"I saw on Instagram that Kal started a nonprofit in Uganda. He's happy." She kept her voice light to let Devi know that he wasn't the reason for her lack of interest in that area of her life.

"What about Cass or your other friends?" Devi asked. "Do they know anyone they can introduce you to? They must know more local people, friends from your school days."

Perfect. "How come, um, I mean, *you* never dated? After my father died." She avoided eye contact to give her mom time to adjust to the shift. Devi was less likely to sidestep if she thought Tulsi was simply making conversation.

"I was busy raising you," Devi said. "And my second focus was Rasa. Ba and I worked hard to make it into what it is today."

Tulsi nodded. Devi picked up her brush again and stirred it into a jar of white paint. She waited a few more beats to give Devi time to reset.

"What about after? Once I was grown and Rasa was doing well."

Devi's back was to Tulsi as she stared at the blank canvas. "I was thinking, we should make a list of possibilities for our mother-daughter trip," Devi said. "We're already in the busy season and won't have much time when October comes around."

Tulsi didn't hide her sigh. "We usually go somewhere warm. But maybe something different this year?"

"Maine? Acadia is lovely, and it will be low season, so we could afford to stay somewhere nice," Devi said.

Tulsi didn't care about their annual Thanksgiving vacation. Not right now. "Chicago." She let her frustration push her into goading her mom. Her stomach ached when Devi froze. A sign that she was emotionally uncomfortable. Her mom had a tie to Hema Patel. It was confirmed in the stiff stillness.

"What made you think of Chicago?" Devi dipped her brush in the canister to get rid of the paint. "Didn't we talk about coastal North Carolina? You were watching that show *Outer Banks* this winter, and it looked lovely. We could sit on the beach and listen to the water move in and out."

"We live on the North Shore. We can do that here. Plus, Chicago has great restaurants and museums. It's not too far to cross into Wisconsin. And we've never been." She told herself to stop doubling down but couldn't help herself.

Devi put her brushes away. She wouldn't meet Tulsi's eyes.

"We've done the west and south, but not the middle. It might be fun," Tulsi added.

"Late November isn't the best time to be there," Devi said. "We won't be able to do much. And there is always the risk of a snowstorm canceling flights. It could become a hassle."

"We're used to winter, Mom. We have all the right clothes."

"I'll think about it, but also add somewhere warm to the list." Devi wiped her hands on the washcloth she kept in the pocket of her painting apron, then tucked it back in and unbelted herself out of it. "I don't believe inspiration is going to hit tonight. But forcing myself to paint has given me a mild headache. Nothing to be concerned about. I'll sip warm water until it ebbs."

Her mom had reached her emotional threshold, which meant there wasn't going to be any more conversation about anything.

"Oh, I almost forgot." Tulsi decided she needed to finish what she'd started. "The day of the fair, when I went to Rasa for more supplies, someone stopped by to see you."

Devi paused on her way out of the sunroom. "You didn't mention it."

"It was so busy. Then I was exhausted from being the mascot. And we had a busy weekend at the shop. Sorry I didn't get around to it until now."

"A new client?" Devi asked.

"He said he was a childhood friend of yours." Tulsi kept eye contact with Devi. "His name was Ashish. Ash."

Her mother froze. There was the slightest movement where her hand reached out to touch the doorjamb for support. "I see."

"Do you remember him?" she asked. "He thought maybe not, since it's been a while."

Devi shook her head. "The name, maybe, but . . . I'm not sure. Good night, beta." She turned and left the room. Her mom had lied. Maybe not directly, but her actions didn't match her words. She'd been shocked at the mention of him.

Tulsi glanced around the sunroom. Her mom mostly painted landscapes with edges. Shorelines. Each of her pieces had a boundary, the other side of which was unreachable whether it was a shoreline, the edge of a cliff, a glacier, or a roaring river. She'd always wondered why that was what Devi preferred. Maybe her mom released drama through her art so that she could keep it contained around others.

Nervous, Tulsi wavered. She really shouldn't push her mom outside of her comfort zone. Particularly with a stranger who claimed a former friendship. One that seemed to bother Devi. She leaned her forehead against the screen of the porch. It was as if everything were just slightly out of reach, and she could almost grasp it, if only she could stretch a little farther.

Instead of giving up, she'd keep moving. First, the letter. Then, she'd learn more about Ash.

CHAPTER NINE

Hema—

If this letter finds you, it means I've simmered enough to reach out. I pray for peace but it eludes me. I have yet to find a way to accept all that has occurred between us.

I still have trouble with saffron. I can't reach for it without thinking of the day we decided to pool our meager coins together so we could have a taste of home, just once. We met when we were both adrift, trying to make it in a country so different from the one we left behind. Ten years. I thought I had finally found a family when I met you.

I had lived through so much heartache, and we bonded over our shared losses. The tragedies of our past had shaped us, but together we had found a path to a better future. Sisters of the heart. Best friends.

I can barely write out these words without anger heightening the tremor in my hand. It has taken root, deep within each cell that makes up my body. I am afraid the heat of it will never leave me. Some days, I take comfort in the fact that I will never see you again. Yet, I yearn to reach out. Not for friendship but to show you that I don't need you. That I am a survivor and even your actions failed to destroy me.

It was my dream you stole.

I have no proof. Even noting the dates of all that transpired, I don't have the means to challenge you. Money was always your main object. So much so that you were willing to lose the only person who had been by your side when you were abandoned by your husband.

Now you've lost me. And I hope you suffer. The money that was to be used toward a better life for both of us now serves me. A city that I thought had become my new home will never again be mine. I have started again. In this new place.

I descend from the goddess of Earth. I will find a way to plant roots again. I will make sure to keep away from anyone who offers friendship. I will rebuild. What is it they say in sports? Three strikes? You are the second person who let me believe they cared for me, only to use me. I will not put myself in the path of another one. It has been almost a year and still forgiveness eludes me. I worry my resentment will consume my energy, prevent me from being the healer that would honor all those who came before me.

I hope your greed was worth the devastation you left in your wake.

Aruna

Tulsi sat cross-legged on her bed. Her cheeks wet from her tears. She could feel her grandmother's pain in those words. There was a rawness, a vulnerability, she could never imagine. Aruna ba had a hard shell. It never cracked. And maybe this letter was the reason.

"Tulsi, your phone is vibrating," Aruna ba called out from downstairs. "It's shaking so many times it almost fell from the kitchen counter."

She put the letter back between two sweaters, wiped her face, drank water, then headed down. Her ba was wiping down the island. Tulsi wished she could go and simply hug her. Then she did. Awkwardly.

"What are you doing?" Aruna pulled away from her.

"I was trying something." She scanned the room for her phone.

"Try studying." Aruna put the towel to dry and left the room.

Tulsi retrieved her phone from next to the sink and saw almost forty text messages. All in her friend-group chat. Someone must have news. She grabbed a glass of water, then headed up to her room before settling on her bed.

Cassie: Tulsi, finally! I just followed.

Kir: What's up?

Cassie: Check out @RasaMagic on Instagram.

Mercy: OMG!! Welcome to the 21st Century, Tuls.

Cassie: 50,000 followers!!!! WHAT?!?! You're famous.

Kir: Great hashtag game.

Juls: I don't think it's Tulsi. Did you hire a social media person to promote the shop?

Malik: As if the Guptas would ever add staff.

Cassie: Right?! No Gupta. No Rasa. TULSI ANSWER!

Malik: She probably left her phone somewhere.

Mercy: The only person I know who doesn't carry her phone around with her. Or she lost it. Isn't this like her 8th phone in four years?

Malik: That's why she's only allowed the oldest version. Refurbished.

Kir: At least it's finally an iPhone. Hate those green text bubbles.

Cassie: Don't be the phone police.

Malik: Any bets on how long before we hear from Tulsi?

Cassie: This evening.

Malik: Too vague, Cassiopeia, that's cheating. I'm thinking by eight am.

Kir: Pacific? Eastern? Central?

Malik: All times Mountain because I'm in chaos and need you all to do some math. Closest gets their bar tab covered next reunion.

Mercy: I miss you all. And it's been five years since all of us made it to one place.

Juls: Three. My wedding!! It was so fun.

Mercy: Good chatting, all. Have to get on a conference call. I say tomorrow by 2.

Cassie: How's Hawaii, Kir?

She scanned through the rest of the messages, all with their different guesses on how long it would take Tulsi to respond. She checked the time, and it was 9:00 p.m. ET, 7:00 MT. If she responded now, the closest guess would be Cassie. But she was more distracted by the link that her friend had posted. She clicked over, and it was the Instagram account for Rasa. She hadn't checked it in a few days, and now there was another post. What was more concerning was that her friends had found it. She didn't know how or who had made it, but the fact that it was spreading didn't seem like a good thing.

She looked at the followers and didn't recognize any names outside of her friends. Who was doing this? And why? Tulsi went in search of her grandmother.

"Ba." Aruna was in the living room, reading a Gujarati novel.

"What was all that buzzing about?" She didn't look up.

"One of my friends sent me a link to that Instagram account for Rasa." Tulsi plopped into the leather chair on the other side of the coffee table. The room was warm because the AC was set on low, and the backs of her thighs, below her shorts, stuck to the seat.

Aruna, on the matching sofa across from her, put down the book. "I told you to get rid of it. We are not that kind of store. Rasa is pure and for our customers. Personal, not for faceless masses. We don't want the wrong kind of attention."

"It doesn't seem to be malicious," Tulsi said. "All the posts are about how to use spices. A little misguided, maybe. Like this one that says ghee is a superfood. Ha. I mean, it's good for some things but not universal."

"We don't sell ghee," Aruna said. "This is false advertising."

Tulsi held up her phone. "I'm not the one posting."

"Tell them to stop."

"I sent messages," Tulsi said. "No one has replied."

"Can't you report it? Maybe the police can help."

Tulsi viewed the posts again, tried to find anything familiar that could help.

"Is it one of your friends? Did you ask them to do this?" Aruna asked.

"If I had, why would I pretend I don't know anything?"

"You've been doing a lot of acting lately," Aruna said.

Tulsi looked up. Her grandmother didn't look away. Her heart raced. Aruna knew that she was up to something. "I'll try to get it deleted." She heard the fart-like sound as she peeled her legs off the leather.

She left the room and went out to the back steps. There was a mild breeze in the air, and it helped her calm down. If Aruna was onto her, realized Tulsi was faking being incompetent, she would have to act fast. Her grandmother was formidable when determined and wouldn't allow Tulsi to abandon the role she'd been created to play.

Forget Instagram, for now. Tomorrow she planned to get in touch with Ash.

CHAPTER TEN

The next morning, alone at Rasa, Tulsi wrote, crossed out, found different words, scrunched up the paper, and started fresh. Texting a stranger was hard, especially when you wanted something from them. Ash had likely left Boston by now. Instead of beating herself up for waiting so long to reach out, she kept her head down, tried different phrases. Was "hi" appropriate, or should she go with a more formal "hello"? Ash or Ashish? And then what? How do you ask someone if they are available? Though not for her. Well, to see her, but also, he'd mentioned daughters, so maybe he was married. Except the way he said Devi's name made her wonder.

She started again. A blank piece of paper would clear her mind. Luckily it was a quiet Tuesday afternoon, and Aruna had gone to one of her suppliers, an independent merchant that only her grandmother knew. Aruna liked to keep her local sources mysterious, at least from Tulsi. Her grandmother often came back with a satchel or two of the "special ones." Apparently all would be revealed, along with other healer-only secrets once Tulsi passed the test. She suspected it was a ruse by Aruna ba to motivate her. But Tulsi didn't really wonder. She knew of the ones they bought from in bulk, along with everything Rasa needed to keep the doors open. The truth was, what they sold was curated, not mysterious. It was all part of the aura that her grandmother had created around Rasa. People wanted the extraordinary, the uncommon. It was much to her grandmother's credit that Rasa had survived for over twenty-five years.

The letter had implied that Tulsi's ba had had to start over. Even though she didn't know the whole of it, Tulsi appreciated what Aruna had done here. The guilt of what Tulsi was doing became heavier, deeper. The last few nights, instead of sleeping, she'd toggled between giving in to her heart and accepting it all or staying the course without breaking her grandmother's. For now, she rationalized, she needed to take a few more steps. For herself.

She'd added a step to her morning routine and scrolled through Instagram. At first it was simply to check on the Rasa posts. Then she'd discovered other accounts. There were people who were doing all the things. Mostly women who were young, blonde, and photogenic. They looked like models who never experienced lost luggage or secondary screenings.

She'd also come across Savasana Skye's account and followed her. She posted mostly about wellness and tips on how to seek out remedies and retreats in interesting locations. Skye's most recent one was curing jet lag with hot water and ashwagandha. Tulsi almost commented that it was the wrong use of the plant, that buttermilk with rock salt would be more restorative. She didn't because Cassie had given Tulsi some social media tips, and one was "don't engage." It was safer to lurk.

Then Tulsi messaged Skye privately, offered her a better recipe that would be effective. It was the least she could do, and Skye had seemed open to wanting to promote natural healing. Once she closed out the app, she got back to drafting her text to Ash. Unfortunately she was interrupted when a few people came into Rasa. Tulsi smiled and greeted them. No one she knew, so they were likely tourists. Two adults and two teenagers. The man stayed by the door and scrolled on his phone, while the woman and teens looked around. They looked like a family. Parents, siblings.

"Hi." The woman approached Tulsi. "I'm wondering where you keep the magic spices. My daughter is having some problems with focus and concentration, and maybe there's a blend that can help her with schoolwork. You know, the special ones."

Tulsi furrowed her brow. "You can try saffron, make a milk drink with sugar and almonds, which can help with memory. We have a variety in the glass case." She tapped the glass counter to show the vials of various saffron threads. "We have sargol, which is more common, negin, which is richer, and also pricier. My favorite is Kashmiri because it has a lovely fragrance."

The woman straightened. "I see. But which ones have a spell cast over them? Or is there a secret code or password that I'm missing?"

Tulsi almost laughed. "I know this area is known for things like that. There's a crystal shop around the corner, and Gemma could point you to something that may help. Our spices are for Ayurvedic healing. It's more homeopathy than magic."

"Bailey?" the woman called out to one of the teenagers. "Are we in the right place?"

Bailey approached the counter. "Rasa. Salem, Massachusetts."

"That's us," Tulsi said.

"Here." Bailey held up her screen for Tulsi.

It was a TikTok video. An account that claimed to be Rasa and talked about spice magic. The video showed a glass with powders being added, then filtered water. The voice-over was a robotic voice that said, "For all that ails you, the magic will cure." Tulsi tried to keep steady even though she was panicking on the inside, not knowing who was doing this or why.

"I'm sorry," Tulsi said. "That must be a mistake. That's not our account. In fact, we're not online at all."

"You have a website," the older woman said.

"Yes, just . . . um . . . only that," Tulsi said.

"Is there a manager here?" the woman asked.

Tulsi rolled her shoulders back. "This is my family's shop. I assure you, what you see is all that we have."

"Really? Because I also saw a post about mixes for 'special customers.'" Bailey used finger quotes.

"It's, yes, we do," Tulsi said. "But it's not . . ."

"Oh, so just not for us," the woman said.

Tulsi didn't know what was happening, but she wished her grandmother would hurry back and deal with these people. They were too loud, and she worried that their frustration was morphing into anger. "We cater to everyone. Our blends require consultation."

"See, Mom," Bailey said. "I told you they have special stuff they don't tell people about."

"It's not a secret," Tulsi said.

"Then give us one for focus," the woman said. "From the special stash."

Tulsi shook her head. Did they not hear her?

"Oh, I think I know what you're saying." The woman pulled Bailey closer and wrapped her arm around the teen. "It's because we're white, right?"

Tulsi was completely taken aback. "What?"

"Is there a problem?"

Tulsi spun around at the voice behind her. She'd never been so happy to see Lucas. She didn't care how he'd appeared but was grateful for the backup. "Honestly, there is no magic here."

"Don't worry, I'll be posting about this rudeness." They glared at Tulsi and Lucas, then left.

Relieved, she unclenched her fingers. "Thanks. How did you . . . ?"

"Oh, your mom wanted me to bring over these paint swatches." Lucas held them out to her. "For redoing your office. I heard raised voices. Came to check it out."

"Swatches?" She took them from him.

"You okay?"

They'd spoken at the same time.

Tulsi laughed. "All good."

He glanced at her shirt. "Peanuts peeking out in their shells?"

She looked down. "Ha, yes, 'in a nutshell.' Get it?"

"Sure."

Though his expression said he didn't. "I like clichés."

He turned to leave.

"Wait." Tulsi didn't know why she called out. "Thanks."

He nodded. Waited.

She looked down at the swatches. "What color did you pick?"

"Something called 'breath of fresh air,'" he said. "Blue."

"Oh, this one." She held up a swatch. "It's pretty."

"Your mom," he said. "She's been coming by. I don't mind it."

"She has a way of making everyone feel taken care of," Tulsi said.

"She brings me lunch every day," Lucas said.

"I'm sorry." The thought of Devi's feeding her barely edible recipes to someone opening a restaurant made her laugh.

"It's not bad," he said.

"And that means she's won you over," Tulsi added. "It's what she does best. She's so sweet and kind that you can't help but adore her."

"You're lucky to have her," he said.

She swallowed the lump in her throat. "Yes. I am. What about your mom? What's she like?"

"Absent." Lucas shifted. "I have to get back."

"Right," she said. "You're not a people person."

He gave her a look, then hesitated. "I spend a lot of time by myself."

As if that explained everything. "I can talk to anyone about anything." As long as it's not to her mom or ba. "Was it because of the marines?"

He leaned against the doorjamb. "No. I've always been like that."

"More a listener and observer," Tulsi said.

He gave her a little smile. "I have better chats in my head."

"Oh, what about?" She leaned against the counter, her back to the front door of Rasa.

"Mostly music, recipes," Lucas said. "Best place to hide a body."

"That's awesome. Wait, what?"

"Kidding," he said.

"Lucas Sharma, did you just make a joke?" Before she could help herself, Tulsi was charmed.

"Anyway, all good here?"

She said yes. She'd kept him long enough. "Thanks."

She meant it. Lucas had snapped her out of the mood that family had put her in. And even though he was hot and might secretly be funny, it was a good reminder that he wasn't interested in prolonging the conversation. She had enough of living in silence, each in their own room, without adding another person into the quiet.

And she had messages to send. She picked up her cell phone. Enough of overthinking it, she needed to hit send and see where things stood with Ash. If he wasn't an option, then she'd have to find another way to get her mom settled into a relationship. She was more convinced than ever that if Devi had someone, it would be easier to leave her.

CHAPTER ELEVEN

After she closed Rasa, Tulsi walked along the cobblestones of Essex Street, then turned the corner onto the major artery she crossed to get to the residential side. The air was less thick, and a soft breeze ruffled her hair. The short walk home helped clear her mind from the day as she meandered through people who would come to a sudden stop for a photo or to read a sign. Based on the backup at the intersection, the traffic was heavy, and cars slowly rolled through the light when it was their turn. How many times had Tulsi crossed this road without noticing anything? Her surroundings were so familiar that she no longer took notice. The CVS on the corner, the restaurants, some that changed names, but she couldn't remember when.

Luckily, the rest of the day had passed without any other incidents. Ash had responded to her text immediately, which Tulsi took as a good sign. Even better, he'd asked about Devi. Tulsi traded a few messages with Ash, and he promised to reach out next time he was in the Boston area. She hoped it would be soon.

She rubbed her breastbone with her thumb. All afternoon she'd been dealing with indigestion. Even a palmful of ajwan seeds with water didn't help relieve her discomfort. Her mom was right—Tulsi's kapha was out of balance. She couldn't remember the last time she had even meditated. But maybe this was what it was supposed to feel like when searching for an alternative to passive acceptance.

The letter her grandmother had written to Hema Patel had inspired Tulsi. She'd assumed so much about their life before her. That they'd always been in Salem, for example. She'd studied the letter more than the *Charaka Samhita* at this point. They'd left Chicago. Aruna and Hema had known each other for ten years. They must have been close if the betrayal caused her grandmother to leave, start somewhere else. That was what gave Tulsi hope. She and Aruna ba were similar, and if her ba could do it, so could Tulsi. Venturing out on her own was possible.

Maybe she'd underestimated her grandmother. She might even understand Tulsi's need to explore. If only Aruna and Devi were more open about their lives and their past, then she could ask all the questions and know more answers. The sound of bumper-to-bumper traffic muted as she turned the corner onto a tree-lined street. Tulsi stroked the bristly spikes of a hedge she passed. When she reached their house, Aruna was in the front yard. It was an evening ritual for her. While Devi prepared dinner, her grandmother watered the yards in the front and back. Ba had divided and reserved the street-facing plot for flowers, and the large yard behind the house was tilled for vegetables and herbs. No pool or big deck for them.

"How are the roses doing?"

"This heat is making it impossible for them to stay lush." Aruna adjusted her wide straw hat. "Dried petals everywhere."

"Hopefully the new fertilizer helps." Tulsi stood on the steps. "The white and yellow are thriving."

"It's the red that's giving me trouble." Aruna pinched a dead stem. "Pricking my skin when I try to untangle the vines. I don't know why I bother."

"Because they're pretty and you love gardening," Tulsi said.

"Sometimes. When your effort is rewarded by nature, it makes sense." Aruna pinched off a dead bulb. "But when the bushes are like this, it's wasted energy."

"You're not giving enough credit to your special soil mixture." Tulsi pulled her tote off her shoulder and let it rest on the stoop, the strap in her hand.

"It's the same I use every year." Aruna adjusted the chin strap of her hat.

Tulsi sat on the stoop. "It's a nice evening. I can smell the sea all the way here."

"Rain is coming."

Tulsi grinned. "You sense it."

"Go ahead and roll your eyes," Aruna said. "If you focused on your healing work, you would be able to hone such skills."

She did not want to go down this path. "You've had a lot more years of practicing."

"I had no choice."

Tulsi nodded. "Because your mother, my great-grandmother, died young." It was all Tulsi knew, no further details.

Aruna wiped her forehead with the edge of her sleeve. "I was barely eighteen. I prepared her body for the funeral pyre."

Tulsi let the silence sit. "I can't imagine not having you or Mom. I was so naive at eighteen. I don't even think I knew how to file taxes, much less run a business. How did you figure it out?"

Aruna paused in her work and opened her canteen to sip water. "Didn't have a choice. I had no one else."

"And you came to America," Tulsi said.

"More like sent here." Aruna recapped the bottle and tucked it into her gardening basket.

That was new information. "But you said you didn't have a family."

"Why all these questions?"

Tulsi kept her eyes on the house across the street. "I guess it's a night for it. The two of us have been so busy between the lessons and Rasa. We haven't spent much time together in a long time."

Aruna reached over and patted Tulsi's hand. "Fine. Let's talk."

It stunned her, this frankness and invitation. Tulsi didn't even know where to begin. "Why were you sent here?"

Aruna went back to clear the dried leaves from the rosebushes. "I was pregnant with your mother. Unmarried. Lived on charity. Then I was handed a one-way ticket on Air India."

So much in such few words. Tulsi couldn't process much less formulate her next question.

"I never said I was a conventional sort of woman," Aruna added.

Tulsi shook her head. "No. It's just, I didn't know. Does Mom?"

Aruna ba nodded. "She does."

"And the man, Mom's father?"

Aruna sighed. Didn't answer.

Tulsi prepared for a change in subject when her grandmother picked up shears.

"My mother rented a room from him, one room where we both lived," Aruna said. "She had been unmarried when pregnant with me. When she died, it was a way for me to have a roof over my head."

The idea of what her grandmother had been through at eighteen made it difficult to talk. Ask any questions. This was more than Tulsi had ever imagined. "Did he, my mom's father, did he die? Was it his family that gave you the plane ticket?"

Aruna didn't say more as she focused on detangling rose vines.

Tulsi sat with this new knowledge. "I always imagined our ancestors like the paintings of Krishna frolicking with the milkmaids. All the spice healers dancing and singing by the river, sifting through grain, picking herbs to grind."

"Not that I ever knew," Aruna said. "This is what I've been trying to teach you. Our work, it's selfless. I see you looking for something more, something that will bring you pleasure. We're not meant for such things. We have a duty to heal others' ailments using our traditional methods. My mother instilled that in me. She told me how important it was for our spices to be known for more than seasoning food. That nature should not be forgotten or replaced by processing and manufacturing."

"Why didn't you explain it to me like that?" Tulsi thought back to all the lessons where it was stressed that she just learn the things because it was what she was born to do.

"I was showing you," Aruna said. "With the way we live and how we work."

Tulsi didn't know what to say. This was the deepest conversation she'd ever had with her grandmother. "Thank you. For sharing this with me."

Aruna nodded. "Maybe now you will stop pretending not to learn."

Tulsi made a fist and released her fingers. "I'm not ready."

"Whatever you're waiting for," Aruna said, "it won't come."

Her chest constricted at the plainspoken words. "I want more." Then she realized she might have admitted something her grandmother wasn't ready to hear. "Time. I need a little more time."

"Sharad Purnima," Aruna said. "The most auspicious full moon in the Hindu calendar. This year it falls on October 15. You have until then."

"What? That's less than three months."

"You're ready." Aruna dropped the shears in her basket. "It's time you accepted it. Our sole responsibility is to preserve and spread the healing power of nature. If you're searching for fulfillment, take your place. We are the descendants of Dharti. Ours isn't a frivolous life. Happiness is reserved for Krishna's milkmaids."

Tulsi stayed on the stoop as Aruna ba gathered her things and went from the side of the house to the backyard. She could understand more fully now. It wasn't a curse. This solitary, single life was the shape of her family. Three thousand years, or so the story goes. Yet Tulsi thought that *she* would be the one to break the cycle.

Except. She had to believe it was possible. People weren't allotted roles in life from goddesses. They had choices. One was to perpetuate the status quo, which had caused at least three generations of suffering that she knew about. Who knows how many more. She would destroy the cycle.

CHAPTER TWELVE

Tulsi sat at a small round table near the back of the busy coffee shop. Boston was typically more crowded and louder than her little corner of Massachusetts. A constant stream of people came through for their orders of coffee or an occasional pastry. If her nerves were calmer, Tulsi could settle in and imagine herself as one of them. Places to go, people to see. She wished she'd worn that T-shirt, but this meeting required a little more effort, so she'd put on one of her two summer dresses.

Even with traffic down 93, she'd arrived early. A tall man, with a backpack and a Boston College T-shirt, asked if he could share her table. Apologetically, Tulsi told him she was waiting for someone. In high school, she'd gone on a few local college tours with Cassie and Mercy. Only to keep them company, knowing she would never attend one. When they came back to Salem during their freshman years, both of her friends had bought her sweatshirts with their university logos as a present. Tulsi never wore them. They were still in a box in her closet. She couldn't even pretend by walking around in them.

At least she never had to worry about choosing a major. She glanced up and saw Ash enter. He gave her a small wave as he made his way toward her table.

"Can I get you anything?"

She shook her head and told him she had time if he wanted to grab something for himself. When he went to the counter, she saw that he was dressed in a nice suit that fit well. He wore no rings, especially not a wedding band.

"I'm so glad you reached out." He sat across from her, his small black coffee in his hands. "I thought maybe your mother would have joined you."

"Um . . . Rasa is closed today, so she's working on some client stuff." Tulsi explained about their regular customers and the way her mom made special healing blends.

"And you?" he asked. "Do you have your own clients?"

She shook her head. "I'm better with the bookkeeping and the business part. I haven't officially leveled up." She didn't openly talk about her family lineage, because it was complicated and sometimes people laughed at the idea of it. Tulsi suspected outsiders thought her family was pretending or performing a part to be more than what they were.

"I see. I imagine Devi has." Ashish sipped his coffee. "She was really good with that stuff when I knew her. One time I had a cold that wouldn't go away. I was so congested. Sounded like a cross between Darth Vader and Batman. But I was an awkward teenager. Let's just say I was not cool enough for that to work. Devi made me take this steam, my face over the hot water, a towel over my head. There was stuff in it, I think, ginger, salt, maybe black pepper. Anyway, it cleared everything out in two days." His eyes crinkled when he talked about Devi.

"I add ajwan and turmeric to it as well. To boost immunity."

"Did Devi not want to see me?" Ash asked.

Tulsi sat on her hands to keep from fidgeting. She'd already ripped up the straw sleeve while she'd waited for him. "I haven't said anything to her about meeting you today."

He raised his brow.

"I'm protective," Tulsi said. "I wanted to know a little about you first."

He nodded. "Smart."

She relaxed, glad he understood. "Thanks."

Ash twirled his half-full coffee mug. "I can start with the basics. I am gainfully employed, which requires me to travel more than I'd like. I drink, but socially. Don't smoke, never have. I'm diligent in getting my annual physical. And I've never been arrested."

Tulsi laughed. "Are you giving me your biodata?"

He looked up at her. "It's been so long since I've heard that term, but it sounds like it, doesn't it? Let's see, what did I leave out? I'm five eleven. Only child. I have no idea what caste I was born into. Oh, and I have two daughters. Twins."

"Are you married?"

He sipped his coffee. "Widowed."

"I'm so sorry for your loss." She almost reached out to touch his hand.

"Thank you. It was sixteen years ago," he said. "She died in childbirth."

Her heart broke for his loss.

"Raising Bina and Lina helped," he added. "I had, have, a big family from their mom's side. Lots of support. Sometimes too much."

"I don't," Tulsi said. "It's just the three of us."

"Devi isn't married." Ash relaxed against the back of his chair. "Your father?"

Tulsi shook her head. "Never had one. I mean, I don't mean to sound casual about it. He died in an accident before I was born."

"I'm sorry," he said. "That has to be hard. I've made sure my daughters know as much as possible about what their mother was like. They have pictures of Shefali. Whenever I spot something, like Bina's allergy to tomatoes, I tell her Shef had the same. I hope your mom did that for you, for your dad."

It was painful to know Devi hadn't. Tulsi didn't even have a name. "How do you know my mom? You said you met in elementary school?"

"I was eight, Devi was a year behind me," he said. "She had pigtails, one on each side of her head. I, of course, couldn't resist tugging them.

Most girls would have retaliated. Not Devi. She just changed her hairstyle to braids down her sides."

"She still wears it long," Tulsi said.

"We didn't have the same classes but always ate lunch together. We lived in opposite directions from our school, but I would walk her home. Then we would do homework together. Math was the hardest for her."

"Me too," Tulsi said.

"I can't tell you how many times I had to break down algebra. The x and y always stumped her."

"You knew her in high school too?"

He nodded. "Yeah, until I went off to Stanford. It's hard for me to picture her now. I have glimpses from growing up together. We went to her prom."

"You dated?"

He blushed. "No. It wasn't an option for us."

"Why not?"

"It's different now," he said. "When we were young, there were still expectations in terms of arranged marriages. We weren't exactly free to have girlfriends or boyfriends. It was still biodatas and matrimonial dates, fix-ups. We liked each other, as friends. I had a crush on her but couldn't do anything about it. I can't believe I'm having this conversation. It's taking me back."

"Sorry," she said. "I'm a curious person. Cassie, my best friend, calls it that whenever I say I'm nosy. She doesn't like negative self-talk."

"That's a good friend," he said.

"My mom is still beautiful," Tulsi said. "Barely has any wrinkles."

"No grays like me?" He rubbed a hand through his salt-and-pepper hair.

"You wear it well."

"Lina, my younger daughter by six minutes, has been pestering me to get it dyed," he said. "Says she's not ready for her dad being an old man."

"I don't think of my mom like that, but she only has a few gray hairs here and there," Tulsi said. "She's very young looking. Occasionally a customer will think we're sisters."

"I don't mean to rush things," he said. "No pressure. But what do you think? Would you be okay with me coming by Rasa sometime?"

She had only one more question. "Did something happen between you, or did you sort of drift apart?"

He finished the last of his coffee. "The latter. Devi and I never had any sort of fight or even an argument. She never engaged in that. If she was irritated or annoyed with me, we wouldn't see each other for a few days, and then it was like nothing ever happened."

Same as now. Tulsi wished her mom would yell, get it all out. The icing out was the worst. "How long are you in Boston?"

"Actually, I came here just to meet you," he said. "I could stay an extra day or so."

"You don't live nearby? I figured you were in Providence or maybe New York."

"No," Ash said. "I'm in Chicago."

She took a minute to sip her drink. Focused on the sweetness of the strawberries to process her twirly brain. Chicago. That made sense. "Right, they lived there for a while. My grandmother and Mom."

"Your grandmother. She's still with you?"

"You knew her as well? I mean, of course you did, since you and my mom did homework together at her house."

Ash nodded. "They were always close, a package deal in every way. I didn't realize they'd moved here," Ash said. "Not until I saw you that day."

"Do you know why they left?"

He shook his head. "Like I said, I'd gone off to Stanford. When I came home for the summer, they'd already left. It was before Facebook and cell phones. Devi was just gone."

"You cared about her." This time she did reach out and put her hand on his forearm.

He put his palm on top of hers. "I did. Devi had this way about her that made me feel . . . it's tough to explain. It was like I wanted to keep her safe and bring her joy. I lived for the moments when she would laugh at a joke I made."

"I get that," she said. "When she's proud of something I've done or the way she brushes my bangs out of my face, it fills my heart with joy. When she's happy, I'm ecstatic."

His phone vibrated, and Ash ignored it. "What do you think? Do I pass the test?"

"With flying colors," she said. "I think she would love to see an old friend."

CHAPTER THIRTEEN

Tulsi watched her grandmother from across the kitchen island. She had softened toward Aruna since the letter and their conversation on the stoop. Maybe her ba was mellowing with age, though according to Mrs. Bishop, seventy was the new fifty whenever she referred to her age.

"Are you paying attention?"

"Yes," she lied.

"Now this is to balance the vata dosha," Aruna said. "What else would you add to this mix for a healthy tea?"

The answers were never at the tip of her tongue; she had to think. There were so many spices, so many concepts. "Vata is air and space. If turmeric is the base, then black pepper and fennel. No, cinnamon."

Aruna stayed silent. No hints. No help. "Black pepper and cinnamon. Final answer."

"Good." There was a small smile on Aruna's face. "How would you use this blend?"

"Milk, add it to warm milk." Wrong. And she was tired of pretending to not know. "No, that's not right. Vegetables. Make a shaak and use the mix as seasoning."

"Excellent," Aruna said. "Which kind?"

Torn, Tulsi calmed herself with a few deep breaths. Ba had been onto her plan of faking it. What she didn't know was that Tulsi had a new one. "Okra."

"It's remarkable how much you've improved. Would you add potatoes to the okra to add a little heft and ease digestion?" Aruna pushed the bowl with the mix toward Tulsi.

There was a hint of snark in her grandmother's tone, and it made Tulsi happy to see this side of Aruna ba. It was almost as if they were back in the garden, picking herbs and chattering away those long-ago early mornings.

"Sweet or regular?" Tulsi asked.

"You tell me."

She gave in. "No potatoes."

"Correct."

The pride in her grandmother's eyes dashed her happiness. Made her feel suffocated. The image of a teenage Aruna standing next to her mother's funeral pyre as it burned hurt her heart in a way that made her want to cave and take her place in line.

"Name four dry fruits to avoid for those who want to keep the vata dosha in balance."

"I can think of only two. Figs and dates," Tulsi said.

"Prunes. Raisins," Aruna added. "It's not enough to memorize. You have to know instinctively. Ayurveda is not like Western medicine, where you write out a pharmacy prescription. This is for the individual, customized based on balancing the doshas and healing a specific person."

"Is this how you learned from your mother? Did she quiz you all the time like this?"

Aruna used a small spoon to gather coriander powder that had spread around the small tray. "No. She preferred to tell stories, ones she'd heard from her own mother. Mostly to share how remarkable we are. That we may not be seen as worth anything, but our power was in our craft. Ma would explain a few things here and there, but for me, it was mostly watching her. My knowledge grew while teaching Devi. That's when I found books like *Charaka Samhita*."

"You didn't have any reference books when you learned?" Tulsi waved her hand toward the bookshelf behind the big dining table.

Aruna shook her head. "Gujarati or Hindi collections were hard to find in America. We didn't have Amazon back then. I had to learn English first, then how to translate what I knew. Devi helped."

"And I never have."

"You used to pick herbs with me," Aruna said. "Dry them. You loved the way your hands smelled of thyme and rosemary after we sorted and bottled them."

"Decades ago," Tulsi said.

"But it's not too late," Aruna said.

The pressure made her tense. "I'm not ready."

"You have until mid-October, Tulsi," Aruna said. "Figure out a way."

It was the hardest question she'd ever asked. "What happens if I . . . don't?"

"Then you'll have to tell your mother that it all ends with her."

Tulsi cast her eyes down on her lap. Her heart ached because of the choice she faced.

CHAPTER FOURTEEN

Tulsi heard the lid of the dumpster clang open and rushed out to see if it was Lucas. Once in the alley, she flagged him down. He was in his usual uniform—long gray T-shirt with paint-splattered cargo shorts.

"Hey." She was slightly out of breath and told herself it was because she'd run to catch him before he headed inside.

"Between the lines." He read her pale-green T-shirt. "That's a song, right?"

She glanced down. "Oh, uh, not sure. I don't know a lot about music. Ba, sorry, my grandmother, listens to ghazels and old Bollywood movie songs. My mom prefers classical cello when she's painting. I don't even have a paid Spotify account. Sorry, I'm babbling."

"You apologize too much," he said.

"We've only had three conversations," she argued. "How would you know?"

"You've done it in each of them." He lifted a black garbage bag and hurled it into the blue dumpster. She got distracted by the way his stomach flexed with the movement.

"Anyway, I wanted to talk to you." Lucas caught her staring, and she quickly looked away. "About your publicity."

He frowned.

"I was just wondering," she said. "Are they—have you asked them to do anything for Rasa?"

"Do you want me to?" He tossed another bag into the bin.

"It's like they weigh nothing to you," Tulsi murmured. "The bags, I mean. Sorry. I mean not sorry. What were we talking about?"

He laughed. "Pick that one up." He pointed to a bag propped against the base of the metal waste container.

She did. "Oh, it is light." Then she tossed it in just like he had.

"Mostly packaging that you can't recycle," he said. "Publicity?"

"Right." Tulsi grabbed her phone from the back pocket of her jeans. "I was wondering if you'd asked them to promote Rasa by setting up some social media accounts?"

He shook his head. "Why?"

"It's strange." She opened an app and turned her screen toward him. "This account and other ones, someone started them. They're using similar hashtags as the Pearl. See this one? #RasaSalem, it's the same as #PearlSalem."

"Yeah, that's just a coincidence," he said. "I have a small marketing budget, and the publicist is mostly doing outreach to bloggers and restaurant reviewers."

She tucked her phone back into her pocket. "I thought maybe since you and my mom have been spending some time together—"

"She brings me food and compliments my work," he said.

"No, it's great. She's like that, remember I told you? I meant that you may have been trying to be neighborly."

"I'm not the type to go behind someone's back," he said. "Even if it is to be nice."

Disappointed, Tulsi let out a loud sigh. The accounts had become a series of frustrations. More and more posts were popping up from Rasa, and she had no idea who was behind it. She'd even messaged Skye to ask if there was a way to find out. But her online friend hadn't offered any suggestions. Though *friend* was a stretch. Mostly Tulsi answered Skye's questions about which spices could be mixed together for cures.

"What do they post about you?"

"Mostly half truths," Tulsi said. "Yesterday it was about how turmeric is an anti-inflammatory, which is right, but then it goes and says it can prevent cancer, which no. There is a connection between inflammation and disease, but we would never make that sort of claim."

"And you've told them to stop?"

"Several times." She squeezed her fingers into her palms. "Zero response. I've even reported them. Nothing works."

"You're worried," he said.

Tulsi released her fingers. "We're getting more and more people coming in to ask for homeopathic treatments for serious medical conditions because of our, or those, posts. We try to correct them. I even made a sign that says we are not responsible for what's posted. That those aren't our accounts, but people ignore them."

He crossed his arms in front of him.

She wanted to lean on Lucas's broad shoulders. "In a way, it means more foot traffic and sales. I suppose that's a good thing," she said.

"But it feels wrong. Because it's not for the right reasons or the right way."

"Exactly." She wanted to reach out and touch his arm. Instead, she tucked her hands in her front pockets. "What's worse is that I don't know why. Like, are they trying to help or hurt us? Who is it and why Rasa?"

"I'm sorry."

It calmed her. The way he said it. His voice soft. She glanced up, and their eyes met. His gentleness didn't match his looks or pose. The way he stood, his feet firm. There was little fidgeting or shifting. A steadiness Tulsi didn't believe she could ever achieve. "Thank you."

"You want me to ask my publicist to look into it?"

Tulsi said no. It was her problem to solve, and she didn't want him to spend more of his small marketing budget on her problem. "I'll figure it out."

He gave her a nod and headed toward his door. She wanted to stop him, invite him to lunch or a walk along the water. But Rasa was busy, and Tulsi needed to go back inside and relieve her mom. She gave a small wave that he didn't see, her stomach heavy with attraction and fear. Tulsi didn't know if the latter was because of how drawn she was to Lucas or the secret social media accounts.

CHAPTER FIFTEEN

A steady stream of customers moved through Rasa, and Tulsi scrambled to restock and get organized. The influx had been good for business, and their profits looked similar to previous years. Tulsi still had to do the math, but the number of sales made her feel better, even if some of them had come from rogue social media. The account, while giving out misinformation at times, was actually helping Rasa. Since her chat with Lucas, she'd come to believe that whoever was behind it didn't seem to have malicious intent.

"Hey, Mom."

"Honey, I'm so sorry I'm late." Devi tossed the dupatta of her white cotton salwar over her shoulder and pinned it to keep it in place. "I can't believe I slept in. You should have woken me before you went downstairs."

"I'm glad you got some rest," Tulsi said. "We've been busy."

"Isn't that great?" Devi gave Tulsi a side hug. "I told you things would improve."

"Don't tell me you're catching Ba's sixth sense," Tulsi said.

"We all have it, beta. You need to believe."

Tulsi was glad to see her mom in a great mood. Devi seemed lighter. They spent a few hours helping customers until there was a lull. Then they silently organized what had been misplaced in the chaos of shopping.

"Have you gone next door lately?" Devi asked.

"No," Tulsi said. "Is it coming along?"

"Very nicely," Devi said. "The paint I helped Lucas choose is perfect for what he's making of the place. He's such a determined man. He works so hard and pushes himself to make it exactly how he wants it. He's such a determined and ambitious man."

Tulsi tested the waters and teased. "Ma, is that why you keep going over there? To make a match between Lucas and me?"

Devi waved her off. "He's lonely, and I think he likes the fact that I check in on him and bring him lunch. He doesn't seem to have any family, at least not any close by. If you gave him a chance, you never know. He is very likable."

Tulsi diverted her mother. "Speaking of . . . what about you?"

"Me?"

"You're trying to set me up, but never consider it for yourself. I know you don't date, but you're still a woman. You must find people attractive." Tulsi kept taking inventory so Devi wouldn't feel as if this was a deep or important conversation.

"You know I don't think about those things," Devi said.

"You should. You're always telling me to get out there again. Why not you?"

"It's different," Devi said. "I'm not young. I've already had my big love, and now I have you. That's all I ever wanted."

Tulsi registered the hitch in Devi's voice. "Really? You never think about having someone else, a romance?"

Devi said nothing, and Tulsi decided to back off. She needed to bide her time, give her mom some space. "But you're right about Lucas. He's very attractive."

Her mom perked up. "And has a great personality."

"He's not much of a talker, though," Tulsi added. "We barely know anything about him."

"Then you should change that." Devi straightened the vials of saffron under the glass counter. "He's shy and you can be persistent. You treat some customers like you're a reporter on *60 Minutes*, getting their whole life story out of them before they can leave with bottles of Himalayan salt or cardamom pods."

"What was it like?" Tulsi asked. "When you had your big love?"

Devi looked away, glanced toward the street through the wide window. "Is this about Kal?"

Tulsi was caught off guard. She gathered herself and pushed away the dull ache of past mistakes. "Maybe. I wonder if I actually loved him." She'd believed she had, but with distance she'd wondered. She had cared about him enough to let it go, but she didn't carry Kal in her heart. Sometimes she believed her reason to end things was more selfish than not. She'd been relieved to let him go. Maybe the curse had been a crutch so she wouldn't have to be responsible for doing the hard thing for herself.

"Only you can know for sure," Devi said.

"How did you know with my . . . um . . . father?"

Silence hung heavy in the shop. Tulsi didn't believe her mom would respond. She braced herself for the change in topic and mood.

Devi clenched her hand around the edge of the counter. "Is there a reason you've been bringing him up recently?"

An actual question for Tulsi. She breathed in and out. "I've been . . . it's been on my mind, I suppose. I know it's hard for you to think about him, that it brings a lot up. I don't want to upset you, but even if you could tell me a little bit about him. The two of you. How did you know you loved him?" She regretted the quiver in her voice.

Devi steadied herself. "He held my hand. The two of us, we walked everywhere. Neither of our families had cars, so we wandered wherever our feet took us. I remember never running out of things to say. He was as talkative and open as you are. I thought he was the smartest person I knew. One day it was bitterly cold. There was ice everywhere. We were crossing the street, and the light turned green. I slipped a little as I stepped off the curb, and he took my hand. When our palms touched, my whole body came alive. I had this incredibly vivid sense that I never wanted to let go. And he kept ahold of me until we got to my house. I knew in that moment that his was the only hand I ever wanted to hold."

Her mother still grieved, and so did Tulsi. "Thank you for telling me."

"Is that how it was for you? With Kalpan?"

Tulsi shook her head. There had been intensity between them. An instant attraction that led to immediate attachment. Within a few months she'd been ready to spend the rest of her life with him. It had been heady, and her thoughts were only ever about Kal. "I don't miss him the way you do my father."

"It's okay," Devi said. "You have time. You'll find your big love."

Tulsi stared down at her clenched fists. "The curse."

"Stop it."

Tulsi glanced up as Devi raised her voice ever so slightly.

"There isn't anything supernatural," Devi said. "Curses, it's not part of our history or our belief. You know better."

"Then how come the men die after leaving us with the next generation?" There. It was said out loud. The thing she feared.

Her mother grabbed a cleaning cloth from under the counter and wiped the surface. "You should go check out stock. More customers are coming through the door."

Tulsi swallowed her tears and did what Devi asked. Grateful for people who entered. She pasted on a smile and focused on the work. At least she'd gotten her mom to open up, even if it was only to share a memory.

At closing time, Tulsi was glad to flip the lock on the front door and turn over the OPEN sign to CLOSED.

"You did so well today," Devi said. "Your knowledge of our work has grown so much. You're ready. Take the test."

Tulsi was tired, and her heart still chafed from their earlier conversation. More the abrupt end to it. "We'll see."

"I don't want to pressure you," Devi added. "But it is time. Remember we do this for the greater good. We can't end what started so long ago. Each of us is a link on an infinite chain."

Maybe Tulsi was a solitary ring, an ear cuff, a bracelet. "And there is no other way? What if we train someone, expand so more people can do this?"

Devi came over to Tulsi and put her arm around her shoulders. "You know what makes me happy? You. My heart is full because I have you and I have Ma. And I have all of our clients that come in over and over again for their health needs. We help ease their pain, give them comfort. That's what *we* were made to do. That's why each generation from the first in our line is important."

"You never wanted more?"

Devi turned away. "I thought about it—of course I did. I was young once too."

"You're not old," Tulsi said.

"No, but I didn't have the maturity." Devi went to the wide window. Stared through it. "Ma was the one that helped me. She told me how we didn't live the way society dictated. That not all women were destined for marriage. That was a different kind of servitude. To one man, his family. We defined our terms, helped hundreds, thousands. I took that to heart. It helped me find peace."

"If you hadn't lost my father, do you think things would have been different?"

Devi turned away from the window and went over to her place behind the counter. "The past is fixed. There's no point in wondering. We live in the present with an eye toward the future."

"I'm glad you said that, about the future," Tulsi said. "Remember I told you about that man who'd stopped by? Ash? Well, we texted."

"What?" Her mom's voice was panicked.

"Don't worry," Tulsi said. "I just wanted to know a little more about how you knew each other. And he's very friendly."

Devi's hand rested on her stomach. "What did he say?"

Tulsi grinned. "Ma, are you nervous?"

"It's only right," Devi said. "Someone comes looking for you after all these years. It's not common, is it?"

"Well, rest assured." Tulsi put her hand on her mom's shoulder. "I vetted him, and his intentions are pure. And even though he mentioned that he'd once had a crush on you, I honestly think he wants to catch up. And you should."

"Stop." Devi's voice shook. "It's not . . . proper or appropriate. You must stop this, Tulsi."

"Please," Tulsi said. "You're always encouraging me to make friends. Meet someone. Just see him. That's all. Nothing more. He hopes to stop by the shop to say hi. And if you want to go out with him for lunch or a coffee, I can cover."

"Oh." Devi let out a rushed breath. "Did you say anything to Ba about this?"

Tulsi frowned. "No. Why?"

"Text him back," Devi said. "It's not a good time. I'm very busy this week. I have a meeting with the organizing committee for the fall art festival. It's not a good time right now. And Tulsi, stop. This matchmaking, texting this man, it's not good. I told you; I don't want any of it."

Her mom was visibly shaking. Tulsi wondered if it was more than nerves about meeting up with an old friend or the idea of another romance. She couldn't handle Devi in any sort of discomfort.

"Okay," she said. "I'll tell him not to come."

Devi centered herself. "Thank you. Please, I want you to really understand this. That part of my life is over. And as far as friends from the past, I don't like to revisit that time. There are too many memories, and I can't. I simply can't." She put her hand over her mouth.

Tulsi noticed Devi's hands tremble. "Ma, are you okay?"

"I need water," she said. "If you don't mind closing up, I'll head home."

Before Tulsi could agree, Devi left through the curtain toward the back. She didn't understand what had just happened. Tulsi knew her mom would be hesitant, but there was genuine fear there. She leaned over the glass counter and put her head on her crossed arms. This was bad. The one plan she'd had, to offer her mom another mooring to keep Devi steady, had just turned to dust. She was well and truly stuck here. Then she gave in and let the tears deepen her exhaustion.

CHAPTER SIXTEEN

Lucas's kitchen was almost finished. The floor was covered with tarps, and there was a sharp odor of turpentine, but overall it looked ready as appliances gleamed, and the standing shelf was stocked with flour, sugar, and other pantry items. She admired the prep station with its thick reclaimed wood butcher blocks.

"It looks so different," Tulsi said.

Lucas looked up from where he was slicing some sort of cheese. "Thanks."

She ran her hand over the smooth surface and traced the dark whorls with her fingertip. "Is this handmade?"

He nodded. "Yeah. I met a local named Jack. No last name. He hooked me up with beautiful pieces of walnut and let me work in his shop up in New Hampshire."

"It's gorgeous," Tulsi said. "And Jack is pretty famous around here for his woodworking and his cantankerous personality. I bet you two got along well, neither one saying a word to the other."

"He's my new best friend." Lucas grinned.

"I came by to drop off lunch, courtesy of my mom." Devi placed the repurposed yogurt container on the counter next to the wide fridge. "It's dhokri."

"Huh," he said. "I don't know what that is, but I like her food."

"Ha!" Tulsi cupped her mouth to cover her outburst. "Sorry. I love my mom, but her food is barely edible. It's because she doesn't believe in salt or seasoning. Ironic, I know, given our shop. But she makes food for sustenance and health, not pleasure."

"I will deny it if you ever mention this, but I use whatever she brings me as base, doctor it up. Especially since most of it is new to me. Like dhokli?"

"It's not an *l*, more like a guttural *r*," Tulsi clarified. "And, yeah, unless you're Gujarati, you wouldn't know a lot of these dishes. But Sharma is an Indian name, right?"

He nodded. "Apparently Punjabi. On my dad's side. Don't know much about it, but they landed in San Francisco in the early nineteen hundreds."

"What about your mom's side?" She leaned against a metal counter stool.

He shrugged. "Part Mexican. There's also French, Irish, and English."

She was envious and wondered if he'd done any of those DNA tests to see all that made him. She'd done it once in secret, but it came back as majority North Indian with a small percentage of Eurasian and Tibet-Burmese. Lucas's breakdown would be much more interesting. "You have so many cultures."

He laughed. "I'm American—that's all I know."

"Is that the menu here?" Tulsi shifted so she fully sat on the stool. "Roasted chicken, turkey sandwiches . . ."

He added diced tomatoes to a metal bowl, then grabbed a red onion. "I'm thinking of expanding it. Your mom's lunches are inspiring."

Tulsi realized that it would make her mom happy. These past few days, Devi had retreated into herself, and Tulsi regretted everything she'd pushed for with her and Ash. She should have taken more care, remembered her mom's nature. It had been a silly thing to do, and for selfish reasons. She'd already sent Ash a message to say Devi wouldn't be at Rasa on Friday, and she'd reach out for another time. She wouldn't, but it was the easiest way to let him down.

"My mom is going to be ecstatic if you tell her the inspiration part," Tulsi said. "We usually make sure that her turn to cook is on nights that might be late so we can pick up takeout instead."

He moved around the prep station and picked up the container Tulsi had brought in, opened it, and smelled.

"It's whole wheat dough that's flattened and cut up into diamond-shaped pasta. Then you boil it in watered-down dal and flat green beans." Tulsi described the dish. "It smells bland, but my mom does add mustard seeds to give it some pep."

He gave her a little wink, which, with the dimples, well, Tulsi was glad she was already sitting down in case she swooned. She clutched her tote a bit tighter against her. She should leave. Yet she sat and watched him.

"Is it supposed to be warm or cold?"

"Usually warm, with rice," Tulsi said.

Lucas grabbed a pot and turned on the stove. He moved fluidly, grabbing jars and spices. He heated a bit of oil, added finely chopped shallots, minced garlic, and ginger paste. The space exploded in aromas. The way he used a knife, stirred the pot, and grabbed whatever he needed with such speed; it was mesmerizing. She'd watched chefs on TV and in videos, but in real life, there was an energy to his pace. Not frantic, more a combination of speed and fluidity. The way he tossed the herbs and spices with confidence. His muscles flexed and bunched as he stirred. Tulsi wanted to sit here all day, every day, as he moved around this space, creating something from scratch. The pot sizzled as he added the dhokri and mixed everything together. He grabbed a metal spoon, dipped it in, tasted, then added more seasonings and salt. Then he grabbed fresh cilantro from the fridge, rinsed, chopped, and put it to the side along with a quartered lemon.

Lucas found two ceramic white bowls, ladled dhokri in each, topped it with herbs, and squeezed a bit of lemon on top before handing it to her along with a spoon.

"Try that," he said.

She tentatively took a bite. Her whole body came alive as flavors exploded on her tongue. The dish had everything, perfectly balanced with the six tastes. Lucas's version was not just edible but extraordinary. "OMG. Is this how dhokri is supposed to taste?"

He shrugged. "No idea."

She kept eating. "If you put this on your menu, you'll have a line out the door."

He grinned. "Devi's Dhokri."

Tulsi was grateful for him. The way he considered her mom and how he made Tulsi feel. It wasn't only the food that warmed her belly. "It would make her day, her year. How did you learn to do this? Your dad?"

Lucas ate a spoonful from his bowl. "No. I grew up on canned soup, boxed mac and cheese, jar sauce, and store-bought pasta."

"I wasn't allowed processed food," she said. "School lunches were when I learned that I had taste buds."

His laugh was deep, and Tulsi's skin prickled.

"I thank whoever taught you." Tulsi scraped the bottom of the bowl.

"Mable Salifu," he said. "She had a diner in town. Hired me to wash dishes when I was fourteen. She was Gullah and taught me to cook by using whatever was available. She'd say, 'Stay flexible, Lucas, creativity needs an open mind.'"

It was that way with spice healing. Understanding them at the foundational level and experimenting to create a unique blend for each client. Except Lucas was doing it. Tulsi was pretending to not know how. She watched as he rinsed their bowls and placed them in the dishwasher. He was more than a shy, quiet neighbor. More than his body and looks. She could feel herself being drawn toward him.

"I have to go." She jumped off the stool. "Thank you. For lunch. And this, the kitchen, it looks great. Your menu is going to be incredible, whatever you go with. I mean, I'm sure your roasted chicken is as delicious as the dhokri." Her hand and brain couldn't get it together, and it took several tries to get the door handle to flip. It was Lucas who came behind her, removed her hand, then turned the knob. In her rush to get away from the warmth of his back, she pushed the door with so much force that she tripped out into the alley. She didn't turn to see his expression, merely steadied herself and kept walking.

She was out of breath and not from exertion. She turned left out of the alley, then remembered she'd been on her way to the post office before popping in to drop off lunch. It was in the other direction, and Tulsi circled back. This wasn't good. She needed to spend time coming up with another plan to escape her future, not become distracted. The arousal, the attraction, needed to be buried. Anything between her and Lucas would play into her grandmother's plans and give her mom hope.

For a few hours after she'd hurt her mom with questions about Ash, Tulsi had considered giving in. It would be easy to take the test, take her place. She couldn't. These past few weeks, even with small actions like the letter and Ash, she'd made progress. If nothing else, she'd become brave enough to push her family into having some difficult conversations. If she kept at it, she might actually find the courage to use her words instead of schemes.

Tulsi took the long way around the waterfront and stopped at a bench. She sat to slow her racing heart. Seagulls hovered menacingly as they waited to pounce on a dropped ice-cream cone or an unattended sandwich. People walking past her were on their phones, either going somewhere with purpose or stopping to take pictures of docked boats.

She closed her eyes. Centered herself. Focused on her breath. A big part of her training with Aruna ba was to know the elements of nature, to understand how heat felt at different temperatures, the strength of the wind, the weight of raindrops. Tulsi meditated to calm herself. Open her mind. She sat until the sun stung the skin on her bare arms. She needed to channel this newfound strength. And in the process, she would help her mom become tough enough to handle Tulsi's rejection of their way of life.

CHAPTER SEVENTEEN

The next few days were such a whirlwind at Rasa that Tulsi barely had a minute to herself. A constant stream of customers required all three Gupta women to be on hand. Even then, there was very little time for Devi and Aruna to devote to their regular clients.

"You're still going." Mrs. Bishop came through the door. "I finally closed up. Not sure where all these people are coming from. Not that I'm complaining. But I tell you, I'm tired. My feet need a good soak."

Her mom finished gathering a variety of spices and herbs for one of the few remaining customers. All day long people had come in for ingredients from recipes they'd found on Instagram and TikTok. They were selling out of almost everything.

"I can't wait to use these." A customer placed a half dozen bottles of various seeds and seasonings on the counter. "I'm so ready for the magic to kick in."

Tulsi rang up the woman's purchases. "These help with minor ailments. It's not magic, only natural properties."

"Wink. Wink. Am I right?" the customer said. "I mean, you have to say that, don't you? But, like, my friend got some special tea from here a few weeks ago because they saw your videos about rose hips and joint pain. They put the bags in the tub and soaked in it for a few hours and said they haven't had pain since then. I get a lot of migraines, so I'm hoping this stuff has the same sort of effect."

"Oh, this is not right for headaches." Devi approached the register. "Here. These are cloves. Crush a few in a cloth napkin, then hold it to your nose. Breathe in the cool heat, and it will ease the throbbing."

"Awesome," the woman said. "Man, getting a magical formula from one of the spice healers. It's my lucky day."

"Again, not magic. Ayurveda," Tulsi said.

"Nature's magic," Devi said.

"My mother is joking," Tulsi added. "Please use these carefully and as intended."

Once the person left, Tulsi approached Devi. "Ma, you have to be careful and not encourage the magical talk."

Devi waved her off. "It's fine, beta. People expect it in Salem. There are witches, oracles, and ghosts all around us."

"This is different," Tulsi argued. "We never imply that these spices can do more than their intended purpose."

"You are being unnecessarily dramatic," Devi said.

Not a word that would ever describe Tulsi, but her mom had a slight bite when she and Tulsi spoke. There was an undercurrent that she believed was there because of Tulsi's overstep when it came to Ash. "I am trying to prevent anyone thinking any of those half truths around curing or preventing cancer could be tied back to something we said."

Devi turned away from Tulsi and greeted another customer. Her mom at least began to taper back the talk of magic for the rest of the day.

Finally, after the last customer left, Tulsi locked the front door and swung the sign to CLOSED. Her legs hurt so much that she regretted wearing her canvas wedges today. And since Aruna was here, it wasn't as if Tulsi could go barefoot. She saw the exhaustion in her grandmother and mom too. Their trips back and forth to help customers had gotten slower by the end of the day. It took strength to move the bigger glass jars full of kokum, dried ginger, and chili. Luckily Lucas had popped in, and when he saw the crowds, he had made time to help them. Tulsi kept her distance, and the brisk business helped. Once she'd caught him looking her way, and when she automatically smiled, he gave her one in return. The warm glow from that small exchange stayed with her for hours.

It wasn't fair. To him or herself. Lucas had to stay an acquaintance. She'd decided that the looming October 15 deadline would be her day to leave Rasa. It was time for concrete steps. She'd even bought a planner and circled that date. Then she'd done some simple math of her savings. If she scrimped, she could manage a trip. A way to figure out if Tulsi had any passions, to find a direction in life. She could manage a few months away.

Then she'd come back and hope Devi and Aruna had forgiven her enough to support whatever Tulsi wanted to do with her future. There was so much uncertainty, and Tulsi knew herself well enough to fear that she'd give up if it became too upsetting. For now she would stay the course.

That meant Tulsi had about seven weeks to prime her mom for her departure. Watching Lucas in the kitchen, hearing of his background, tasting his food that was an amalgamation of his experiences . . . she wanted that for herself. The doctored-up dhokri had become a driving force. Like the dish, Tulsi didn't want to be bland anymore.

Before turning away from the doors, she saw a few people taking selfies in front of the store as they posed with their Rasa bags. Rasa's social media posts were becoming more popular. There were several hundred thousand followers when she looked at both Instagram and TikTok.

"I'm still amazed at all of this." Devi propped her elbows on the counter and leaned on her forearms.

"I asked Gemma if it was the promotions we've been doing," Mrs. Bishop said. "Remember how we paid a few bloggers to write articles about our shops? Then there was that piece in the *Globe*, a whole spread on the North Shore and a full page about Salem."

"That was in June." Aruna wiped the table by the window.

"Here, Ba." Tulsi rushed over. "Sit for a bit. I'll clean up. I'll get us all waters too."

They paid for a professional cleaning service to come in the mornings before Rasa opened, but Tulsi needed to make sure the space was picked up some beforehand.

"You're good people, Tulsi." Mrs. Bishop took a seat at the table opposite Aruna.

Tulsi got a stool for her mother and handed her water before bringing over two glasses to the others. Her legs throbbed, but she was hardwired to serve. She finished picking up the dropped garbage, then the cups people brought in and left on shelves instead of tossing them, and she swept the dirt from the day's worth of feet shuffling in and out.

Finally she plopped on the floor between the table and the counter, took off her shoes, and placed the soles of her feet on the cool tiles. Hopefully that would ease the throbbing. "Has Gemma been doing social media too?" Tulsi had asked her friend, but Gemma said she hadn't set up Rasa's accounts.

"I'm not sure," Mrs. Bishop said. "I don't even have a way to look it up. I do everything old school. Sarah gets annoyed because I still write checks, but I don't want my identity stolen. There can be only one me."

"I find it odd," Tulsi said. "Someone is using Rasa and implying that we're doing some kind of sorcery in here. It's not good, especially when they're misleading people on how to use spices."

"They're learning," Devi said. "At least when they come in, we can guide them to the right usage. The more people understand Ayurveda, the more they will benefit from it."

"We're not in the business for popularity or fame. Tulsi is right to be worried," Aruna said. "We are here for our community, to serve their needs. As long as we have enough to live, we don't need to be greedy."

Tulsi sat up at the use of her grandmother's word. It had been what Aruna had written in the letter. *I hope your greed was worth the devastation you left in your wake.*

"Why can't it be both, Ba?" Tulsi asked.

Her grandmother looked down to where Tulsi sat. "Ayurveda is not for capitalism. It is our birthright. We founded it. It belongs to us, and only we can be the healers. Those videos you showed me, the way those young blonde women talk like they're the authority, like they made up the recipe for turmeric milk, it's offensive to our origin. How can people who can't even pronounce ashwagandha properly claim it as their own discovery?"

"She has a point," Mrs. Bishop said.

"I agree that they shouldn't claim it as their own," Devi said. "But if they use it properly, offer history as part of it, then isn't it better for everyone? It feels unfair to keep it just for us."

"It depends," Mrs. Bishop said. "In this country, it's about who gets to profit."

"Money," Aruna ba said. "I came from nothing, will leave with nothing. My sole responsibility is how I must live my life. For that, I need only food, shelter, and clothing. Rasa doesn't have to reshape itself to be more than it is. It doesn't need to become a franchise."

"Like House of Spice," Tulsi said. "I hear they're opening one up in Andover."

"Just what we need. Another Indian grocery store. That is the worst possible news to end my day." Aruna stood. "I'm going home."

Tulsi rose. "I can walk with you."

"I'm fine," she said. "I'll heat up the leftover green curry from yesterday. You take your time. See what stock is left for tomorrow."

Tulsi watched as her grandmother shuffled to the back.

"She worries too much. Who cares how they use it?" Mrs. Bishop shifted in her chair. "You're selling responsibly; what they do with it is up to them. You're in the retail business. Make the sale when you get the chance."

Tulsi agreed with all three of them. Another reason she wasn't meant to be a spice healer or shop owner. She didn't feel strongly about who used what, how. Her only worry was people using Rasa's name to tout uses that were not based on Ayurvedic science. Mostly to protect her family more than the shop.

"I'm off too." Mrs. Bishop rose. "Sarah's on dinner duty, and maybe, if I'm sweet to her, she'll rub my sore feet."

Once she left, Tulsi relocked the door; then she and Devi worked in silence. Her mom went to the back to bring out more inventory, and Tulsi added stock to the empty shelves. From the corner of her eye, she saw someone at the door. Then a gentle tap on the glass.

Ash. Oh no. Oh no. Oh no. She glanced over at Devi, hoped her mom hadn't noticed him. Too late. Her mom saw Ash through the glass. Devi froze, her hand at her throat.

"I'm sorry, Ma. I don't know what he's doing here. I told him not to. I swear." Tulsi pushed past her and opened the door. "I told you I'd get in touch. Why are you here?"

He couldn't take his eyes off Devi. "I'm sorry. You said it was a busy time, but I thought I would chance it and see if I could catch you, Devi." Ash's voice was almost a whisper as he came through the open door.

As the three stood in tableau, the energy in the room changed. Tulsi sensed the invisible current of connection between Devi and Ash. It felt intimate and heartbreaking. Tulsi stepped toward her mother and took the box from her.

"I didn't mean to interrupt." Ash saw only Devi.

"Ashish."

Tulsi heard shock, yearning, and aching in her mother's voice. Confusion and panic warred within her. Devi hadn't wanted to see Ash, and now they couldn't look away from each other. All she could do was stand next to her mother, be ready to throw him out if Devi began to shake or cry.

"I can't believe it's really you," he said.

"You . . . haven't changed as much." She cleared her throat.

"You're still kind." He rubbed his hand over his head. "I've filled out a bit, added a lot of wrinkles and grays."

"I don't see it. Your eyes." Then she stopped talking. Looked over at Tulsi.

"It's fine, Ma," Tulsi assured her. "I'm right here."

"Your daughter told me she was very protective of you," Ash said.

"Yes." Devi clasped Tulsi's hand. "I'm blessed to have her."

Tulsi squeezed her mom's hand.

"Are you free? Maybe we can catch up over dinner?" Ash tucked his hands in the pockets of his suit pants.

"We've had a long day," Tulsi said when she saw her mom tremble. "I don't think tonight is the best time. Perhaps in the morning? You can come over for cha."

"No." Devi released Tulsi's hand. "I'm fine. I need some air. Maybe we can walk by the water?"

"I'd like that." Ash moved toward the door. Held it open.

"Mom." Tulsi stopped her. "I can come with you if you'd like."

"No, beta." Devi's voice was steady. "We're old friends. I'm sure Ash has a busy life; it's better to catch up tonight so he can get back to it."

Tulsi saw Ash's face fall a touch, but he recovered quickly as they walked out together. She gave them a wave as they headed toward Congress Street. Tulsi worried. They both had seemed more surprised, hesitant, to see each other. She considered following them, keeping a little distance, but close enough to run interference if her mom became upset. No. It was better to have Devi handle this. To get her accustomed to not having Tulsi as a crutch.

CHAPTER EIGHTEEN

Before she left Rasa for the evening, Tulsi replaced her painful wedges with flip-flops she kept under her office desk. Instead of walking home, she paused. The Pearl's back door was open, and she peeked in. Lucas was sitting on the stool at the prep counter with papers in front of him, a pen between his teeth. He'd changed the deli so much, it looked unrecognizable from when it had been the Gallaghers' place. They were a sweet couple who always talked about settling somewhere warmer year-round. If Moira Gallagher still lived here instead of in Tucson, Tulsi would have popped in for an iced tea.

Just then Lucas noticed her.

She should go home. Exhaustion would only weaken her defenses to keep her distance, to not let him mean more to her. She should thank him, though, for lending a hand earlier in the day.

"Hey." She stepped through the door. "Thanks again. For earlier. It was a big help."

"Not a problem." He rose. "Hungry?"

"Your kitchen is too clean to mess it up," she said.

He moved the stool over by her. "Sit. I'm mulling over a recipe and need a taster."

"I'm not really a foodie," she said. "I grew up on my mom's cooking, remember?"

"That reminds me." Lucas pointed to a paper grocery bag under the small corner table. "Empty containers to return to your mom. Once I'm up and running, I'll send lunch to you all."

She put her tote on the ground. "From loner to providing us lunch in less than a month."

He laughed. "I tried to resist, but the HSBA is persistent with their help, advice, and nosiness."

"Mrs. Bishop calls it being neighborly," Tulsi said.

"She would." He grabbed potatoes out of the pantry and mushrooms from the fridge. "Vegetarian?"

She nodded. "All my life."

"Because of Ayurveda?"

Tulsi watched as he diced the potatoes, then put them in a bowl of cold water. "No. I mean yes. It's how I grew up. But it doesn't require a meat-free diet. In fact, in Vedic times, when Ayurveda was first practiced, they did eat meat. All things are allowed as long as it helps the body stay balanced."

"I thought it was a religious thing." Lucas diced portobello caps. "The vegetarian part."

"Ritualistic Hindus, sure," Tulsi said. "But those rules came about over time, when sects of Hinduism formed, like Jain or Swaminarayan. My family are Vedic practitioners, which is very broad and bound within nature."

"The God I believe in isn't short of cash," he said.

Tulsi didn't understand.

"U2? It's a line from 'Bullet the Blue Sky.'" He turned on the stove and heated a stainless-steel skillet, then peeled and minced garlic.

"Another recommendation," she said. "I listened to 'Between the Lines.'"

"And?"

"I like her voice." She didn't tell him how many times she'd listened to it, like a teenage crush who'd given her a mixtape. "You look almost ready to open."

He added a big slab of butter to the pan, then tossed the garlic around before adding the washed potatoes. "I'm sending invites for next week. Nothing fancy, just a card with the date and time. It's a preopen, or rehearsal. Mostly neighbors. Also sent them off to local bloggers, reviewers, and food journalists, critics."

"That's great," she said.

"That's what I was jotting down." Lucas tossed the potatoes, added a splash of red wine, then covered the pan. "A tasting menu for that night. Your mom gave me cardamom and saffron, along with cinnamon bark. I might try a barfi of some kind."

Her mouth salivated, not only from the aroma explosion in the small kitchen, but from the dessert. "It's my favorite."

He looked over and smiled. "Your mom might have mentioned something about that when she gave me a few ideas."

She was overwhelmed at the idea of this man making her favorite dessert. "Lucas, I just want to warn you."

He checked on the potatoes, then added salt, black pepper, and a splash of soy sauce.

She didn't know how to have this conversation. "My mom, if she's pressuring you, I mean implying . . ." She forced herself to say it directly even as her face warmed with embarrassment. "She might be trying to set us up, but feel free to tell her you're not interested."

He grabbed a tube of polenta and cut a few thick slices that he added to the grill pan he'd had on the stove. "She's not exactly subtle."

"I know," Tulsi said. "I'll talk to her."

He flipped the grilled polenta. "Don't worry about it. It doesn't bother me."

She didn't know how to take that. Did it mean he was open to her mom's attempts? Or that he wasn't bothered because he knew Devi's ploy wouldn't work? It shouldn't matter. She knew that nothing could happen between them. "This must be a big change from the military. Why did you decide to open your own restaurant?"

He plated the polenta slices, then stirred the mushrooms and potatoes before turning off the stove. "It's different, but there's still a routine to it, which I like."

"Gemma says you run every morning. Early."

He added chopped herbs to the pan, then topped the polenta with the mushroom mixture. "She tried to join me once. Couldn't keep pace." He handed her a plate and kept his in his hand before grabbing forks.

"Thanks, this looks delicious." She took a small bite and closed her eyes to appreciate the sensory experience.

"I like the way you eat."

Her eyes snapped open. The timbre of his voice jolted her spine. Her face warmed even as her taste buds came alive. She tried to defuse whatever was happening between them. "Like it's my first meal in a week?"

He shook his head. "The surprise in your expression, the way you close your eyes to focus and revel in the taste. Makes the chef in me proud."

She looked away, hoped he didn't notice her blush. "It's delicious."

The energy crackled between them, but all he said was "Thanks."

She had to regain control and changed the subject. "My mom is out catching up with an old friend."

"Good for her." Lucas ate standing up.

"I sort of connected them." She gave a little shake of the head. "It's funny. Because while I don't want her in my business, I was trying to set her up with him."

"She's kindhearted and gentle," Lucas said. "I hope he's worthy."

Tulsi remembered the way time had stopped when Ash and Devi first saw each other. "I didn't think it through. She was really upset about the idea, didn't want to even see him. Now they're out for a walk together, and I feel bad because I sort of pushed this on her without considering whether she even wanted to reconnect with an old friend, much less date him." She ate a few more bites, savored them. A part of her never wanted this meal to end. She didn't dissect whether it was because of the food or the company.

"You're worried," he said.

"She doesn't date. Never has."

"Nothing wrong with that either," he said.

"I was being selfish." Tulsi laid her fork across her empty plate. "I want her to have someone else, so that when I—" Tulsi stopped talking. She was revealing too much. She barely knew Lucas.

He gave her a curious look.

"I think it would be nice for her to have someone in her life," Tulsi said. "What about you?"

"Your mom is strikingly beautiful," Lucas said. "But she's too good for me. Too sweet, and I use language that might not sit well with her."

Tulsi felt the pressure ease with laughter. "Not even the mildest expletive in our house. I was taught that cursing showed a lack of respect for whoever you were talking to and yourself. Words mean things."

"I don't think I can live up to that kind of standard," he said. "You don't cuss?"

She grinned. "When I stub my toe, when I have to calculate estimated taxes, as long as no one is around, I find it cleansing. A way to release frustration."

"In the marines, it's a necessary part of our language," he said.

"I read this essay once about ownership of certain words and how meaning could change based on whether it was an in-culture language or if you were outside of it." She stopped talking, embarrassed. "Sorry. I'm not trying to sound smart. It just made me think of it. I couldn't even tell you the theories the writer mentioned."

"It makes sense," Lucas said. "There are words that mean something different based on where you are or how you grew up."

"You must have that with your dad," she said. "A way that you communicated with him."

"We don't talk much," Lucas said. "He does his thing, I do mine. It's been like that since Marianna left. If he needs me, he'll get in touch."

It was so matter of fact that Tulsi admired him for it. To be able to live life on his terms, without the weight of parental expectations. That was freedom. "Marianna?"

"My mother," he said.

Flat. Emotionless. Tulsi was shocked at his detachment. "I don't know the name of my father. But I miss him. Isn't that weird?"

"Not really," Lucas said. "It's like the idea of someone. There was this kid I served with on my last tour. Amari. Every mail drop, he'd find a way to be somewhere else. Sometimes I'd keep him company. He told me he'd never gotten mail, knew he wouldn't because he didn't have anyone except the marines, but it still hurt. He said it was the idea of it, that it reminded him that there was no one out there who had enough regard for him to know his address."

"I think my father would have loved me," she said.

"And I know my mother doesn't," he said. "Makes it easier to not miss."

She wanted to reach over. Wondered what it would be like to be held in his arms, to wrap herself around him. She stood and picked up her tote and the bag with the containers. "I need to check on my mom. I'm sure she's back home by now. Thank you. For the meal. It was amazing."

He walked her to the door. The sun had set, and she could see the moon emerge.

"You okay to get home?"

She felt the warmth of him behind her. It took every ounce of energy she had left to not lean back against him. Without looking his way, she nodded and turned into the alley. Only her aching feet kept her from running, as her heart wanted to turn around and stay with him for as long as he would have her.

CHAPTER NINETEEN

Tulsi slept through her alarm and jolted when she noticed that it was almost ten in the morning. She rushed around to get dressed and go through her morning routine. When she'd gotten home last night, Aruna ba had already gone up to her room, and her mom's door was closed. She'd wanted to go in, check on her, ask how it went. Instead, Tulsi let her be. And also avoided her mom's tears. Then she'd spent most of her night tossing, her brain on overdrive with what-ifs and rationalizations.

She ran downstairs and found her grandmother in the kitchen. "I'm so sorry. I'll run to Rasa. Mom's there by herself?"

Aruna stopped her. "Take it easy. Devi is fine. It's still early for a crowd. I'm heading there now."

She took the travel mug of cha from her grandmother as they locked up the house and headed toward Essex Street.

"What time did Mom get home last night?" Tulsi asked.

"I heard her come up shortly after I went to my room," Aruna said.

Tulsi wondered if Devi had said anything to her grandmother about Ash.

"And you?" Aruna asked.

"I stopped by to see Lucas," Tulsi said.

Aruna patted her arm. "He's a good choice."

She counted to three before speaking again. "It's not like that, Ba."

"For the sake of our future, what is the problem?" Aruna said sharply, loudly. "I'm losing my patience with you."

Tulsi had never heard her grandmother raise her voice. No one in their home did. She stopped at the crosswalk as they waited for a driver to notice enough to stop. They walked in silence for a few minutes.

"I'm going to put in an order for more stock." Tulsi heard herself—just like her mother, she'd changed the subject. Disappointment in herself that she was doing the same. Yet she stayed the course. "If it's busy, I'll cover the front after that. You did call your supplier, right?"

Aruna nodded. "I'll go see him at two."

As they waited to cross another intersection, Tulsi mentally admonished herself. If she couldn't have a hard conversation with her own grandmother, what made her think she could travel around by herself? People who traveled solo were brave. They leaped. She'd simply cowered, right there on Washington Street.

"Did you ever pressure Mom to date, after my father?" Her voice shook, but she'd made herself ask.

"No."

While Devi's go-to was to change the subject, Aruna's was silence or one-word answers.

"Why not?" Tulsi knew the answer. It was the reason she'd ended things with Kal.

"She'd already done her duty."

"She had me," Tulsi finished. "Our curse."

Aruna glanced over. "It's not a curse. It is how we live our lives. On our own, not tied to anyone but each other. There is no such thing as a curse, just like there is no magic."

"What else would you call it?" Tulsi kept pace with her grandmother's short strides. "We fall in love. Have a daughter. The man dies. There isn't a happily ever after for us. It seems like that's how it's always been."

"It has," Aruna said. "But curses are destructive. We do not cease to be who we are destined to be because of loss. We gain strength, empowerment. There is achievement in doing things on your own. A fulfillment of sorts."

Tulsi stopped in the middle of the sidewalk. It was the one answer she'd never gotten. "Who decided that? Because every culture pairs people up. We live in a world where love is the biggest milestone in life."

"Each generation that came before us informs how we live," Aruna said. "This is our tradition. We are not followers of the way society is set up; we take what we need and stay who we are. Independence gives us power."

"That is used for the greater good," Tulsi finished.

"Take the final test. Choose Lucas or someone else. And take your rightful place," Aruna said. "I don't know how much longer I can last."

Tulsi stopped in the middle of the sidewalk. "What do you mean?"

"No one who has come before me has survived to see my age," Aruna said. "I think our ancestors are keeping me here until you take over."

"You want to die?"

Aruna shook her head and turned into their alley. "Don't be ridiculous. We don't decide when it's our time; fate does."

Tulsi let her grandmother go into the store. She stood frozen, under the heat of the late-morning sun, surrounded by the smell of garbage. Maybe it had been better when her mom and grandmother *didn't* tell her anything.

An ambulance siren in the distance snapped her out of her thoughts, and she went into Rasa.

Her mom was in the middle of a rush of customers. Aruna ba took off her hat and headed to help. Tulsi hoped they'd have a lull so she could catch up with Devi about Ash. She was about to join her mom and grandma out front when the phone rang.

It was a producer from a local news channel. One of their future segments had fallen through, and they'd heard the buzz about Rasa. Sonia O'Shea featured lesser-known places and activities, and wanted to interview the local spice healers. Tulsi told them that Rasa didn't want to be featured. Her grandmother was already short tempered this morning, and news like this would ruin Ba's entire day.

"What was that about?" Devi came into the back office.

"Weird," Tulsi said. "A local news program wants to do a story about Rasa, but I turned them down."

"Why?" Devi put on a gray apron. "It sounds exciting. And we would be able to tell people our way of using spices."

Devi had a point. "It feels like too much attention, and you know Ba. She hates publicity of any kind."

"I know." Her mom was quiet. "Maybe, though, it wouldn't be too bad if a few more people knew about Rasa."

Tulsi was confused. "I thought you two agreed to keep a low profile."

"Yes," Devi said. "Just like I told you I didn't want to see Ashish."

There was a snap to the way Devi spoke to her. She'd never seen this side—mostly it was tears or change of topic, never even a slight hint of temper. "Did things go okay on your walk?"

Devi didn't meet Tulsi's eyes. "It was fine. He's . . . more mature than I remembered."

"Is that a good thing?"

Devi finally glanced Tulsi's way. "Good or bad has nothing to do with anything. He has his own life, and I have mine."

"I see. Do you plan to stay in touch?" She couldn't believe she'd pushed it by asking the question.

"We exchanged contact information," Devi said. "More to be polite than anything else."

"He seems to come to Boston a lot," Tulsi said. "Maybe—"

"For business." Devi opened jars and measured powdered mustard into her small white mixing bowl.

"I'm sorry if I badgered or rushed you to reconnect with him," Tulsi said.

Devi nodded, then shifted her focus to the blend she was creating.

Tulsi headed out to the front to prep for another day. This was a different kind of torture, but maybe it was better to create distance between them. Six weeks. That was how much time she had. Not that she'd booked a ticket or even knew where she was going, or if. Then Tulsi stopped herself. She wouldn't waver. She would go regardless of where her relationship with her mom would end up.

Whether she would enjoy it was a different story. Maybe Lucas had advice on how to not need people. Even moms.

CHAPTER TWENTY

"I didn't peg you for a Beyoncé fan." Tulsi dropped her tote on the floor, then pulled out the counter stool to take a seat. Lucas was spreading and smoothing something in a chilled metal tray.

"I served with a guy who was a big fan, and he'd play her music on repeat, along with Mariah, Whitney, Missy Elliott, and Queen Latifah. We were there so long that I know most of their songs by heart." He glanced at her, then refocused on his task.

"What's that?"

"Barfi. It's my third try," he said.

She jumped off to look over his shoulder. "Can I have a taste?"

"Yes. But it needs to settle first." He brushed her hand away.

The tiniest of touches and Tulsi wanted more. "What happened to the other batches?"

"The crew," he said. "If you're hungry, there's a Spanish tortilla in that glass container by the stove. Your mom dropped off tarragon from your grandmother's garden. Whatever she's growing is potent."

Tulsi served herself a sizable piece and sat at the small table. "Whew. I'm exhausted. We ran out of anise, marjoram, and poppy seeds. I still can't figure out who's behind these social posts. It's not Gemma. I've asked everyone, even Jemele at the post office. People have seen the posts, but no one knows anything. I've been messaging Skye—remember the influencer from Summer in the Park? Maybe not. She keeps telling me to just go along for the ride, that it's a good thing. She said this is normal and wished she was getting that kind of traction with her posts. I'm not sure."

Lucas said nothing as he chopped pistachios and almonds to sprinkle over the milk mixture settling in the pan.

"Now we have reporters calling." Tulsi spoke between bites. "Sonia O'Shea left four messages today, talking about a feature on Rasa. My mom is excited and thinks we should, but Aruna ba is very much against it."

"And you?"

The simple question startled her. For the most part, Aruna and Devi decided everything. "I usually do whatever they want."

"You don't get a say?"

"I'm not sure. I don't know if my mom and ba have ever been on opposite sides before. I usually do whatever they decide." Even as she said it, Tulsi was embarrassed for how she must come across to him. Lucas did what he wanted, opened this restaurant—even the menu was on his terms. She'd been standing still for so long, she had forgotten how to use her legs.

"Why did you leave the marines?" she asked.

"It was time."

"And?" Tulsi laid her fork down. Her appetite was gone.

He glanced over at her and shrugged.

"You wanted to, and you did it," she said.

"I had a choice to re-up or do something else," he said.

"I don't know what that's like," she said, more to herself. This was what she needed. Advice on how to just go without worrying about her mom or Aruna. "When you first left home, was your dad okay with it?"

"I don't know," he said. "I was eighteen. It was my call."

She wondered if it was a male thing. "And you didn't have regrets or miss him?"

He laughed. "I was too physically and mentally tired."

"Were you scared?"

He faced her, the tool he was using to evenly spread barfi in his hand. "What's bothering you?"

It was easier talking to his back. His expression was one of concern. For her. "I'm making conversation. You were so young. I couldn't imagine leaving everything I knew when I was eighteen."

"Because you liked where you were," he said. "I didn't."

She wanted to go over and hug him. Curl herself into his chest, know what the fabric of his gray shirt felt like against her cheek. Instead, she stayed where she sat. "Why Salem?"

He carried the tray to the fridge. "Why anywhere?"

It was funny how two words could tilt an entire worldview. "Most people live within fifty miles of where they were born."

"Pub trivia?" Lucas grabbed a few jars and spread out cashews, pistachios, and cardamom on a chopping block.

"I read a lot of random things and watch a lot of TV," she said. "What do you do when you're not working?"

"I read too," he said. "Nonfiction, mostly. I'm halfway through a biography of cod."

"The fish?"

He laughed. "It's actually pretty interesting."

"Weird," Tulsi said. "I guess I only think of you being here as a chef. I mean, of course, there's more, like Beyoncé and books. I had you in this specific box. You must think of me like that, only at Rasa."

"We see what we want to," he said.

"I should get that on a T-shirt." She noticed that he hadn't expanded on her comment.

"How many of those T-shirts do you have?"

"Last count was twenty-four," Tulsi answered.

"Slow your roll." Lucas read her pink shirt.

She looked down. "I overslept this morning."

"I get it now," he said. "That's your way of communicating. Displaying the quiet part."

"It's a hobby." Tulsi tensed.

"I run," he said. "It's a release valve from pressure."

"I was a cheerleader," she said. "Middle school. Not like gymnastics cheering. I had purple pom-poms."

"Bet your cartwheels were perfect," he said.

She stared down, unused to the compliment. "I can't do them anymore, but yeah, I was really good at it, and air splits. It was a lot of fun."

"Why did you stop?"

"I lost interest," she said. "I get distracted easily and always want to try new things."

"Because you're curious."

The urge to reach over, lean in, almost overtook her. She felt she'd do anything to experience the warmth of his skin, listen to the beat of his heart. She got up and rinsed out her plate before putting it in the dishwasher. "I'm sorry I keep coming over, talking your ear off. Wait, not sorry. I am trying not to apologize so much. Except I know that you're busy. Anyway, I've taken up enough of your time."

He didn't fill her awkwardness with questions or comments.

As she passed him, Lucas was gathering chopped nuts in a bowl. She stopped close to him and watched him wipe the blade of his knife with a finger. His hands were strong, and she saw the edge of ink peek out from under his sleeve. She resisted the urge to touch him. "Why do you wear long sleeves? Doesn't it get hot in here?"

He turned to face her. Leaned his hip against the edge of the station. "Habit. At the diner, I got cuts and burns all day long."

"That sounds painful."

"Kitchens are hazardous," he said. "It's a safety thing."

"High insurance deductible."

He smiled and she returned it. All it would take was a touch, a kiss. She stepped back. Then another. Too risky. Dangerous. "Thanks for feeding me again." She moved past him to grab her tote.

"Anytime."

She refused to read anything into his thick voice.

"Don't say that." Tulsi tried to ease the heaviness in the air between them. "It could become a habit."

He grinned. Leaned against the station and crossed his arms. "I hope so." Tulsi cleared her throat and rushed out and into the alley. She had to keep her distance. Unfortunately, she didn't know if she was strong enough to stay away.

CHAPTER
TWENTY-ONE

A few days later, instead of being tempted to stop in at the Pearl, Tulsi went home with her mom and ba. It was her turn to cook, and Tulsi decided to see if she could add a little more to their boring meals. She'd picked up a few things from watching Lucas in the kitchen. She chopped parsley and tomatoes, diced garlic. The water boiled on the stove, ready for the pasta. She added olive oil, then garlic and tomatoes, fresh peas, and asparagus to a pan. Her version of a primavera. She hoped.

"It smells good." Devi came into the kitchen.

Tulsi let out a small sigh of relief. Things were no longer frosty between her and Devi. As usual, time was all they needed to brush it off.

"Our vegetables?" Aruna came in and helped Devi set the table.

"Except for the asparagus." Tulsi added the fresh pappardelle she'd also picked up from the market to the pot and stirred the veggies.

"That news producer called again," Devi said. "While you were at the post office."

Tulsi concentrated on lifting the pasta from the pot with tongs and adding it to the pan. "They'll stop calling eventually."

"I think we should do it," Devi said.

Both Aruna and Tulsi gaped at Devi.

"No," Ba said.

"We are doing well," Devi said. "Helping more people. On TV we can reach so many more, hundreds of thousands."

"We have more clients than we can handle right now, and Tulsi doesn't seem to be in a hurry to pass the test to help." Aruna filled glasses with tap water. "We're always out of stock; people are traipsing in and out, disrupting the energy. We need to do less, not more."

"What do you think, Tulsi?"

And you don't get a say? Lucas's words popped into her head. Her mom had hope on her face. Her grandmother's reflected frustration. Her head agreed with Ba, but her heart—it was rare for her mom to want something. If Tulsi sided with her grandmother, Devi would be deflated. She and her mom were back to normal, and October 15 was getting closer each day. "It might be worth trying."

Aruna ba shook her head. Devi clapped in joy. Tulsi concentrated on plating their meals.

Over dinner, Tulsi and Devi decided her mom would be the one on camera. Tulsi would call in the morning and offer Monday, their one day off, as the only option. Tulsi and Aruna both stressed that Devi needed to use the time to dispel the magic part and talk about the benefits of Ayurveda. Then they spent the rest of dinner practicing potential questions and answers.

"It's not sitting well." Aruna had voiced her concern over and again. "I have a bad feeling about this woman."

"You've never met her, Ma," Devi said. "She looks friendly and happy on the news."

"The woman nods a lot," Aruna said. "That's a sign of someone pretending to listen."

After they finished dinner and cleaned up, Devi lit a chamomile-scented candle to wind down from all the tasks of the day.

"Maybe it's not sitting well because it's different, Ba," Tulsi said. "We don't have any experience with this kind of attention. To exist is to change."

"Don't quote me from your T-shirt. You two are lacking sense. I'm going to meditate, see if I can channel positive energy for all of this." Aruna left them.

Tulsi took a mug of hot water from her mom and sipped. "Peppermint tonight."

"It will help settle nerves," Devi said. "I'm thinking the pale-blue salwar. Or do you think silk is too fancy? We don't want to pretend we're something more. Maybe it's best to stay with cotton."

Her mom always wore pale colors, whites, and muted pastels. Tulsi believed it was because it was the mark of a widow, though Devi and her father had never married. "The silk is pretty, and it's very simple. No embroidery or epaulets. The color makes your skin glow."

Devi sat straighter in her chair. "It is my favorite color."

"You should wear more," Tulsi said. "Branch out."

"Maybe," Devi said.

Her mom had been lighter lately. Happier, less resistant. She'd even gotten her creative mojo back and painted whenever she had a few hours of free time. "I'm surprised that you want to do this interview. It really isn't like us."

Devi stirred the mint leaves in her mug. "I was nervous at first, but Ash has been so supportive and encouraging. He said that it was good for branding, would help us be known by name, not just in Salem but possibly New England."

Tulsi was glad she was seated; otherwise she would have fallen on the floor from shock. Instead of peppering Devi with all the questions, Tulsi breathed. "I didn't know you were in touch."

Devi waved her hand. "I shouldn't have mentioned it. We text. Talk on the phone. It's not a big deal. You know he lives far. And he has his own life. His twins keep him busy, and his business is demanding."

"He mentioned that he was in retail," Tulsi said. "When he came in that first day, he said he was looking for boutique spices."

"His family has a chain of grocery stores." Devi was quiet and hesitant. "He's the head of the whole company."

Tulsi noticed Devi's hands tremble. "Why are you whispering?"

Devi looked out into the hallway. "Ba wouldn't approve."

Tulsi laughed. "You're an adult, Ma. Besides, I think it's nice that you have a . . . friend."

"Just don't say anything," Devi said. "She wouldn't understand."

Tulsi was surprised at how young her mother sounded. "How often do you talk or text?"

Devi hesitated. "A few times. More than I expected."

Just like she stopped by the Pearl at the end of her day. "That's wonderful."

"Tulsi, I . . . there is something." Devi paused. Sipped. Paused again.

She understood how uncomfortable this was for her mom. They'd never really talked like this. Sure, Devi had helped her through the Kal breakup, but mostly with platitudes of "it's for the best" and "there will be others." She didn't want to do that, so she simply said, "Ma, I approve."

"I don't know what that means," Devi said.

"Your friendship with Ash," Tulsi clarified. "And if it turns into something more, that's good. I like seeing this side of you."

"Oh no," Devi said. "You misunderstood. That is not what we're doing. It can never work with Ash. Too much time has passed, and there are things you can't go back and change."

Now she was the one who didn't get it. "You always say to stay in the present and look toward the future. What does the past have to do with it?"

"Some wrongs can never be fixed," she said. "But none of it matters. Ashish and I are acquaintances, and that's how it must stay."

There were still so many things about her mom's history Tulsi didn't know. She'd always believed that the sadness Devi carried under the serenity was grief. "I know that, historically, spice healers are meant to be alone. Maybe that doesn't have to be the case. There is still plenty of time to try a different way."

"Your ba taught me that there is power in being free. Independent."

Free. That wasn't how she would describe their lives. Tethered to each other and to Dharti. "That's why I let Kal go. That's why I avoid relationships. I don't want to bring another person into this life and know what they will have to sacrifice."

Her mom gripped her mug. Devi's eyes began to dampen. Which meant the topic would change.

"You learned the wrong lesson," Devi said. "Those were circumstances. Fate, perhaps. Ba is happy; she knows who she is and has purpose. Fulfillment isn't always dependent on romantic love. But it's not that healers have to be alone."

"Then why did you never date again?" Tulsi asked.

Devi closed her eyes. When they opened, there were tears. "I'm sorry."

"For what?"

"So many things," Devi said. "I'm sorry."

Tulsi stood to give Devi a hug, but her mom pushed away from her seat and left the kitchen. Tulsi let her be. She hated it when Devi cried. She rinsed out their mugs, then headed up to her room.

Her phone was on the charger on her nightstand, and she wondered what it would be like to text Lucas. Would he even respond? She didn't know if they had a friendship or if he saw her as the person who worked next door.

A few minutes later, she mustered the courage to write.

Hope you're all ready for tomorrow's pre-launch.

There. She sent it. He might not even have her phone number.

It's Tulsi by the way.

Then she added another message.

From next door.

Then she threw her phone on the bed away from her, her face warm with embarrassment. He was likely thinking she was message bombing him. She should shut it off, pull the sheet over her head, and pray for sleep.

Her phone vibrated. And her heart swelled when she saw his response.

Thanks. All set. And there's an extra tray of barfi for you. This is Lucas by the way. From next door. ☺

She hugged the phone to her chest. Read the message a few more times. Eventually she fell asleep with a smile on her face.

CHAPTER
TWENTY-TWO

That next day the Gupta women made a unanimous decision to close Rasa a few hours early. For one, they were all worn out from a long and hyper-busy day. It took a bit of coaxing to convince Aruna, but she finally relented. Her grandmother had developed a soft spot for Lucas. What started as vetting him for Tulsi had turned into a genuine admiration, and they all wanted to support the preopening night of the Pearl.

At Tulsi's insistence, her mom and Aruna had changed and gone ahead to the restaurant, while she'd stayed back. Once she finished cleaning and organizing the shop and closed out for the day, she went to their small bathroom and washed her face and wiped her armpits. She'd brought a dress for the occasion and changed in Rasa's staff-only restroom. It was the fanciest item she owned, from a boutique a few doors down. She was celebrating Lucas's night—that was the only reason. Plus, she'd get more than one wear out of it. It was a statement piece, a navy-and-yellow print that made her think of Paris. While it hung loose and didn't add curves to her slim frame, the hem twirled when she moved, and it made her feel feminine.

Just like the makeup she applied, this was for her. Not Lucas. Though Tulsi was sure Mrs. Bishop would make some sort of remark about her dressing up like this more often. She finger- brushed volume in her hair, added a bit of spray to keep the hold. She batted her eyelashes to dry the mascara. The dark eyeliner added drama to her angled features. She finished the look with a shiny lip gloss, then slid into ballet flats. No way was she wearing heels after the torture her feet had gone through this week.

Tulsi took one more look in the mirror and spontaneously blew herself a kiss. It was silly, and she was glad no one had seen her, but she liked her reflection. It wasn't often that she thought about her looks. Her mom, Aruna ba, they taught her to focus outwardly and live without judgment of others or herself.

A little over a month ago, she'd been wallowing, thrown by a tattoo. Now she felt different. Less wishing and more doing. She had a plan, however loose. Instead of passive existence, she said what was on her mind more often. She'd learned more about who her ba and mom were and pushed them too. She had enough confidence to even admit that she liked a boy. She would enjoy this feeling of having a crush. The future wasn't something to dread as much.

Tulsi let herself out from the back but went around the corner and to the front entrance of the Pearl, so as not to disrupt the kitchen staff. It was a lovely evening for early September, clear with a cool breeze. The Pearl's facade was welcoming, with gold hardware gleaming on a white door. The large front wall was clear glass, no writing on it, but you could see inside. The sign was simple and understated. As she walked in, she noted most guests had already arrived.

Her mom was with Mrs. Bishop and her wife at a large table in the corner by the window. Tulsi did a lap around the room first, saying hello to the people she knew. The others she stepped around. A man with a camera snapped a photo of the event. Two servers dressed in white shirts and dark-gray slacks moved through the room with trays filled with specialties.

She chose a small puff pastry topped with shaved tandoori paneer. In one bite, she fell in love. Whatever was in it, she'd never tasted something so divine. She knew her spices—if not used in balance, they could overwhelm. With the paneer Lucas showed he knew spices too.

Tulsi looked behind the counter. The kitchen door was open, and she saw Lucas move around as he cooked, plated, and directed his staff. It was the first time she'd seen him in his white chef's coat, and her belly fluttered as attraction came to the forefront. Unlike the chefs on TV, he didn't shout orders, just kept doing the work alongside his team. Then Lucas looked up, and their eyes connected. Even at a distance she could see his surprise at seeing her dressed up. Hopefully he liked what he saw. Then he offered a small smile and a wink. It made her laugh.

"Tulsi."

Devi was calling her, and she went toward her mom's table.

"You look lovely, beta," Devi said.

"Honestly," Mrs. Bishop said. "When you make an effort, you're really quite beautiful."

Tulsi laughed, then reached her palm out as Sarah put a five-dollar bill in it.

"What's that about?" Mrs. Bishop said.

"We had a bet as to whether your first comment to me would be about my looks. I won."

Mrs. Bishop turned to her wife with exaggerated shock.

"Look at it this way, my love. I had faith in you," Sarah said. "Yet I'm out five bucks because you just can't help yourself."

"When I see a pretty woman who lets herself go, I have to say something." Mrs. Bishop sipped her dirty martini. "Now that's done, feed yourself. Everything is delicious. I need Lucas to make fresh paneer for me to sell at Cheese Are Us."

"Oh, that would be a great addition. I haven't tried everything, but I adore the green mango salad. That reminds me." Devi opened her small black purse for her phone. "I need to take a picture of the shrimp skewers on your plate, Betty."

"He has a photographer," Tulsi said.

"Oh, it's for her 'friend.'" Mrs. Bishop put the last word in air quotes.

Her mom actually blushed. "He's in the food business. And only a friend."

"Last time, he was an acquaintance, so things seem to be moving along," Mrs. Bishop said. "But I still don't get why you won't tell us his name."

"Because I don't want any gossip," Devi said.

Tulsi hadn't realized her mom confided in Mrs. Bishop about personal things. She was seeing Devi a little differently. Like a person, separate from being her mother. Tonight she wore a sari that was more coral than pale pink. The color added brightness to her eyes. "Are you wearing lip gloss?"

"My lips have been dry," Devi said. "I haven't been drinking enough water."

"Tulsi." Mrs. Bishop tugged at her arm. "What do you know about all of this?"

"Not as much as you," she replied.

"The suran pakora are great." Devi held up her small plate. "Has a lot of Ayurvedic benefits."

"Fine, change the subject," Mrs. Bishop said. "I'll ask you again after you have another glass of wine."

Tulsi bit into a pakora and discovered elephant yam inside. "Yum."

"Suran is a tuber, right?" Sarah asked.

"Yes." Devi sipped white wine. "Good for colds and coughs and for the liver."

"I need to make a note of it." Sarah popped another pakora from the platter.

"Or just come in when we're not so busy," Devi said. "We can figure out the best way to prepare it for your needs."

"Don't forget to mention this place and our HSBA during your news interview." Mrs. Bishop ate another wedge of paneer.

"I plan to talk about all of us," Devi added.

"And the magic," Sarah added. "That's the hook."

Tulsi twisted the gold band on her second finger. "Maybe not that part."

"Beta, it's fine," Devi said. "People can tell the difference. You have to trust them to understand. Besides, the health benefits to Ayurveda are real and based in facts, nature. If some want to refer to it as magical, what's the harm?"

The harm was they risked being taken less seriously. Tulsi didn't think it would be good for Rasa to become some sort of gimmick or get-better-quick type of place. Aruna ba would hate that. She glanced over at the table where her grandmother sat with Mr. Rhodes and Gemma. "I want to make sure people respect what you do. That's all."

"They will," Sarah said. "Devi is so knowledgeable; it will come across naturally. It's that the audience wants something different. You have to give them a reason to buy Rasa and not supermarket brands like McCormick's."

Tulsi left them to their conversation. "I'm going to get a glass of wine. Can I get anyone anything?"

They all ordered another round, and Tulsi made her way to the bar. Seeing so many familiar faces warmed her. It reinforced what she hoped for on her discovery trip. Three months of new experiences and different people. Seeing places not just through pictures and videos. She wanted to know whether the food tasted differently from what she'd imagined. She wanted to try new things, like the garbanzo beans soaked in pani puri water she was currently enjoying. She wanted more.

She had yet to figure out what cities to visit or how to get from one place to another, but in her planner, she'd started lists. Her plan was to start closer. Montreal. Toronto. Baby steps, familiar language and culture. She could take the bus from Boston. Then figure it out as she went. Tulsi glanced over at her mom and ba. They would be okay. She had to believe it. She sipped the fruity white wine, afraid to even think about what would happen if she gave up this time.

She still hadn't told anyone. Was it really to avoid confrontation with her ba or hurt her mom, or was it because it would be less shameful if she didn't go through with it? Confidence was one thing; her track record told the truth. She'd never actually followed through on anything. College, for instance. She'd wanted to go, had filled out applications, but never mailed them.

After the interview, she would tell her mom and Aruna. All of it. Including that she didn't want to be a spice healer. It was going to be hard; they would need convincing. But it needed to be done. For herself more than for them.

CHAPTER TWENTY-THREE

It could have been the two glasses of wine, a full and satisfied stomach, or that she felt pretty. Tulsi didn't want to overthink her decision to stay well past the event to help Lucas clean up. Not that there was anything left to do. The restaurant had been readied for the morning's opening, and the kitchen sparkled thanks to Lucas's staff. Now it was only the two of them in the back as she made herself comfortable on the barstool. The small piece of furniture was beginning to feel like it was only for her. Which was nice. As if she had a place here, in his space.

"How do you feel?"

"Relieved." Lucas wiped the doors of the stainless-steel fridge. "Ready to open."

"If it was me, I'd be doing a happy dance," she said.

He stopped, towel in hand. "Let's see it."

"You first," she challenged. "I could play Beyoncé on my phone."

"I'm good," he said. "Maybe in a year. That's when I'll know if this is going to work out. Sixty percent of restaurants fail before then."

"I'll light a success candle for the Pearl." Tulsi wondered where she would be in a year. It felt good to not know the answer.

"There's such a thing?"

"Totally," Tulsi said. "Missy sells them. Also, love, money, and other types of hope. Not that you need it. You have nothing to worry about."

Tulsi put her empty wine flute on the small round table beside her. "You should be proud of what you've done."

He came around and picked up her glass to rinse it, then added it to the industrial dishwasher that he had yet to run.

"I didn't see your dad here," she ventured.

"He doesn't like to leave Texas," Lucas said.

"Oh, a homebody, huh?"

Lucas didn't respond.

"My mom and I went to the Grand Canyon once. That's as close as I've ever been to Texas. But we did have Tex-Mex in Phoenix. I prefer Mex-Mex." She laughed at her own joke. "Do you think you'll add some dishes from the diner to your menu?"

Lucas checked to make sure everything was done, then grabbed a bottle of beer from a small fridge next to the pantry. "Maybe."

He held another bottle. "Drink?"

"No. I can handle max two glasses of wine. I learned the hard way that anything stronger or more means a night of throwing up." Tulsi winced. "Sorry, shouldn't have said that after eating here. But I will toast to you with . . . my hand."

He bent and grabbed a bottle of sparkling water, added ice to a glass and a squeeze of lime, then handed it to her. Then clinked his bottle against her glass.

"Thanks," he said. "For sticking around. The adrenaline from tonight is going to take a bit to level off."

She kept her face neutral even though everything inside her warmed. "Of course. It's good to celebrate with friends. Even for those who aren't people persons."

"Touché." He tilted his bottle toward her.

"How does it feel to want something for so long and then make it happen?"

He gave her a curious look. "Not sure. I don't think about it like that."

"Oh, sorry." She shifted in her seat. "I assumed this might have been a dream of yours from when you worked as a dishwasher."

He laughed. "Back then all I could think about was the next day. There were things I enjoyed. Baseball, video games. When it came to the future, I did whatever was next. Graduated high school. Enlisted. It wasn't until I decided not to re-up that I thought about what I wanted to do."

"I'm trying to figure that out myself. What's next for me." His words gave her the courage to say her own out loud. "I always hear people say they're living out their dreams. I just don't know what mine is. I know I want to travel for a bit, but after that, what?"

"It's not Rasa."

It wasn't a question, only a simple statement. He saw her. Deep inside, not just what she presented to the world. "What if I had the freedom to do anything? What would it be?"

"Your family expects you to take over," Lucas said.

"It's who we are," Tulsi explained. "Spice healers, descendants of the goddess of Earth."

"What's the answer to your own question?" he asked.

She looked down at her hands. "You'll laugh." She hated to admit it or even think it.

"I might," he said. "You shouldn't care."

"If you think I have your level of confidence, you're mistaken."

"Try it."

Tulsi wanted to be the person he saw. "When I was little, I would take all my stuffed animals and put them in rows. I was their teacher." Her face warmed. "I'm not qualified. At best, I was a B student. No one would ever imagine me as a teacher." Not even herself.

"Don't sell yourself short," he said. "You should get a T-shirt with that on it."

This man overwhelmed her. "You're good people, Lucas."

"That's what Mable used to say. She was the one who owned the diner," he said. "She wore a pearl necklace every Sunday. She'd come in after church and ask me to make her something to eat."

"Were you close?"

He took another sip. "All I know was that she was the only steady woman in my life. I saw her every day for three years. When I told her I enlisted, she gave me a check. A gift. It wasn't much. I set that money aside. Added it to the down payment on this place."

"That's incredible." To have support like that from someone who wasn't a relative floored her. "Did you invite her tonight?"

He finished his beer. "She passed over a decade ago."

Tulsi did something she'd wanted to for a long time. She moved toward him, reached out, and touched his arm. The cotton on the chef's coat was soft, but she resisted the urge to stroke it. "I'm sorry."

He took her hand in his and toyed with her fingers. "It was a long time ago."

They stood there. Her hand in his. Tulsi could see little flecks of green in his light-brown eyes. His lashes thick. In the silence, her heartbeat seemed loud. She tilted her face, leaned closer.

"It's late." His voice was soft. Husky.

Her body vibrated in anticipation. "It is."

Then they met each other halfway. His lips brushed against hers. She hesitated. Hoped she remembered how; then all thoughts left her as heat took over. She matched the gentle pressure of his mouth, and her confidence grew as she heard him moan. His hand gripped hers, fingers squeezed as if to keep control. Of himself. Her. Tulsi had no idea.

Then he broke their kiss. Stilled as they caught their breath. Her feelings unsettled her. "I'm leaving," she blurted out.

He let go of her. "Yeah, okay. You good to walk back alone?"

She nodded. He'd misinterpreted her comment, but it was for the best. "I do it all the time. It's only a ten-minute walk. I stay on the main streets anyway. I'll let you close up." She reached the door, then turned toward him. "Congratulations again, Lucas. I hope you are proud of what you've done here."

His dimples deepened into his cheeks. "I appreciate you saying so."

She gave a quick wave and left through the alley. Once she was a block away, she cupped her cheeks with her hands. She'd kissed him.

And it was good, shockingly so. Her heart began to race again. She needed to temper these feelings. It was nice. She'd planned to have a fun night, and she did. It was how things were done. Sometimes kisses happened, and they didn't have to mean more or anything. She should see it for what it was, a nice end to a great evening.

They were friends. And she wouldn't mind repeating the experience. Her mind went to joining him at the counter stool after she closed up Rasa. Him feeding her. Them sharing a kiss. As she waited at the light, Tulsi laughed at her silly fantasy. Tomorrow the kitchen would be open, and his staff would be there, preparing and serving. The evenings of just the two of them were over.

CHAPTER
TWENTY-FOUR

Tulsi checked her watch. The television crew was set to arrive shortly, and since Rasa was closed, it gave her the chance to set everything up, to showcase the shop.

"It looks lovely," Devi said when she entered. "Fresh flowers are a nice touch."

"Gemma dropped them off." Tulsi ran her fingers gently over the white-and-pink dahlias. "They're from the HSBA."

"That's very thoughtful." Devi checked over a few places. "Does this display of the bottles on the counter make it seem crowded? Maybe we can move the computer screen of the register."

"It's to create balance so that the counter doesn't look empty and stark in the background." Tulsi understood her mother's nerves. In a little while, Devi would become the face of Rasa to the broader public.

"Do you think there will be enough light? It is a gloomy day." Devi looked outside.

Tulsi wrapped her arm around Devi's shoulders. "Ma, they'll have equipment. I thought you were going to come a little later. Relax at home a little longer."

Devi patted Tulsi's hand, then pulled away to pace. "I was ready, and honestly there isn't enough mint or calming tea to settle me. What was I thinking, agreeing to be interviewed on TV? What if I freeze and don't know how to answer a question?"

"It's not going to be live," Tulsi said. "You'll be great. Pretend you're talking to a customer. That's all. Forget about the camera or the reporter."

"You're right," Devi said. "This is good for us. I'm proud of what we've built here, our work, the community we take care of. So why am I terrified?"

"If you don't want to do this . . ."

Devi took a few full breaths. "I am fine. Besides, it would be terrible for us to change our minds. They are already on their way. If we pull out, that will be more work for them to find something else to film. Are you sure you don't want to wear a little makeup in case you're captured on camera?"

"I have mascara on." Tulsi exaggeratedly blinked. "Besides, you're going to be so amazing, you'll have everyone's complete attention."

Devi stroked Tulsi's cheek. Her mom wore the blue silk paired with simple hoop earrings and a gold chain around her neck. She'd left her hair long and straight, and her eyes were highlighted with liner. "You are so beautiful," Tulsi said. "I forget that sometimes."

Devi laughed. "It's because you see me every day."

Tulsi hugged her mom. "I'm proud of you for doing this."

Devi patted her back, then pulled away. "I think that is the nicest thing you've said to me. I know I haven't always been strong or a good role model."

Tulsi wanted to automatically shut her mom down. Except Devi was acknowledging what Tulsi had been ashamed to think. "I love you, Ma." That's really all that needed to be said.

"And I you," Devi said. "I want you to know, this, all of it, it's for you. Now, let's breathe to center ourselves." Devi closed her eyes. "This is the right path for us. More people will benefit from our work. We are intentional and purposeful. We are fulfilled."

Tulsi waited for her mom to finish her quick meditation, then adjusted a few bottles, made sure all the labels faced out and could be easily read.

"I told Ba to stay home." Devi adjusted her dupatta so that it draped over her left arm. The sheer fabric was the same color, but the material made it appear lighter.

"Good. I hope she has her feet up and a novel in her hand."

"She was fiddling in the garden when I left," Devi said.

"Hey, the back door was open." Lucas came into Rasa.

"Oh, I'm so happy you're here." Devi clasped Lucas's hand. "Especially since you had such a busy weekend."

"It was great," Lucas said. "But I'm glad to be closed today. You look beautiful."

Her mom blushed. "That's really sweet of you to say."

"Thought you could use some cha." He put a thermos and a couple of mugs on the counter against the wall. "The way you like it. Lots of ginger."

Devi claimed a mug Lucas filled. "My cha will never be good enough now that you bring us yours every morning."

"It's the least I could do," he said. "I put it on the menu. As a special."

"I'll be sure to mention it during my interview."

Tulsi watched as they chatted. He had a bit of scruff around his jaw this morning.

"I hope you didn't open the Pearl just to make this for us," Devi said.

He shook his head. "I have prep to do, inventory." He glanced at Tulsi. "And paperwork, your favorite."

She laughed. "Wait until you get to invoices. It's a party."

"If you need help," Devi said, "Tulsi can give you tips. She does Rasa's books, and she has a great system."

Tulsi scrunched her nose. "Ma. I'm sure Lucas knows what he's doing."

"And in return," Devi continued, "you can teach her how to cook. She knows the basics, but it would be nice for her to learn a few more dishes besides pasta primavera."

Lucas moved to stand next to her. "Happy to do that anytime."

"Are you going to stay when Sonia O'Shea is here?" Tulsi asked.

He put his hands in the front pockets of his jeans and leaned against the sales counter. "Don't want to miss your mom's debut."

An hour later, Tulsi stood next to Lucas and watched as Sonia began the interview. She chewed on a cuticle, then tucked her hands into the back pockets of her jeans. Her mom was calm and cheerful as she spoke on camera. Sonia asked about the history of Rasa and how the spices worked. For the most part, Devi stuck to the rehearsed answers. Then Sonia mentioned magic and the increasing popularity of Rasa. Tulsi prayed her mom would defuse the whole thing; it was the perfect opportunity.

"Well, Ayurveda is an ancient science . . ."

Tulsi relaxed when Devi started off right. Then the front door of the shop opened, because Tulsi had forgotten to lock it. Ash. He stood off to the side and watched Devi.

Her mother noticed him and became distracted by his presence.

"But this is alchemy, right? Like Hindu sorcery," Sonia said. "I see so many mentions of people being helped by your magic. Hundreds of comments about how your spices heal them because they are infused with a special something."

Devi pulled her gaze away from Ash and faced Sonia. "Magic. Yes. Of course. But it's how you define—"

"Well, you heard it from Devi Gupta, the spice master." Sonia took the mic away from Devi and looked into the camera. "Rasa spices are magical. On your next visit to Salem, make sure you stop by and get your own special cure."

Devi waited off to one side as the news team packed up and left. Then she rushed to Ash. "What are you doing here?"

"I came to support you." He took her hands.

Devi tugged out of his grasp. "I told you there was no need."

"I want to be here for the big moments," he said. "We talked about that."

Tulsi looked at Lucas. "I should . . ."

"Give them a minute?" He tilted his head to indicate that they should go to the back office.

"My mom looks upset with him," Tulsi said.

"What are *you* doing here?" Aruna's voice filled the room. She stood in the doorframe, while Ash and Devi stilled by the front door.

"Ba," said Tulsi. "I thought you were resting."

Aruna glared at Ash. "Leave. You're not welcome here."

Tulsi was confused. "Ba. What are you talking about? This is a friend of Ma's." She gave Ash an apologetic look.

"It's okay, Tulsi." Ash finally spoke. "Hello, Aruna auntie."

CHAPTER
TWENTY-FIVE

The thing about growing up the way Tulsi had, she knew what to expect in charged situations. Even with the progress she'd made with Ba and her mom, it was still easier to revert to their way of doing things. Devi was already twisting her hands; tears filled her eyes. Ba was ready to turn away, disappear from where she'd come. Tulsi decided to break the cycle. Even though Lucas and Ash were here, Tulsi wanted answers and didn't want to wait. She would channel Lucas's directness.

"Ba? Why are you asking Ash to leave?" Tulsi took her grandmother's hand. "He's an old friend."

Aruna didn't answer. So Tulsi asked her again.

Aruna glared at Tulsi. "No good will come of this. That's all I'll say." Then she slipped out of Tulsi's grasp and left.

Tears rolled down Devi's cheeks. Ash had his arm around her mom. The sense, the gut she'd pretended she never had, told her to run. That she shouldn't be here for whatever was about to happen. Tulsi steeled herself. "What did she mean? I don't understand."

Devi closed her eyes, wiped her face with the edge of her sari. Then she stepped out of Ash's arm and went to Tulsi. "There are things you don't know." Her voice quivered.

So many things. Tulsi gripped the counter to keep from balling her fists. "Start somewhere. Anywhere."

"I can't," Devi said. "Because you will hate me."

Tulsi moved out from behind the counter and clutched her mom's hands. "Never. It's not possible. Even if you killed someone, I would know it was because you were doing what you felt was best." Her stomach roiled. "Not that I would ever believe you capable of something like that. You don't cause harm. If there is one thing I know about you, it's that. You would never deliberately hurt anyone." She was stalling because whatever came next would be painful. She knew that. Wasn't sure she wanted to hear it.

It was Ash who moved to stand beside Devi. "Just like your mom and I were friends, so were our mothers. They had a falling-out. We were torn apart because of it."

Chicago. "Is her name Hema?"

Ash nodded.

"How do you know?" Devi asked. "What do you know?"

The panic in her mom's eyes scared her. "I found a letter a while back. From Ba to a Hema Patel. It didn't say much, except that Ba felt betrayed and something about stealing dreams."

"They were close," Ash said. "All four of us were."

"They wouldn't have approved," Devi said. "There was so much anger between them."

"That's why you were taken away," Ash said to Devi. "Aruna auntie knew I would try to stop you. I knew you didn't want to leave me."

It was as if her brain was being poked by the scalding blade of a knife. "You were more than friends."

Tulsi saw the shock on her mom's face. The knife twisted, and Tulsi squeezed her hands into fists to stay focused. It was difficult to breathe. In the distance a warm palm rested between her shoulders. She took a gulp, then another. She couldn't form clear thoughts. Only snippets. Her mother had only ever loved one man. Or so she'd said. Over and over again. She looked from Ash to Devi. It was undeniable that he was the one Devi had meant. "I don't understand. You said you loved my father; you grieved him. But it was Ash you were talking about."

Devi clutched Tulsi's hands. "I'm sorry, beta."

"It's . . . fine." If this was all it was, Tulsi could handle it. "I get it. You wanted to make sure I had a happy story about my father. I understand." So what if she'd written stories about the great love between her parents, that she'd grieved alongside her mother for all those years. She wasn't a child. Her mom was only protecting Tulsi. Maybe the man was horrible, and Devi had to rewrite . . . the panic rose. Something wasn't right. She needed to leave.

Tulsi pulled out of her grasp. She didn't want to hear it. It was all wrong. There were too many thoughts in her brain, and none of them made sense. Her instincts warred with her head. Her father was dead. She repeated it again to herself. She could handle everything as long as that stayed the truth.

"I let you believe something that wasn't true."

Tulsi closed her eyes, shook her head. She wanted to put her hands over her ears. Then she felt a warmth behind her. A wall of strength at her back. She straightened and let herself be supported by Lucas. "Like I said, it's fine. I don't need to know any more. Whatever your reasons, I'm glad that you two reconnected. I need some air."

"What is going on, Devi?" Ash's voice trembled. "Her father, who was he?"

Devi closed her eyes. "You."

The whispered word broke Tulsi from the inside. Cells became shrapnel that tore apart her muscles and singed the inner layer of her skin. Outwardly everything was in its place. The spices were still lined against the wall; the fresh flowers on the counter had all their petals and leaves. There was stillness.

It was Ash who spoke first. His voice trembled. Tulsi didn't know him well enough to understand if it was because of anger or shock. "What did you say?"

"I . . . I'm sorry," Devi said.

"I don't understand," Ash said. "We . . . that one night. Then you disappeared from my life. *You left.*"

"I didn't know," Devi pleaded. "We were already here, in Salem, when I found out."

He hadn't known either. At least there was that. Tulsi looked at Ash. His face reflected her pain. Then she understood what betrayal felt like. From the one person she'd never expected it from.

She couldn't look at Devi. Didn't know if she would be able to ever again.

CHAPTER
TWENTY-SIX

It was Lucas who had helped her up the back steps to his small apartment above the Pearl. He'd handed her a glass of water, which she now held in her hands but couldn't remember how to drink. "I took this online contemporary lit course. One of the books we read was *The Kite Runner*. 'Better to get hurt by the truth than comforted with a lie.' I wrote it down in my notebook. Thought it was so profound. I was so inspired by that quote. I kept thinking that's the type of person I want to be. Strong enough to handle the pain of truth. I lived with omissions. My ba, my"—Tulsi cleared her throat—"my mother. There was so much we never said. I kept thinking, What would happen if we just said the things, you know? How much could we really hurt each other if we spoke up?" Tulsi hiccuped, then sipped water. "I can't . . . she lied to me."

Tulsi wanted to curl up on his sofa and stay there. Everything she knew about the woman who loved her, raised her, was wrong. Tulsi had been so careful to avoid causing Devi pain, and yet . . . Tulsi curled inward. Made herself small enough to contain her anguish.

Lucas sat on the coffee table, close enough for their knees to touch. "Maybe take a beat. You're in shock."

Tulsi ignored him. "Every time she avoided answering my questions, she was lying to me. My whole life was built on this one lie. Or are there more?"

Lucas took the glass from her grasp and placed it next to him. "What do you need?"

She stared into his eyes. Had anyone ever asked her that? She'd spent her life around what her mother needed. Eggshells and emotional distance. Yet Tulsi could remember only remedies and cures. Hot water with mint. Never asking. Always prescribing. "This past week, I tried so hard to be like you. WWLD." Her bitter laugh bounced off the wall. "I don't think I know what Lucas would do in this situation. Tell me how to make it stop." Tulsi put her hand over her heart as if to keep its shattered pieces intact.

"I can't." He took her hands. "As for what I would do, hard to say. I'd go for a run. Play video games to keep my mind occupied. Sleep. Those are my go-to coping methods."

"I don't run," she said. "And I only play *Candy Crush*, but I don't know where my phone is right now. Why did she do it? That's what I can't figure out. He doesn't seem like a bad person. He didn't know either. I thought my mom and I were so close, no secrets between us." Even though Tulsi had never voiced her own wants, they weren't blatant lies. "I can't turn off my brain."

Lucas stroked the tops of her hands with his thumbs. "Okay, option three it is. How about a nap? Half an hour."

Tulsi pulled out of his grasp. Anger replaced the ache, and she could no longer contain it. Tulsi stood and paced. "I'm so mad. All these years she'd cry if I even tried to ask any questions. I stopped. I didn't want to hurt her. Turns out she cried so that she wouldn't have to keep lying to me. Not that it matters, because the original one was big enough. It didn't make it less because she'd only said it once. Or was it all because they wanted me to be alone? Like them. Dependent only on them. Because they need me to fulfill my destiny." And in that moment, Tulsi knew only one thing. She would never follow in their footsteps. Dharti's rule over their lives was finished.

"I've been so careful, all my life. No more." Tulsi paced from the tiny kitchen to the wall of the living room. At least there wasn't much in the way of furniture to trip on, and the plain rug that covered half the hardwood floor was taped down. "You don't have life stuff."

He followed her gaze. "What do you mean?"

"Nothing on the walls, no books, art, or photos of people. It's like a college dorm before students move in."

"I travel light," he said.

"There isn't even a fruit bowl or anything on the counters except a toaster and a teakettle."

"Everything I need is downstairs," he said. "I spend most of my time at the Pearl."

His voice was calm. She needed something from him, but it wasn't this "there, there"–type comfort. "Fine. Come take a nap with me."

At least that got a reaction. "Not a good idea."

"Do you want me to spell it out?" She put her hands on her hips.

"You're going through stuff; adding more to the mix isn't a good call." He stood.

She shrugged. The idea of sex with Lucas as a distraction took hold. It wouldn't fix everything, but at least she could escape for a bit. "I'm over it. So my mom lied, and my father, who I thought was dead, is actually next door." She saw his pity and turned away from him.

"Well, if you're already past it." His voice was light.

Their eyes met, and Tulsi saw what he wanted from her. Which was not sex, but to handle this, face it. "I'm sorry. I don't know why I'm being like this. You're trying to help. Except I don't know how to be in my own skin. Can you just fight with me? Or teach me how. Isn't that wild? Passive-aggressive, that's where I live. God, I'm such a mess."

"The only kind of arguing I know is the way my parents yelled at each other," he said. "I don't think they ever had a conversation that wasn't loud. I'm trained to take a person down. But I don't think that's what'll help."

"Physically?" Her brain focused. She imagined rolling around on the floor with him. Though no hitting. Maybe playful wrestling.

"Marine, remember?"

"Can you kill someone with a paper clip?" She really wanted to know.

He laughed. "No. Can you?"

"I wish," she said. "Why didn't I ask more questions, Lucas? Why wasn't I persistent? I didn't get to have feelings. Like, ever. If I was sad, I was told to balance my dosha and avoid spicy foods. This anger, it hurts. My skin is on fire; my chest feels like it's being pressed in a vise; my legs ache."

He pulled her down to the sofa, sat next to her, his arm stretched across the back. "You're doing okay. Getting it out instead of holding it in. You may not have practice, but you're handling it."

"You really think I'm someone I'm not." Tulsi leaned her head against his arm. "Strong. Nope. Smart. Not really."

"Stop beating yourself up," he said. "Those things aren't constants. There are times when we all do dumb things or give in when challenged."

"I can't imagine you weak." Tulsi craned her neck to look at him.

"I've cried at every funeral for a fallen marine," he said.

"That's a sign of strength," she said.

"Fine," he said. "I haven't talked to my dad in over a year because it's too hard. We exchange occasional emails."

She snuggled against him. "Why?"

"He's a victim of life," Lucas said. "Believes others are responsible for his circumstances. Marianna for leaving him. The oil company for forcing early retirement. He doesn't see that he can do something. Meet new people, find another job. He'd rather stay where he is and be bitter."

"I'm sorry." She patted his thigh, then rested her hand on the warm denim. "I can relate, though. I'm not bitter—at least, I don't think so. But for a long time, I accepted that I would live a boring life because of fate, and there wasn't anything I could do about it."

"Nothing about this day has been boring," he said.

Tulsi smiled at the irony. He was right; she'd wanted change and here it was. "Even though I'm mad at her, I still feel bad worrying her. I know I should let her know where I am, but I can't make myself." It was petty and selfish the way she felt toward Devi, and the guilt of it would swallow her, suffocate her.

"I told her when we headed out," he said. "You didn't hear me."

"I wonder if she and Ash are still talking. I hope he isn't being too hard on her." She sat up. "I should go check, make sure she's . . ." Tulsi forced herself to stop, to breathe. For now she wanted to be the kid and let her mom be the parent.

She settled back against Lucas's chest. "I should have recognized him, right? I haven't studied his face, but if I had tried, maybe I would have noticed if we had the same nose or chin."

"There wasn't any reason to," he said. "This isn't on you. It will get sorted out. For now, close your eyes and breathe. Shut your mind off for a minute."

"Has my grandmother been teaching you her ways?" Tulsi snuggled closer to his heat.

"I learned it during combat," he said. "A way to focus."

He'd lived this whole other life that she barely knew about. "I guess you think this is silly compared to life and death."

He wrapped his arm around her. "I think that loss, pain, grief, don't have a scale. It's not about who has more reason or less. You're suffering. Don't devalue it or push it aside. It's yours, and you get to feel however you want."

His words soothed her, and Tulsi let herself sink into her exhaustion.

CHAPTER TWENTY-SEVEN

She woke up in a strange bed. As she stared at the ceiling, Tulsi scanned her body inside and out. Her mind wasn't in a swirl, her chest had loosened a bit, and her legs were no longer sore. Her heart, well, she didn't dwell too much on that part. She was alone in the huge bed, twice the size of her own. As she looked around, the room was sparse. It suited Lucas in a strange way. He was as uncomplicated as this room. The bed was warm and comfortable and had his unfussy smell. Pine maybe from his aftershave. Soap from his shampoo. She curled to her side and saw him come through the door. "You take minimalism to a whole new level, Lucas."

"I hope that's a compliment."

He was in a towel. And she let herself look in a slow and appreciative way. His hair slick and damp. His jaw shaven clean. His skin taut around muscles that were defined even in a relaxed state. It was his massive chest that fascinated her. Ink. So much of it. The right side of him was covered with different symbols, places, dates, images she couldn't decipher from a glance. All threaded together and cohesive, like a painting. A string of circles curled around his left hip. "You're so hot. I mean attractive. Handsome?"

"Are you asking *me* for the right word?"

She pulled the sheet over her head. Then dropped it. "You do know that beds have two sheets, right? A fitted on flat. I am sleeping on one sheet, and it's all bunched up, so half of me is on the mattress."

"I haven't made it to Target yet; the place came with these." He crossed to a small dresser, his back to hers.

It was bare, no tattoos, only muscles. They flexed as he pulled on a T-shirt. It was then she noticed his arm. "Buddha wrapped in barbed wire."

He turned. "What?"

She crawled up on her knees. Shifted to the edge of her bed and grabbed his arm. "This. I saw this. It changed me." She examined it up close and traced the lines. It had been imprinted in her mind, but now she saw it in detail, the shading that gave the statue dimension. "I wondered what kind of life the person with this tattoo lived, and wished I could have something like that to mark me. It kind of sent me into an existential tailspin." She looked up. "It was you."

"I don't know what's happening right now," he said. "But we can get you one if you want. I'm sure there are some artists around here."

She shook her head and grabbed his shoulders to get down from the bed and stand up. "It has to be earned. Routine doesn't deserve this level of permanent marker."

His fingers tightened on her hips, pulling her closer.

"It was you," she repeated. "A sign from the universe."

"A coincidence," he said.

Tulsi disagreed but didn't want to talk about it. She just wanted him. This moment. As if his well-lived life could make up for her own. Her heart pounded in a staccato rhythm. Being with him was an adventure that she wanted, that she needed more than anything else right now. Her life was messy, and she decided to make it messier. Tulsi cupped his face and pulled him down to her for a kiss. His lips coursed over hers, and she sighed when he took control. The featherlight touch of his mouth became more insistent, more demanding, and she sank into the sensation of his touch. She didn't know when or how, but they managed to slip out of their shirts, their pants, and then they were skin to skin. The room filled with their sounds of pleasure. Tulsi's fingers laced with Lucas's as they lost themselves in each other, tipping over to the point where there was no return.

They were both out of breath when they heard banging on the front door. Lucas moved first, pressing a soft kiss against her temple before he shifted off her. "I'm going to clean up and dress. Stay here."

And she did. Instead of beating herself up over what had just happened between them, she let herself be happy. It was him. From that very first day, it had been Lucas's arm. Fate. As he came out of the bathroom, the knock was louder. Tulsi got dressed as he went to answer.

"Beta." Devi rushed in. "I've been so worried about you. You left your cell at the shop. Thank you, Lucas, for taking care of her, but it's gotten so late, and when Tulsi didn't come home . . ." Her voice faded.

Seeing her mother, everything she'd released in the past few hours boomeranged back. She couldn't meet Devi's eyes; then she did. Her mom needed to see the result of her lie on Tulsi's face. "I'm an adult. I don't have a curfew."

Devi put her hand over her mouth. Her voice wobbled. "I know this is upsetting for you."

Tulsi saw Lucas go back into the bedroom. She appreciated the privacy even as she yearned for his support. "Not sure *upsetting* is the right word."

Devi wrenched her hands together. "Come home. We can talk there."

"Ha," Tulsi said. "Hot water, mint leaves, and avoidance. No thanks."

"Tulsi," Devi said.

"I'm surprised you came looking for me," she said, cutting Devi off. "I thought you'd be in your sunroom with your paints or closed up in your bedroom."

Devi wept, her face in her hands.

Tulsi pushed aside the urge to wrap her arms around her mom. "Where is Ash?"

Devi steadied herself. Dropped her arms to her sides. "He . . . he left."

His rejection was a gut punch, and Tulsi moved away from the door, back to the couch that had given her rest. "Guess he didn't want to see me?"

Devi came around and sat next to Tulsi. "He needs time."

She nodded. "I don't want to talk in circles, Ma. No more. Tell me. All of it."

Devi cleared her throat and twisted her fingers together. Because love won even in betrayal, Tulsi brought her mom a glass of water. Handed it to her, then sat again. This time her mom would have to get it all out, regardless of how hard it might be for Devi. "He is my father. You lied to me."

"Yes."

"And to him," Tulsi said.

Devi sipped. "Yes."

Tulsi waited. Let the silence linger. She was determined to hear the whole of it.

"Ashish," Devi said, then halted as if to search for the right words. Toyed with the glass in her hand. "Your ba and I had left Chicago. We were settled here for a couple of months when I found out I was pregnant."

"There were phones, the postal system." Tulsi didn't hold back her simmering temper. Stopped measuring her words for her mom's sake.

"We were in a new town far from anything familiar," Devi added. "At first I was so scared I couldn't even tell Ba. I knew how angry she was at Hema, Ashish's mother. So I kept quiet for as long as possible. I knew that if I told Ashish about you, he would want to be in your life. He would have taken me away from my mother. Your ba might have disowned me. I couldn't leave her. When I started showing, I had to tell her. She wasn't upset. Told me she had no right because of her own past, how she'd been only a few months older than me when she got pregnant. I asked her what we should do, and she put her hand on my stomach. Told me you were a blessing. Fate. Our future."

Tulsi shut her eyes to keep steady. "She's the one who told you not to tell me about him or him about me?"

"It wasn't like that," Devi protested. "There was no plot or plan. I knew she and Hema would never reconcile. That the four of us could never be a family."

"Five of us," Tulsi said. "Guess I didn't count, though."

Devi reached out, and Tulsi recoiled from her touch. Devi dropped her hand. "You counted more than all of us. If I said anything to Ashish, you would have been raised in an environment full of anger and hatred between your two grandmothers. Ashish and I were both so young—he had big dreams. All of that would change. But if we started here, in this town, just the three of us, I vowed you would never lack for anything. I promised to dedicate my whole life to you."

Tulsi couldn't accept those reasons, not when she knew Devi as well as she did. "You were protecting yourself, not just me."

"You're right," she said.

"And it fit within the narrative of spice healers and our solitary lives," Tulsi said. "Convenient."

"I did what I believed was right."

Tulsi stood. "For you." Her voice rose. "It wasn't about me at all. It was about your inability to handle any hard emotions. It wasn't about what it would be like for me to believe my father was dead, even though he wasn't."

"I could raise you," Devi said. "Like Ba raised me. We did fine without fathers."

"That is not the point, Ma." Tulsi ran her hands through her hair. Tugged. Then let go. How could she explain when she didn't know how? That there had been a gap, a missing part that had always made her wonder. It was the unknown that had beckoned her. She sat again. She didn't know what she wanted in life, because she'd known only half of who she was. "I had a secret notebook when I was little. I used to draw an outline of a face. Just a circle with ears and a chin. I wondered about the color of his hair. Was it like mine? The shape of his eyes, nose. I left them blank because I couldn't see him. And I couldn't ask you. That was the worst part."

"I didn't know," Devi said.

"You wouldn't have wanted to," Tulsi said. "I knew even then that talk of him was forbidden. To save you from mourning. The pastels . . . you've dressed like a widow my whole life."

Devi wept. "I'm a horrible mother. I failed you in so many ways."

Tulsi ached to the core of her being. She couldn't even be mad without her mom falling apart. "I'm upset. So are you." Maybe it was better to stop here.

"I really believed it was better to protect you from that kind of friction," Devi said.

What an understated word to use as a reason for such a big lie. "Go home, Ma. I'll ask Lucas if I can crash here."

"No," Devi said. "I'm not leaving without you."

"I'm not ready to pretend everything is fine," Tulsi said.

"I'm sorry," Devi said. "I never wanted you to be hurt for my mistake."

Tulsi turned away from her mom. Waited for her to leave. She stayed by the closed door between them. Lucas came up behind her. Enfolded her in his arms. Tulsi placed her palm over the Buddha on his arm, and while he held her, she wept.

CHAPTER TWENTY-EIGHT

Tulsi watched the sun emerge from the distant horizon. Streaks of red, orange, and yellow glimmered on the water as ripples moved toward her. The early-morning quiet brought her peace, if not clarity. The dew on the bench under her began to evaporate as she brought her legs up, wrapped her arms around her shins, and rested her chin on her knees. The gulls stirred and chirped, but even they were lethargic, knowing food would have to wait until the bustle of the day.

She had a father. And lost the relationship she'd had with her mom. If she was more like Aruna ba, Tulsi would shut down. Leave. If she was more like Devi, she'd go to Rasa, open up, and pretend everything was fine. Neither was the right way. There was one more person in the mix. Ash. What did she get from him? And would she ever get the opportunity to know?

He'd left. Needed time, which was an infinite measure. It could be a week, a year, the rest of her life. She reached for her phone in her tote. Opened the message app to write to him.

Hi.

It's Tulsi.

Coffee? Or tea? Or lunch?

If you want.

No pressure.

Feel free to ignore if . . .

She dropped her phone back in the tote and refused to regret the six messages she'd sent Ash. He didn't seem like the type to not reply; then again, this changed his world as well, and he might want to pretend he'd never seen her in the Viking costume.

A night's sleep had dulled her resentment toward her mother. As much as Devi didn't like to talk about the hard things, she'd still been a loving and nurturing mother.

Approaching footsteps broke through the quiet. Tulsi craned her neck to see Lucas jogging toward her. His T-shirt had sweat splotches. When he came near, he slowed his trot to a walk and fiddled with his watch.

"How's the view?"

Tulsi shifted to make room for him on the bench. "You or the sunrise?"

He nudged her with his shoulder. "Your choice."

She liked that he made things easy, didn't pressure her to talk, which made her want to lean on him even more. But this was hers to figure out. Lucas, well, she didn't know what they were, but for now she liked that they were more than friends. It was better to not define it.

"How was your run?" Tulsi handed him the water bottle she'd put in her tote for him.

"Slower than usual." He took a gulp. "I don't like the heat. I've been in Afghanistan, Iraq, other places in the Middle East, and still my body works better when it's below sixty degrees."

"Not to mention, born and raised in Texas," she added.

"I guess it doesn't matter; sometimes it's biology."

Tulsi watched a seagull circle over the water. "I used to wish I was more like my mom," she said. "Peaceful. Serene. Nothing ruffled her, you know. She inspired people to take care of her, support her, return her kindness. But I guess I was like her, too, in that I always kept all my thoughts, questions, and comments to myself. I couldn't tell her I didn't want to be a spice healer, so I pretended I wasn't any good at it. Mixed up blends and made myself look incapable of being able to handle it all. I got so great at it that I started to believe I wasn't capable of doing anything. Jack-of-all."

"That explains why you're so hard on yourself," he said. "Maybe it's time to be you."

She rested her chin on her knees again. "How?"

He clasped the bottle in his hands and leaned his elbows on his thighs. "I don't know. What do you want? Not forever, but maybe for the next year or two."

Tulsi crossed her legs and leaned against the back of the bench. She looked at him. It was time to say the words out loud. "I don't want to be a spice healer. I don't want to run Rasa." Her heart raced at all she'd revealed. "It sounds ungrateful. They built this for me to carry it on to the next generation." Guilt and shame made her turn away from him.

"It's okay to want something else," he said.

Then even as she feared what it might mean for the two of them, Tulsi said the last of it. "I want to leave Salem and figure out if I can find my passion while seeing some of the world."

He stretched his leg out in front of him, his arm across the back of the bench. "That adds a wrench for me."

Surprised, she looked at him.

He toyed with a strand of hair that brushed her neck. "I didn't know about you, at first. My goal was to keep my head down, open the Pearl, not get involved. 'Not a people person' was a way to keep my distance. Now that the restaurant is open, I thought, new goal. This town is good enough, the people are nice, and everyone is in each other's business, instead of minding their own. Reminded me of Mable's place."

"What is your new goal?"

"Going to HSBA meetings, making paneer for Betty Bishop. You."

Pleasure and pressure collided. He wanted her. She wanted him. He would ask her to stay, and she didn't trust herself not to.

"There's a pull for me," he said. "Maybe it's your big brown eyes. The way you devour whatever I cook for you. Every time you laugh, you look surprised that you let it out. You encourage everyone, from your mom to me. No matter what's going on inside your head, and it's a lot, you keep going. Yesterday, I saw you persevere. Heard you empathize with your mom even after she hurt you. You're amazing."

"Even though I don't have any tattoos?" He was seeing her in a way she'd never seen herself. It was hard to believe him.

He stroked the nape of her neck. "Oh, I'm aware."

"Are you saying I shouldn't go?" She wanted him to ask her to stay and hoped he wouldn't.

The sun was fully above the horizon. She stayed silent. Waited.

"I would never ask that of you," he said. "No one should. It's your life, Tulsi. You have to figure out how you want to live it. Not for your mom or grandmother. For you."

His words hugged and scared her at the same time. "What would you do?"

"I'm doing it." Lucas shifted his body to face her. "I was looking for a place to put my own roots down. I found it."

He was making this so hard for her. His steadiness would help her stay anchored. Tulsi could see what more could be with Lucas. They could start their mornings together, have dinner. On days off, they would go to the beach or explore Boston. Annual vacations.

It would be another routine. It would mean going from one pattern to another.

She leaned toward him. Brushed his lips with hers. Once. Twice. He let her stay in control. Held her neck but only to steady her, no pressure, just a static hold. With one more gentle kiss, she pulled back. Undecided. But tempted.

CHAPTER
TWENTY-NINE

Nothing had really changed at home. Only harmony and serenity had been replaced by unspoken tension. Avoidance was no longer passive, and the three Gupta women lived in silence. Their routine continued, and Tulsi didn't miss any more shifts. Three days had passed since the fateful moment when Aruna walked in and saw Ash. And still Tulsi paid invoices, ordered inventory, and catered to demanding customers. Except her cheerfulness was forced. Her smile dropped when no one was looking. She still hadn't heard back from Ash.

Physically and emotionally exhausted, Tulsi picked up takeout from the Pearl. Seeing Lucas, however briefly, was the best part of her day. He'd dropped off lunch for them these past two days and texted her to grab dinner on her way home. He liked feeding her family. And she was afraid of becoming overly attached to how much her heart wanted to fully welcome him.

In the kitchen, she laid out the baked naan stuffed with paneer, tomato chutney, and fresh herbs. The one change was to not set the table. The food was out, and each would grab their own plate and disband. Aruna ba would sit on the back patio. Devi in her studio. Tulsi at the counter. She refused to be invisible. Her mom had tried a few conversations about things other than what was now between them. Tulsi was civil in her responses but didn't engage.

Just as she was about to grab a slice, the doorbell rang. It was likely Mrs. Bishop, who'd noticed the disturbance among them and was likely here to make them confront each other. She gasped when she opened it to see Ash standing on the front porch.

"I, um . . . hello." Every muscle in her body tensed. "Hey."

"I should have replied to your message or called." He seemed unsure, different from the way he'd carried himself when they'd met for coffee. "I didn't know what to say."

"I can relate," she said.

"I still don't know how to start." He looked at her as if studying her face.

She searched his for resemblance. Perhaps in the sharp arch of his eyebrows, the slightly protruding ears, or in his general lankiness. She opened the door wider. "Do you want to come in?"

"I'd like that," he said.

"My mom and grandmother are home." There. He'd been warned.

He nodded. "That's good."

She raised her brow.

"I believe in putting it all on the table." Ash looked around the foyer.

She laughed. "I have that T-shirt."

"What?"

"Never mind." She led him to the kitchen. "I was about to eat. Can I get you a plate?"

"Just water." He stood with his hands on the back of the counter chair. "It's cozy. Your home. Lived in."

"None of it was intentional." Tulsi handed him a glass of tap water. "If one of us saw something we liked, we made space for it. The quilts, the pillows, most are handmade."

"Your grandmother was always a big knitter," he said. "She made hats, gloves, and scarves for Devi and me when we were kids."

"For me too," Tulsi said. "I think my very first booties are still in the attic. Aruna ba doesn't like to throw anything away."

"I'm glad," he said. "Maybe I can see what I missed. Baby pictures, your favorite toys, how old you were when you took your first steps."

Tulsi drank from her water glass to wash away the tears that rose up. "I can dig those out for you at some point." It was strange that they could make small talk of such big things.

Ash was dressed in dark slacks. His fitted white shirt gleamed as dusky sunlight from the open windows hit just right. He stripped off his suit jacket. Tulsi hadn't noticed that the AC wasn't on. Most people would find their indoor temperature uncomfortable. "I can turn on the air-conditioning."

"No, I'm fine," he said. "I grew up like this. Cool air was for company."

"I've heard that my whole life." She shifted and wished she hadn't changed into her rattiest denim shorts, the ones she wore only at home. At least she wore her "Time Will Tell" T-shirt. An appropriate coincidence.

"Have a seat." She gestured to him. "I'm sorry the counter is messy. I sort of dumped everything I was carrying when I got home."

He waved her comment off. "I know I showed up abruptly. I don't want you to think I'm pushing myself on you. Even though I am." He glanced at the photos on the hall table. They were of Tulsi and Devi on various vacations, a few with Aruna around holidays. "I can't not know this. I can't stay away. I hope you understand."

Her muscles relaxed. She'd been waiting for him to reject her. She wasn't a kid anymore, and he had two daughters of his own. "I'm glad you came."

His whole face opened up, and Tulsi saw that they had the same smile.

"You again? This time in my home." Aruna came into the kitchen.

Tulsi noticed that Ash didn't look afraid. In fact, he bowed down to touch her feet. It was part of the old culture, a way to greet your elders and receive their blessings. Tulsi had never done so, mostly because there hadn't been another grandparent in her life. Until now. She wondered if Hema would expect it from Tulsi.

"He came to see me, Ba. You're welcome to join us."

"Ash," Devi said, coming in from her studio.

Her two parents looked at each other. Ash glanced away. Tulsi saw her mom's pain at his silent dismissal.

"I see that without my influence your mother stopped teaching you manners," Aruna said. "Showing up without being invited."

"You haven't changed either, Aruna masi," Ash said. "You never miss an opportunity to scold me. It used to be your favorite hobby."

"I am glad you're here," Devi said.

Tulsi snorted.

"Another lie," Ash said to Devi.

"Don't use that tone with my daughter," Aruna added.

"The food's getting cold." Tulsi tried to defuse the pressure in the room, then regretted it. Ash had come here to face all that happened, and she wanted to stop avoiding the pain that would be revealed with every spoken word. Luckily no one took her up on the food distraction anyway.

"What was Tulsi's first word?" Ash asked.

"Ma," Devi whispered.

He ran his hands through his hair.

"How old was she when she lost her first tooth? Was she scared of monsters? Is she allergic to anything? My God, I don't even know her birthday." He turned to confront Devi. "You took that away. From me. From Tulsi. Why?"

"To avoid this," Devi said. "Our mothers were always fighting. Eventually we would start as well. Tulsi would have been in the middle of it all. We left because . . ."

"Your mother betrayed me," Aruna said. "Stole from me."

Ash shook his head. "Was that why you kept my own child from me? Revenge? I have to admit, Devi, I didn't think you could ever be this cruel."

"No." Devi approached him. "No. It wasn't like that. I . . ." She looked at Tulsi. "Every morning I would go to the water, sit, and watch the ripples. I was at peace. I decided that it would be better for Tulsi to have this kind of life. That I would love her enough, keep her safe. And I did. I didn't want to raise her around hatred and anger."

"It wasn't only your decision," Ash said.

"You were nineteen," Devi argued. "At your dream college. You had so many plans, ambitions. You would have given that up."

He shook his head and stood. "Some faith you had in me. And you may have rationalized that not knowing about Tulsi was somehow better for me, but it was wrong."

"Then blame me," Aruna said. "I knew she hadn't told you. I agreed with her."

Tulsi hung her head.

"Did you hate me along with my mother?" he said. "You raised me like your own. You would pretend to scold me, then offer me a treat. I still don't know what happened between you and my mother. She's never spoken about it. But I thought you had a soft spot for me. You were a second mom to me. Then you just left."

"I didn't hate you," Aruna said. "But I didn't appreciate you giving my daughter ideas, filling her head with thoughts about California. She even applied to Berkeley because of you. You knew Devi's passion. You knew her responsibility to our work. She would have given up her calling for you."

"Ma." Devi touched Aruna's arm. "It was never going to be permanent. I always knew I was a spice healer. I never thought about doing anything else. I would follow Ash to California and only to get a degree. Then I would return to Chicago so we could do our work together. It was never my plan to leave you."

Ash laughed. The bitter sound made Devi cower. And Tulsi moved to flank her mom from the other side. It was so habitual that she didn't even notice she'd done so.

"At work, we have this conflict training." Ash walked around their kitchen. "The basic principle is that most issues can be resolved with direct and immediate conversations. It's how I raise my daughters. They know that things unsaid can morph, lead to disaster and destruction."

"To be fair . . ." Tulsi felt the need to defend the way she'd grown up. "My mom was eighteen when she had me. Ba was the same age when my mom was born. There weren't any trainings available for them. They did their best."

"Do you believe that?" he asked Tulsi. "Even now?"

"I love them." It was the only answer she could give him. They did do their best. And it wasn't good, the way they all behaved with each other. Still, Devi and Aruna were hers. And she was theirs. It wasn't exactly forgiveness, but she could understand.

He sighed and tucked his hands in the pockets of his slacks. "I've been so angry. I called my lawyer to sue for custody. She reminded me that Tulsi isn't a child."

"I'm so sorry, Ashish."

He made his way to be in front of Devi. "How do I make up for all this lost time?"

"You can't," Devi replied.

"And these past few weeks?" Ash asked. "We talked, messaged each other. We became friends again. Did you ever plan to tell me?"

Tulsi heard the pain in Ash's voice. She related to it because he was speaking her thoughts. Asking her mother questions Tulsi had left alone.

"I shouldn't have." Devi's voice warbled. "I knew it was bad to respond to your messages once you came back. And neither you nor Tulsi had any reason to suspect. I gave you vague answers about her age." She wiped her cheeks. "I got lost. I remembered how much I loved you. I hadn't used my heart in that way for decades. I couldn't. Then you were back and I . . . I was selfish. I wanted what I missed all these years. Even if it was from a distance. I knew nothing would come of it, so I enjoyed the thin reconnection. You married, have daughters, a full life even after you lost your wife. I only wanted to keep the joy I felt at being in your life again."

Tulsi couldn't stop herself from holding her mom's hand.

"You didn't answer my question," Ash said.

Devi looked up. "I wanted to tell you. I didn't know how. And I was afraid to lose Tulsi."

It was the most direct her mother had ever been. Maybe Devi was capable of change. If pushed. And Ash didn't shy away from doing that. She saw how it might have been between them.

Ash cleared his throat and stepped back. "I want time. With Tulsi."

"What do you mean?" Devi said.

Ash looked at Tulsi. "Come with me. To Chicago. Meet my daughters, my family."

"No," Aruna said. "Absolutely not."

Tulsi steadied herself. "I will."

CHAPTER THIRTY

The next day it was all sorted, thanks to Ash's assistant. Tulsi would join him in Chicago as soon as she could. Rasa was too chaotic for her to leave with him, and he had to go back and share the news with his own family. Instead, she did everything she could to get more stock, get ahead on the paperwork and invoices. She'd wanted to get a temp for them, but the conversation was over before it started, as Aruna didn't want any stranger in their shop. "It would upset the balance."

"I can't believe I'm doing this." Tulsi sliced into the polenta cake that was topped with a flavorful mushroom medley. Lucas had saved her a plate of tonight's special. Everyone had gone, and it was only the two of them in Pearl's kitchen. Her favorite time of the day. Her favorite place. And with her favorite person. "It's not like I've never been on a plane. Though not international unless Canada counts. Please stop me from babbling."

"Nope." He'd gotten another stool and sat across from her, a beer in his hand. "Might be better to get it all out now to me and not the person seated next to you on the flight."

"Do you ever think about growing a beard?"

"No."

"Good. You would look scary." She took another big bite. Chased it with her lemony sparkling water. "Things are weird. At home, I mean.

My home. They don't want me to go to Chicago but won't come out and say it. So we avoid the topic. But then my mom helped me pack this morning before we opened. I have to keep reminding myself that she was only eighteen. It'll be good to have some distance, right?" She was chattering again but refused to apologize. He didn't mind. She could see that. When she talked, no matter how inane, he listened. "Rasa is still busy. Maybe I should have waited to go to Chicago. October, except then Halloween takes off." Her fork stopped halfway to her mouth. The fifteenth. She hadn't considered. It would be even busier. On top of what was happening, Salem would soon be inundated with Halloween-itis. From the Salem witch trials to *Practical Magic*, hundreds of thousands of tourists would descend to celebrate the eerie, spooky, magical, and fun holiday that lasted for the whole of October. "I can't go. What was I thinking?"

"I'll check in on them," he said.

"No, not tomorrow, I mean, the whole—" She inhaled, then exhaled. There was no point in bringing that up. Everything had changed. Her plan would too. And it would mean more time with Lucas.

"Never mind. You're right. And it's only for a week. You'll call me if I need to rush back, right?" She liked that he hadn't changed the way he interacted with Devi and Aruna. He didn't hold anything against them.

"Of course," he said.

She grinned. "You are firmly in it, aren't you? Mr. Not-a-People-Person."

"Betty wants me to join the winter festival committee." He took another sip.

She clasped her hand over his. He would be there for the holiday parade and tree lighting. Tulsi could see herself next to him.

He flipped his hand so they were palm to palm and held it.

"I have half sisters. Isn't that incredible?" She entwined her fingers with his. "Bina and Lina. I asked Ash yesterday, when he sent me pictures of them, if he'd been the one to name them. He told me it had been something his wife had chosen for the girls, and he wanted to honor her wish. Shefali, that was his wife's name, liked the way it sounded together. And B came before L, so they decided the birth order would be the same."

"Breathe."

She nodded. Clutched his hand. Then did as he ordered. "This was delicious. Thank you."

He clanked the lip of his bottle against the top of her glass.

"Oh, I forgot to tell you," Tulsi said. "The weirdest thing happened today. These two people came in. They said they knew Sonia O'Shea and that they were excited to visit. I asked them how they knew about it since it hasn't aired yet." She stared down at their joined hands. "They said they'd gotten a sneak peek from someone who worked at the station and that's why they were there for cures."

"That's like most people lately, right?"

"Yeah." Something about them bothered her. "It's just, I got the sense that they were up to something. They took pictures and bought three hundred dollars' worth of things. I asked them what it was all for, and they gave each other sneaky looks. I don't know, it was all so weird."

"Did you mention it to your online friend?"

"Skye? No. I usually just give her recipes," Tulsi said. "At least she doesn't tag our accounts after I asked her not to. It's already out of control with all the followers."

"Trust your instinct," he said. "But also, you can only do what's within your control."

"You're nice." She scooched up, leaned over. He met her halfway for a quick kiss. "My mom knows we're . . . uh, spending time together."

"We're adults," Lucas said.

"My ba." Tulsi shuddered. "I don't know how she'll react."

"She likes me," Lucas said.

"That's the problem." Tulsi knew Aruna would take it as a positive development.

Then she voiced a fear that had settled in ever since she got the email with the tickets and itinerary. "I don't know how to be part of a family."

He glanced at her. "You have one. You can handle this, sweetheart."

She reached up and brushed her lips against his again. "Sleepover?"

"Always."

This. Her whole heart lived here now. In this moment. In this place.

CHAPTER THIRTY-ONE

Ash's cool, white-tiled foyer was the size of Rasa. A wide staircase rose from the center, and a crystal chandelier the size of a wheelbarrow hung from the vaulted ceiling. Tulsi had never been inside a house this big. It reminded her of the type of mansions on *The Real Housewives of Beverly Hills*, but Indian. A bright-green fabric wall hanging embroidered with tiny mirrors took prime position in the living room. A full-size indoor bench swing made of wood and covered in green and yellow silk throw pillows occupied a corner of the room. The white sofa where Tulsi sat could seat six, even though it was meant for three.

She perched on the edge and smoothed her white capri pants. As she wiggled her bare toes on the thick white carpet, she was grateful she'd given herself a pedicure.

"Your flight was good?"

Ash had already asked her that when he picked her up from the airport in his dark-blue Mercedes SUV. It was high enough that she had to grab the overhead handle and heave herself into the passenger seat.

"They made me a cranberry juice with seltzer and lime. First class was definitely an experience." She'd also had a glass of white wine just to settle her nerves but didn't think it was appropriate to mention in front of the twins.

"Your first time?" Lina asked.

"Not on a plane, but we usually travel in coach." The twins sat across from her in two wide chairs with a small round table between them, where they'd set water and pink Starbucks drinks for themselves.

"We only fly first," Bina added. "Lina has been begging Dad to get a private jet, though I worry about the environment. I'm on the fence."

"No plane," Ash said.

"Dad grew up poor and now doesn't know how to spend money," Bina added. "We try to teach him, but he refuses to learn. He's always checking the price on everything and still buys stuff on sale."

Ash laughed. "Look around; nothing in this house is cheap."

"Thanks to us," Lina said. "I have an eye for style. We've already picked out our cars for when we turn eighteen. He's making us wait until then, even though we both have our driver's license."

"It's going to be one car you will share," Ash said. "Used, not new. And your rideshare allowance will be reduced to only for emergencies."

This conversation was so foreign to her. The idea of picking out a car. "My mom, grandma, and I share a Toyota between the three of us."

"Is it new at least?" Lina glanced up from her phone.

"Twelve years old," Tulsi replied. "It still has a CD player slot."

"My first car had a tape deck," Ash added. "Now it's all a giant computer instead of a dash. I wonder if I have a box of tapes in the basement. I had every INXS and U2 album."

Lina rolled her eyes. "You have Spotify."

"And I listen to it," he said. "I'm reminiscing."

Tulsi heard his love for them even through his frustrated tone.

"What's your family like?" Bina flipped her long black hair behind her shoulder. It was smooth and shiny as it hung straight, parted in the middle. The twins were fraternal but resembled each other. They both had dark-brown eyes and black hair, but Lina wore hers up in a fancy twist. Their faces were contoured, their thick eyebrows perfectly trimmed, and their lips bright red. Lina wore a long, silk maxi dress with billowed sleeves, and Bina was in a silk jumpsuit, each in an identical shade of red. Tulsi had searched but couldn't find a single point of resemblance between her and them even though the three of them shared a biological father.

She looked over at Ash, wondered how much he'd told them. "My mom and grandmother are spice healers. We help people be healthy."

"Right," Lina said. "You have a store, right?"

"Rasa," Bina added. "I saw your website."

Lina glanced at Bina.

"After my dad told us," Bina added.

Tulsi wondered what their silent exchange was all about. "If you ever want anything, I can send it to you. We usually don't ship—"

"We have a store of our own," Lina said, cutting her off. "Seventy of them, all over America."

"Oh, right." She knew Ash worked in retail. "Groceries."

"House of Spice," Bina said.

Tulsi was shocked. "I guess I never asked the name." She'd missed it, this whole time.

"We have a lifetime of catching up to do," he said. "The name isn't important."

Except it was. House of Spice was Aruna ba's nemesis. She hated them more than the spice aisles in Market Basket. "Did you have your stores when my ba lived here?"

"No," he said. "Our first one opened about a year later."

"I see." Tulsi made a note to ask her ba if she knew who ran House of Spice or if it was simply the concept of an Indian grocery store that she hated.

"You're expanding to Massachusetts. I heard something about that."

"We've mostly focused on the West and Southwest," Ash said. "It's our first attempt to become established in New England. The market is saturated, so I've been researching ways to set us apart from not just other supermarkets but also Indian grocery stores."

"Dad," Lina said. "You're boring our guest."

Tulsi noticed the emphasis on the last word. No one had mentioned the nature of their relationship. "I'm not bored. It sounds exciting. Rasa isn't a chain or a grocery store, but I have been involved in retail my whole life."

"Healing is all the rage right now," Bina said. "Everyone is into natural remedies."

"All over TikTok," Lina said. "The influencers try to one-up each other on who can make matcha trend. Like, stay out of other people's cultures."

"You and my ba would get along." In a way, Tulsi agreed. She thought about Skye and her interests. Tulsi had seen how Skye misunderstood the mixes Tulsi sent, adapted them to what she wanted to say, left a few things out, like their properties, and played up the curative parts. "Are you on there?" And had they seen Rasa's videos?

Lina sat up. "Most of my posts are styling tips. From fashion to home decor."

"She wants to be an icon," Bina said. "I'd rather watch videos than make them. Sometimes Lina makes me be in hers, which is fine."

Bina was older, but Tulsi got the sense that it was Lina who took the lead. "You have a great eye. I like your choices."

"We've been in this house since the girls were toddlers. Their masi, Shefali's sister, helped with the decorating," Ash explained.

"Toral masi has okay taste." Lina didn't look up from her phone. "We did most of the picking and choosing. She was the one who kept the budget and ordered everything."

"Do you have any siblings?" Tulsi asked Ash.

He shook his head. "On my side it's just my mom and me. Then Shefali and the girls came along."

Tulsi liked that he talked about his dead wife so freely. He didn't treat it as taboo to mention her name or even seemed particularly mournful about saying it.

"Our mom was amazing," Bina added. "I'm going to follow in her footsteps and study biology. She got married before she finished her PhD in molecular biology, and then we were born, so she didn't get to complete it."

Ash nodded. "But you will." He turned to Tulsi. "It's her choice, though, not something I asked of Bina. She's always liked science."

"Can you do magic?" Bina asked, changing the subject. "Like with the spices."

Tulsi shook her head. "No, we practice Ayurveda. It's an ancient science, not magic."

"Oh," Bina said. "Because the videos . . . ow."

Lina reached over and poked her. "She talks too much."

"I don't mind," Tulsi said.

"Lina, no hitting," Ash admonished her.

"It was a poke, Dad. Bina is being dramatic."

Bina poked her back. "Now we're even."

Homesickness hit her in the gut. She was an outsider here, too afraid to even put her glass on the table without a coaster.

"Are you okay with your room?" Ash asked.

"Oh yes," Tulsi said. "I love how it looks over the backyard." *Yard* was an understatement, because it was a huge, manicured lawn that butted up against the woods.

"It's the best guest room," Bina said.

Tulsi heard the emphasis on *guest* again. "Thank you. It's quite luxurious, and blue and gray is such a soothing combination."

She'd made a mistake. How was she going to last an entire week here?

"It must seem very fancy to you," Lina said. "What's your house like?"

"It's home," Tulsi said. "I guess I never thought about color schemes. My mom paints, and her pieces are hung up all over."

"Sounds chaotic," Bina said.

"It's comfortable," Ash said. "Well lived in."

"Which means poor," Lina added.

"Lina." Ash's voice was stern. "Apologize right now."

"What? I was only stating an opinion," she said.

"You were making a judgment." Ash stayed firm. "You know better."

Tulsi didn't like them fighting, not over something said to her. "I didn't take your comment as an insult, Lina. I grew up in a great community, and we never lacked for anything. My house isn't as big as this one, but it has its charm, and there's history. It was built in the eighteen hundreds. Sometimes it'll creak in the middle of the night. I used to think it was ghosts. We do live in Salem, but really, it's just the house settling in after being used all day."

"That sounds cool," Bina said. "I don't believe in ghosts, but I do think there are spirits. My mom is one. She watches over us."

"I agree," Tulsi said. "My friend Gemma is a medium. She talks to spirits."

"Wow," Bina said. "That's so cool."

"It's fake," Lina added. "My sister is gullible. She has, like, three horoscope apps."

"You make me read ours out loud at breakfast every morning," Bina retorted.

"Another friend of mine is into geomancy." Tulsi broke up their verbal skirmish. "It's about planets and how their positions affect our day-to-day."

"You're making that up," Lina said.

"It's true." Then Tulsi got an idea. "Did you know that Salem got its name from a warlock? That's why we have so many witches and oracles."

"What?" Bina said. "I never knew that."

Lina read from her phone. "Salem comes from the Hebrew word *Shalom*, which makes it the city of peace."

Tulsi laughed. "Got you." She pointed to Bina.

"That's not funny," Bina said.

"It was." Ash reached over and tapped his daughter's knee. "I love that you're trusting, but maybe stop and think before immediately believing something."

"Geomancy?" Bina asked Tulsi.

"Real."

She glanced at Lina, who confirmed it by showing her an open page on the phone screen.

"I have a lot planned for this weekend," Ash said. "I took a few days off next week as well so we can spend it together. As a family."

The mood changed at Ash's use of the word. The twins glanced at her, then stared at their phones.

"That's great," Tulsi said. "I'm looking forward to seeing this city. There are so many things to do—maybe we can see the giant bean?"

"It's on the list," Ash said. "I thought tonight, since you traveled, the four of us could have dinner in. Our home chef is making lasagna," Ash said. "And a salad. You mentioned you're a vegetarian."

"I am," Tulsi said. "So are my mom and grandmother."

"Because you're Hindu?" Bina asked. "We are, too, but I need to have a Chicago dog whenever I go see the White Sox."

"And chicken nuggets." Ash patted his small belly. "That's okay in my version of Hinduism."

"Dad," Bina said. "You know better."

"What?" Ash exaggerated his confusion. "My Stanford roommates and I kept a running list of best to worst from every place within fifty miles of campus."

"And you're no longer allowed to have any," Bina said. "It's not good for your heart."

"Bina's my healer." He smiled at his daughter. "She forces me to eat healthy, makes me practice tennis, and badgers me if I have more than one scoop of ice cream."

"He has a sweet tooth," Bina said. "We're omnivores, but our grandmother is pure veg. She doesn't even eat eggs."

Tulsi wondered where Hema was and whether she was even aware of Tulsi's existence. "Does she live nearby?"

Ash cleared his throat. "She lives here. With us. But she's away this week."

"Oh." Tulsi suspected that, really, Hema might not want to have anything to do with Tulsi. In a way, she was glad. "My grandmother is the same. Vegetarian."

"Dad loves Guju food," Bina added. "But we're not big fans, so Chef Jaya auntie makes it for him and ba and something different for us, even though my dad says we should learn to eat our own food."

"My mother is visiting a friend in Milwaukee. She wanted to be here to meet you, but this trip had already been scheduled," Ash said, still looking anxiously at Tulsi.

Tulsi nodded, tried to reassure him that it was fine. And it was. After the way Aruna ba had treated Ash, it was likely for the better to not have Hema around during her visit. If that was how angry Aruna still was, imagine how angry Hema would feel about Aruna having kept her grandchild from her. Though she hoped that Hema understood it hadn't been Tulsi's choice.

"OMG, Beens, check out this video?" Lina handed her phone to her sister.

"What are you looking at?" Ash asked.

"Some influencer-versus-influencer drama is happening." Lina stood up. "Dad, can we go? We'll be back down for dinner."

"For now," Ash said. "No phones at dinner. Leave them upstairs."

They left the room.

Ash apologized for their behavior. "Short attention spans. I blame cell phones."

"It's fine," she said. "It's better not to force it. If it makes you feel better, my phone is in my tote upstairs in the guest room."

"It does. At least I have one daughter that's able to go more than an hour without checking her phone."

A wave of emotion rose within her. She couldn't say anything without letting him hear the quiver of her voice.

"You are, you know," Ash continued. "I know it. Feel it. Your mom, it's complicated between us right now, but thirty years ago, I loved her. She loved me. You are a welcome result of it."

Tulsi blinked to dry her eyes. "Thank you for saying that. You're good with your daughters. The twins," she clarified.

"It was much easier when they weren't teenagers," he said. "Toral, their aunt, says these years are supposed to be painful. I miss the time when they were little. The two of them were so sweet. They weren't even fussy, slept full nights. Shef's influence."

"They're protective of you," Tulsi said. "Like I am of my mom."

Ash clasped his hands in front of him. "Did you let her know you arrived?"

Tulsi shook her head. "She has a copy of my itinerary."

"Send her a message," he urged. "She'll worry until she hears from you."

"She's retreated into her work. It's how she deals with things."

"I remember that about her," Ash said. "She couldn't afford paints then, so she sketched. Hours and hours with her notebook and pencils. I got her a set of watercolors and a nice brush for her sweet sixteen. The handle was made of wood, and the tip at the bottom had a small French flag. I'd saved for months to get it for her."

"She still has it," Tulsi said. "The hair is warped on it, but it sits on her easel, and whenever she gets stuck in the middle of a project, I've seen her play with it. She once told me it was the only thing that unblocked her creativity."

He closed his eyes. Then opened them. "Thank you for telling me."

"It's never been this challenging between my mom and me," she said.

"None of this is easy," he said.

"Because of me."

"No." He took her hand. "This is not your fault."

"I mean that I could just let it go," Tulsi said. "Forgive and forget. That's how it works for us. This time, I can't. And I know she's hurt, but so am I."

He hugged her, then let her go. "You have every right to feel this way. This isn't like missing your birthday. You get to take your time. Devi will have to handle it on her own."

"You're angry with her too."

He sighed. "I'm mellowing. My temper is usually quick, then gone as soon as I say what I need to and release it. What you said, about her not having any training, I've been thinking about that a lot. I had so much support with the girls. And I was older, more mature. Devi had Aruna, who also didn't have support or good role models."

"Given that, I shouldn't be a parent," Tulsi said.

He laughed. "If that's what you want. But not because you'll be bad at it. We're all capable of change. We can unlearn just as much as we learn. Don't repeat this when you meet her, but my mother is more Lucille Bluth than Claire Dunphy."

"How much can a banana cost? Forty dollars?" Tulsi repeated the meme she'd seen so many times.

"Exactly."

"I thought I was going to marry Devi," Ash said.

Tulsi almost fell off the sofa. "What? When? Recently?"

"Back then," he said. "I had a plan. I always do, six months, one year, five years. It steadies me to know what my north is. It was all mapped out. We'd graduate from school in California. Move back here. I'd start working. Even back then, Aruna wanted a shop of her own. Devi would work there as a spice healer. Then once I had enough saved for a down payment on a house, we would get married."

"How did she feel about it?"

He rose. "I never told her. Kept it to myself. Then she was gone."

What if he had? Tulsi couldn't imagine how different her life would have been.

Or she might not have existed.

That was the problem with wishing for a different past.

CHAPTER
THIRTY-TWO

The next four days were filled with activities. Bina and Lina had shown up for dinner that first night but then disappeared to their rooms. While they were thawing, they kept their distance. It was probably a teenage thing. At least it gave Tulsi a chance to spend time with Ash. On Saturday, they spent the morning on the Mile, walked around the Pier in the afternoon, and caught a White Sox game in the evening. On Sunday, Ash hosted a huge family dinner with the twins' aunts and uncles, along with Ash's distant relatives. Apparently he had sponsored visas for his extended family twenty years ago.

The mansion was filled with family, and the whole experience was so new to Tulsi. Younger kids ran around, were told to go play somewhere else, and were fed snacks. Adults laughed, gossiped, bragged, and generally seemed to enjoy themselves. People simultaneously spoke in English and Gujarati. And for once she was glad Aruna had forced Tulsi to learn and practice Gujarati, which meant Tulsi was at least orally fluent. The food had also been a fusion of sorts. There were two grills, one vegetarian and one for everything else. Shef's family were devout Hindus, much more conservative than Ash's side.

At one point, Tulsi had mentioned to Toral's husband that around 1500 BC in the Rig Veda, ancient Indians did consume meat, particularly beef. Primarily for ritual reasons. That was why you could practice

Ayurveda and keep a non-veg diet. He'd walked away. She stopped talking about Rasa and their practice after that interaction. The more she revealed about herself and life in Salem, the more she sensed their disappointment and pity.

"If Ash had known about you . . ." That had been the common refrain for all the ways Tulsi's life would have been better. None of them attempted to believe that Tulsi was glad about the way she'd grown up. That there was no need for this strange sort of pity. Then she became defensive when one of them presumed that Devi and her grandmother hadn't given her the best possible life. And the more she'd been forced to hear about all the ways she'd been shortchanged, the more she resented their wealth and elitism. The mansion, the pool, and the gold and diamonds many of the women sported were fine for them. Tulsi didn't need or want them. She was happy with her cozy home, her tiny back office, fresh vegetables from the garden, and the less-used air-conditioning. Her pillow and mattress in Ash's guest room were more comfortable than her own, but those types of things were nice-to-haves. And shouldn't come at the cost of thinking like these people.

Tulsi had overheard comments about her simple wardrobe, even though she'd been wearing the same dress from the Pearl's preopening. She'd noticed a lot of whispers around her about her lack of college education, single status, and sheltered life. She stayed mostly quiet, stood in corners, and pretended interest in the photos on the mantel. She noted that photos of Hema, even in older photographs, showed her always looking well dressed and perfectly made up.

She'd wondered if Ash thought the same. While he was nice and friendly, did he believe she would have been better off? Not from having a father, but the material life he could have provided. And did that mean he judged Devi, resented her, for the ways he found Tulsi lacking? The night after the party, as they sat on the patio, Tulsi with a glass of wine and Ash with whiskey, she'd asked him.

"Absolutely not," he said. "I regret what I've missed. I'm sorry if my family made you feel as if you were less than. I'll speak to them."

"Please don't," Tulsi said. "It's not worth the friction."

"Beta, you don't have to be afraid of disagreements," he said. "It's healthy to argue, say your piece. Otherwise, things build, stay with you. People need to know when they've caused you pain. After you've made them aware, if they still continue, then you disregard them. That's how you set your boundaries."

That word—*disregard*—had never applied to family, Tulsi thought. There was no such thing. Children obeyed their parents, believed they knew best. "It's strange that I never saw my mom or ba as people. Only who they are to me. Which means that I put their feelings and needs above mine."

Ash added another splash of Johnnie Walker to his glass. "It used to be like that. Parents ruled, kids obeyed. You've met Bina and Lina, how is that working out for me?"

Tulsi laughed. "Fair."

"In a way, I saw my mother the way you see Devi," Ash said. "My father left us when I was eight. Took off. No note, nothing. My mom filed police reports. We searched for him, mourned him. I read so many obituaries in the paper that year. Then she found out, through the Patel network, that he was working as a bartender at a resort in Half Moon Bay and lived with his girlfriend. That was it. She never spoke of him again. I took care of her. Us. Until she remarried when I went off to college."

"You were so young." Tulsi felt for the little boy he'd been.

"Culture," he said. "I am a male, which means it's my responsibility to take care of my mother. Didn't matter that I couldn't write a check or have my own bank account."

"In the photos on the mantel, she looks so determined and put together."

"Oh, she's not fragile, never was. She preferred ordering me to pleading with me, but the end result was the same. Compliance."

"How did you learn to, I don't know, be you?"

"University was big in terms of independence," he said. "Taught me more than business. Then it was work. Met all types of people with different backgrounds. I have longtime friendships with people who know me and can call me on my BS."

"My mom has all of that," Tulsi said. "Though not the call-her-on-things. No one does that, because we don't believe she can handle it."

"She can." Ash placed his empty glass on the small wrought iron table.

"I disagree."

Tulsi whipped around at the sound of an unfamiliar voice, then stood.

Hema. Hema's hair, unlike Aruna ba's, was silver-gray, dyed, and styled in short waves that sat perfectly on her head. Her skin had fewer wrinkles, and her face was fully made up. Hema reminded Tulsi of a much, much older version of Bina and Lina. She looked striking in a white button-down shirt and khaki capris. Her bare toes were painted bright pink, and her nails had a perfect french manicure.

"Ma." Ash stood. "You're back early."

"I changed my plans," Hema said. "You must be Tulsi."

Tulsi was intimidated. She was not at all the grandmotherly type. Tulsi stood, then bowed to touch Hema's feet. She waited until her paternal ba put her hand on Tulsi's head to offer a blessing. "You were taught well. I'm surprised."

Tulsi stiffened. "Our culture is important."

"At least the parts your mother finds useful," Hema said.

"What does that mean?"

"Ma," Ash cut in. "You must be tired from your trip. Why don't we do this in the morning?"

"Your grandmother—"

"She's the best." Tulsi remembered the letter. The pain in her grandmother's words. Caused by this woman. "I've been very lucky to have her. She works more than she rests, which is something I nag her about.

And she knows so much. I'm very grateful for the life she built for my mom and me."

"Hmm." Hema considered her. "You have her bite."

Tulsi didn't want this confrontation but steadied herself. "Thank you."

"How has your visit been so far?" Hema asked.

Tulsi relaxed slightly. "Great. It's different here, but Ash has made me feel welcomed."

"If it weren't for Aruna and Devi," Hema said, "you wouldn't have to act as a guest in this home. It could have been yours too."

Tulsi had no response, so she diverted the conversation. "You were friends with my ba."

Hema went to the edge of the patio. "I am your grandmother as well, you know."

Not yet. Tulsi didn't know what it meant, but Hema was still an adversary to her. "What happened between you? No one seems to know."

Hema approached her, assessed Tulsi. "We argued. Wanted different things, but forgiveness doesn't come naturally to Aruna."

"You're admitting it was your fault?" Tulsi asked.

Hema cupped the glass in her hand. "If someone misinterprets or doesn't quite have the capacity to understand, I am not responsible. And all relationships end, even close friendships," Hema said. "Our lives went in different directions. I like where I'm standing."

"My grandmother loves where she is too," Tulsi said.

"Good for her," Hema retorted.

"You don't sound convinced," Tulsi said.

"She kept you away from my son," Hema said. "From me. No, I don't want to accept that she gets to be happy."

There were so many people devastated by the actions of her mom and grandmother. Tulsi couldn't fault Hema for the anger in her words. "I'm sorry."

Hema dismissed it. "It's not for you to apologize. You didn't do this. Aruna and Devi, on the other hand. I want them to beg."

"Ma." Ash stood.

"What did I always tell you, Ashish? You are a better person than me," Hema said. "Always will be. So I will be the one to fight your battles. I don't have the need to be gentle or choose my words to appease and consider."

"Not in front of Tulsi," Ash said.

Tulsi's face burned with shame. Hema's anger was justified, but her loyalty was with Aruna ba. If Hema came for them, well, all Tulsi needed was a few teaspoons of nutmeg.

"I know you don't want to hear it from me," Tulsi said. "But they did their best."

"They left," Hema said. "Slipped away without a word. Never to be heard from again. With my grandchild in your mother's womb."

There was pain in the way she spoke about it. "You're still hurt?"

Hema clenched her jaw. "Aruna abandoned me."

"Why?" Ash asked. "What caused the rift?"

Hema centered herself, then crossed her arms in front of her. "Aruna's worst quality was her complacency. She only wanted enough, never thought bigger than her small ideas. She didn't want to stretch, explore possibilities. It was offensive how limited she was in the way she viewed the world. America was the land of opportunity. She wanted nothing more than a tiny shop on a street corner. And she hated that I wasn't satisfied. I won't apologize for my ambition."

"But you were friends for so long," Ash said. "You knew this about each other. Something bigger must have happened for it to get to this point."

"Ask Aruna." Hema turned toward the patio doors and left them.

CHAPTER THIRTY-THREE

The following day Ash had to take care of a few things at the office, so Tulsi kept to herself, walked the grounds, spent time in her room. Avoided running into Hema. She reread her texts to Lucas, and his responses. This relationship—if that was what it was—was different from any she'd had before. If Lucas didn't message her back within a few hours, she didn't stress out like she had with Kal. And she didn't feel she needed to unload all her feelings on him all the time. Except last night she'd sent him a flurry of messages after her encounter with Hema.

> She's extreme. Kept insulting my ba and mom. I had their back and so did Ash. I don't like her, but I don't blame her either. I get it. It's just weird that I am the reason for all of this. Like a pawn, no, like the rope in tug of war.

> I wish Aruna ba had been there. Because then it would have been an even match.

> How are you? The Pearl? Rasa?

> Okay, it's late. I'm fine. I will be. Part of me wants to come back home. The other part of me wants to stay and fix things.

Okay bye for real now. God, I hope your phone is on silent.

Good night.

This morning she'd read his responses.

Rasa, Pearl, your mom, and grandmother are good. There's a steady stream of customers but they're handling it.

It's complicated and you're not an object. Don't forget you have a voice.

You are handling it, sweetheart. Know that. And stay or leave, it's your call. No one else's.

She'd hugged her phone to her chest. How could she not fall deeply for this man? And being away from home, even for less than a week, made her miss everything. Even Mrs. Bishop. Though her life was no longer boring. There was drama and discovery. It had all arrived on her doorstep.

Tulsi stared out the window. The desk she sat at was dainty and blue. Colonial design. She scanned the pictures in her messages to her mom. Tulsi had been sending her photos of her visit, from the Bean to a selfie with a White Sox cap. She hadn't written anything, but it was a peace offering of sorts. A sort of return to neutral. Devi, for her part, didn't push, only sent a heart emoji after each photo.

A knock on her door jarred her. "Come in."

It was Bina. "Dinner?"

Tulsi nodded and followed her down to the kitchen. They usually ate at the informal table that sat six comfortably. The formal dining room, which seated twenty-four, was reserved for guests. The scale of this house continued to impress her.

"Hi. I'm sorry I'm late. My last meeting went over, and the traffic was brutal." Ash laid his wallet and keys in one corner of the massive kitchen island. "Smells amazing."

"Guju food," Lina said.

"How was everyone's day?" Ash asked.

"Birth. School. Work. Death," Lina said.

"She's taking poetry this year," Bina said. "Ignore her. I do. I have a ton of homework, but I made a lot of progress, so I only have a little left. Lina made an unboxing video, so she's going to have to catch up after dinner."

"How about a video on five ways to study without your phone?" Ash spoke to Lina.

"Your dad jokes need work," Lina said.

"Bina beta." Ash turned to his other daughter. "You'll always laugh, won't you?"

She nodded. "But maybe try a little?"

Tulsi laughed. "*That* was funny." She liked Bina the mediator. They were alike in that sense. She caught a small smile from Lina, and Tulsi knew that even the slightest progress was good.

Hema served everyone before she sat down. Tulsi was surprised by the very traditional Gujarati thali. There were eight metal bowls on a large metal tray. Each had different vegetable curries, dal, rice, smashed popadam, and ras malai. "This is a lot."

"I wanted you to have this experience," Ash said. "I love a good thali."

"Beens, I'll trade you my potatoes for your cucumber raita." Lina passed her small bowl over and traded with her sister. "I'm off carbs right now. And Beens loves batata shaak."

Tulsi glanced over at Hema, who was quiet as she tucked into her meal.

"It's all really good." And spicy, so she chased each bite with water. This was a whole other heat level, and Tulsi hoped she wouldn't sweat through the meal. That would break Hema's silence for sure. At least the ras malai was deliciously sweet. She wondered if Lina would trade for that too. But then Hema might think Tulsi was being childish.

Ash talked about his work. There were some zoning issues for the Massachusetts store. Tulsi tried to follow along, but somewhere around blueprints and soil grade, she lost the thread. "Are you always this busy?"

He nodded. "I admit, I like work, so I forget the time. My girls remind me when I have to leave the office so I'm home for dinner."

"Then he works for a couple of hours in his office here," Bina said. "The perfect makings of a future heart attack."

"I'm healthy, Bina," Ash said. "I showed you my test results from my physical, didn't I?"

"Stress doesn't show up in the body until it's too late," Bina said.

"She worries about my dying," Ash explained to Tulsi. "I've been meaning to revoke her access to WebMD."

Tulsi saw Bina fidget with her rotli instead of eating it. "I used to worry about that when I was younger," Tulsi said. "It was just my mom, ba, and me. I'd make my grandmother wear a hat whenever she gardened because I'd read about heatstroke. My mom, she forgets to eat when she's deep in her work, so I would leave plates of food on the kitchen island."

Bina gave her a weepy smile.

"Dad would never forget to eat," Lina chimed in. "He loves food."

Tulsi saw Lina pat Bina's arm. The two of them were in it together.

"More please." Ash used a funny voice, then reached for extra rotli that was on the table.

"Bina worries too much," Hema said. "She has me and all of her aunts and uncles."

"It's not the same, though, is it?" Tulsi said. She didn't like the way Hema dismissed Bina's concerns. Bina was sensitive and seemed to take worrying about her father very seriously.

The twins looked at her and their grandmother.

"How would you know?" Hema twirled her wineglass.

"I have a community of my own," Tulsi said. "But parents, even grandparents, it's different. If you're lucky, which Bina, Lina, and I are, you feel safe and cared for in a way that you can take them for granted. No matter what they do, Ash will never stop being their dad."

"Or yours," he added.

That tripped her up. She wasn't ready yet. Not for an immediate embrace. "Thank you." That was as much as she could offer him right now. With time, she hoped it would change.

"My son offered you his heart," Hema said. "Don't be like your mother and treat him as if he was insignificant."

Tulsi stilled. Wiped her hands on her linen napkin. "I'm not. And what happened between them, it's theirs to resolve."

"I remember the way Devi held back with Ashish," Hema said. "Giving the slightest of inches, making him be the one to pursue friendship. Ash is a giver, you see. Generous to a fault. Your mother took. Us only learning about you now proves my point."

"Girls." Ash spoke to Bina and Lina. "If you're done with dinner, go wash up and head up to your room. If you're still eating, go to the dining room."

"We're not little kids, Dad," Lina said. "We want to stay."

He kept his eyes on them until they pushed their chairs back, put their trays by the sink, and left the kitchen.

"Ma, no more little jabs about Devi," Ash said.

"Did you not like my mom, ever?" Tulsi said. "Or is this because of her . . . what she kept from you?"

"*Who*. Not what," Hema said. "And no, I found her weak and manipulative. I wonder if she got pregnant on purpose. She always wanted to be like Aruna. Maybe this was part of all the Vedic responsibility Aruna always went on about."

"This is all conjecture." Ash wiped his mouth with his napkin. "I've spent too much time with lawyers today. This is family, not a trial. Can we not make accusations? Things happened. They can't be undone. We have to deal with it now. I forgive Devi. There. It's done."

Hema leaned back in her chair and crossed her arms. "See? That's your mother's power. She doesn't need to apologize. Devi just waits it out."

"That's unfair." Except it wasn't, not totally. "My mom is a good person. If she believed you thought this way about her, it would—"

"Make her cry?" Hema finished. "Then all the attention shifts to making her feel better."

"You're twisting everything," Tulsi said.

"Enough." Ash's voice ricocheted around the room.

Bina ran back to her father. "Dad, please relax." She clung to him. "He's had a stressful day. Can you both argue somewhere else?"

Tulsi felt ashamed. She'd let Hema get to her, and for what? Criticizing her mother for the same things Tulsi did? It wasn't fair and added to Bina's worry for her father.

He stood and hugged his daughter. "Beta, I don't even have a heart condition. I'm fine. You know that I yell sometimes. That's all it is. Do you want to check my pulse? It's steady."

Tulsi watched as Bina put her fingers on Ash's wrist and counted while checking, staring at her smartwatch. Meanwhile, Lina came back with a bowl of strawberries and took her chair at the table. A silent command to stop stressing their dad out.

"I'll get some whipped cream." Tulsi made her way to the fridge to steady herself. Where was the family that loved each other, laughed, and joked their way through dinner? This version was as warped as what she'd left back in Salem. Except they never yelled. Maybe that was the better option. More comfortable. Silence wasn't always bad.

They ate strawberries dipped in whipped cream. Ash told stories about Lina's and Bina's escapades. He teased them; they told him to stop embarrassing them. And the tension between her and Hema subsided, at least for now.

CHAPTER
THIRTY-FOUR

The original House of Spice was small compared to the blueprints for the Massachusetts store that was slated to open in a year. From the single front door, it was one long room. Shelves covered every inch of each wall. Rows of racks in the middle were laden with boxes and bags, from ready-to-eat chana masala to family-size bags of tapioca, puffed rice, and various types of flour. In the back were two square tables with boxes full of vegetables like methi, okra, and papdi, alongside cilantro bunches and loose lemons.

"We keep this store as close to the original as possible." Ash shifted a sealed box to make room for both of them by the single freezer next to the produce. "Kaka, at the register, he was the first person to come work for us. He's been here twenty-eight years; everyone in the neighborhood knows him. The regulars still come. This was my first job. I wasn't the big boss. That was my mother. I did everything from unloading supplies from trucks to shelving. Sifting through produce that had gone bad, removing expired stock. I kept the books, paid the bills."

"I do all that at Rasa." There was a connection. In that moment, she could see him in her life, understand what it could be like to have a father figure. "I took over the business part when I was still in high school. Aruna ba had done it before me, but she . . . did her best."

Ash nodded. "The books were a mess, huh?"

She laughed. "I didn't know how or where to start. At first I did the things she showed me, but then I spent a lot of time on the internet. YouTube was where I learned the basics. I still search for how-to stuff whenever I'm stumped."

"You and I are similar," Ash said. "We're both resourceful. Find our way, figure things out as we go."

"Except you went to Stanford and have an MBA."

"You're right," he said. "What you've done, are doing, at Rasa is more impressive."

She blinked to clear her eyes. To be seen as being good at something she believed she wasn't cut out to do, the feeling was difficult to explain. Ash looked as if he was proud of her.

"Did I say something wrong?" Ash took hold of her arm.

She shook her head. "I'm . . . I don't think I do anything well, not at Rasa. Mostly I do whatever needs to be done. It's not that hard now because I have systems."

He shifted her slightly to reach behind and open the glass-front fridge. "Do you know the first time I sensed that my mother approved of my work? It was after the opening of the fiftieth store. She said I made her dream come true. From this store to that moment, I had to believe in myself, trust that I was making good decisions. And learn from my mistakes."

If Ash had been around growing up, things would have been different.

After the tour, he led them out. But not before he filled a bag with chips, chiku ice cream, and lassis. He paid for it all, then handed it to her. "I never got to spoil you with treats."

As Tulsi climbed into the car, she said, "I'm glad I came here. That I got to spend time with you."

He beamed. "First of many more visits, I hope."

Later that afternoon, once they got back to Ash's house, he suggested that since it was so nice outside, they should grill and spend the rest of the afternoon by the pool. Bina and Lina would join them once they finished their homework.

Hema came from the kitchen. "Ashish, another day off?"

He nodded. "Yes, Ma." Ash headed up the steps. "I'm going to change. Oh, and we can grill for dinner. Ask Chef Jaya to marinate chicken and paneer? We can do corn and some papdi on the grill too. Oh, wait, Tulsi, did you bring a swimsuit? If not, maybe the girls have something you could borrow."

"She's not a teenager, Ashish," Hema said.

"I actually packed one," Tulsi said. "You'd mentioned that your house had a pool."

A half hour later, she sat in a lounge chair under an umbrella.

Ash sat on the other side of the small table, a book in his hand. He alternated between reading and checking his phone, which vibrated every few minutes. "I thought you had the day off."

He held up his phone. "This makes it impossible."

"Was House of Spice always your idea?"

"My mother's, actually," he said.

Hema had joined them and was perched in a chair on the other side of Ash, dressed in a long black-and-white silk caftan that Mrs. Bishop would think too plain. "Aruna and I worked in a department store. Cashiers. Stockroom. Inventory. She was usually in groceries. I was in the women's department. I didn't like working for other people. Patels are merchants, business owners."

Tulsi was genuinely impressed. "And now you have almost seventy-one stores."

Hema adjusted the brim of her hat. "And Aruna has one. Small dreams. Small achievements, I suppose."

Tulsi stayed quiet. Being in and around Hema these past few days, Tulsi saw that Ash's mother was fiercely loyal to her family. While she enjoyed and wore her wealth, it was Bina, Lina, and Ash that she continued to fight for. Tulsi didn't know where she fit in with Hema, mostly because Hema's anger toward Tulsi's family was barely contained. The past and present appeared to have merged together for the older woman.

"Rasa is terrific," Ash interjected. "The design is so inviting; it lets the shopper browse. The cool colors are soothing so that people don't feel aggravated or rushed. And all of the spices are on display in clear glass so people can see the quality and care. You've all done an incredible job."

"Rasa was Aruna ba's dream. She works hard. We all do. It may not seem like much, but we've become an institution in our town. Locals know us, and recently my mom did an interview for the local news. I'm proud of what we've built." Ash had helped her see that she'd had a role in what they had built together. That two decades of her efforts counted. She hadn't been as passive as she'd once believed, and even the dreaded paperwork was a part of what their shop had become over time.

"That's your accomplishment. You have a good head for business," Ash said. "Your mother used to believe all things that grew—fruits, vegetables, flowers—should be free."

Tulsi sat up a little straighter, proud to be seen. "She fights me every time we need to raise prices. We don't do it often, only when suppliers increase theirs. Our margins are very small."

"Aruna was the same," Hema added. "Profit was a four-letter word for her."

"The Guptas always had good hearts," Ash said.

Hema snorted. "Yes, so good that they kept your own child a secret."

"You're going to have to find a way to make peace with all of this, Ma."

"Have you?" Hema asked.

He looked over at Tulsi. "We're working on it."

"I'm going to see if Jaya needs anything." Hema left her lounger. The flap of her straw hat bobbled as she went toward the house.

"She'll come around," Ash said.

"She has a point." Tulsi couldn't believe she had just defended Hema. "They're so different, your mother and my grandmother. The pool, the house. We don't live like this. I can't picture them here with your family."

"Our family," Ash said. "And don't sell your mom short. Devi can adapt."

She looked over at him. "You've thought about it. What it would be like to have my mom in this house." She left out the "with you."

"I want her to see it," he said. "Not that she would be impressed; you're right about her discomfort with all of this. More to appreciate what I've accomplished. Guess we never outgrow wanting to hear someone you care about acknowledge your efforts."

"Do you . . . I'm sorry if this is personal, and you don't have to answer," Tulsi said. "But do you still care about her?"

He watched Lina dive to the bottom of the pool. Waited until she came back up. "I do. At first I was so angry, not about you, but back then. She'd left. We'd spent the night together, talked about the future. I gave her the words that were in my heart. A week later, I'm back in California, and my mom calls me to say they left, no idea to where. I looked. For months. Time passed. Devi stayed lodged in one corner as I met and married Shefali. And now my feelings for your mother are jumbled."

"She was wrong to not tell you."

"I make all of these excuses for her in my head because of my heart."

"Me too," Tulsi added.

"There is a Gujarati word, *bhutkur*. It doesn't have a literal translation, but it refers to the past. It's embedded in our culture that the past has happened and doesn't need to be revisited. My mother, she rarely goes back in time. This, all of it resurfacing, it's good for her to see that sometimes it is important to go back and understand what happened, who we were when we made choices. If we don't think about it, talk about it, how can we learn from it?"

"You don't. You repeat the same patterns, over and over," Tulsi said. "My grandmother had no father; neither did my mom. They reasoned that it was better this way, not only for them but me. They did just fine, and so would I."

"Then the day-to-day of surviving takes over. Time and distance make it seem okay. Regrets fade," he said.

Tulsi stared at the rippling blue water; a small plastic ball floated at the will of the slight current. "I've been thinking about choices lately. I believed I never had any. Now I know that I choose to believe that, use it as a crutch to not do things."

"What made you hesitate?"

She looked over at Ash, wondered why it was so comfortable talking to a parent she barely knew over the one whom she loved. "I didn't want to hurt Ba or my mom." It was so simple. Everything she hadn't done came from that sentiment.

"My mother and I had a different relationship than Aruna masi and Devi," he said. "Perhaps because I am male, and while it's changing, there is still a cultural deference mothers give their sons. We argue, as you've witnessed. We apologize and forgive. It's important for Bina and Lina to see that."

And running away wasn't the only option.

Her phone rang. She was used to the buzzing from incoming texts, but this was an actual *ring*. "I didn't even know it wasn't on silent." She glanced at it. Lucas. That was odd. It was the middle of the weekday. Maybe he was taking a break after the lunch rush. "Do you mind if I answer it?"

"Go right ahead." Ash went back to his book.

"Hey," she said. "Slow day?"

"Opposite." There was urgency in his voice.

She sat up. "What's wrong?"

"The Sonia O'Shea segment aired. Your mom hadn't been told about the timing. Best I can tell, it was a hit job," he said. "It's not good. Your mom and Aruna need you back here."

She went on full alert. "Oh no." She sat up, began to gather her things. "What happened?"

"Trying to figure it out, but people are coming in, angry about fake magic," he said. "They're asking for refunds on stuff they never bought. Aruna and Devi are doing their best, but I sent one of my sous to stay in the shop to watch over them, because Rasa is swamped."

She nodded, then realized he couldn't see her, so she told him she'd figure it out and get there as soon as possible. Then she explained to Ash that she had to go home and ran up to the guest room to change and pack.

By the time she came downstairs, Ash was dressed, his keys in hand. "My assistant is booking you on a flight that leaves in three hours. I'll drive you to the airport."

That Ash didn't try to dissuade her from leaving, and that he'd already put things in motion, gave her pause. "Can we get a flight out this late?"

"Already sorted," he said. "You'll get into Logan around midnight."

Tulsi filled him in on what little she knew from Lucas. On the drive she concentrated on breathing, but it didn't help. Her chest was tight, and her knee wouldn't stop shaking.

"I can't find anything on Sonia O'Shea or Rasa." She clutched her phone and stared out through the windshield. "I was there for the interview; she didn't say anything bad." Then she paused. "I just looked through socials, and the comments are all lies. Lucas said they want refunds and something about fake magic. At least the shop is closed by now. I called my mom, but she didn't answer, which is normal, because half the time her phone is in her bedroom. The landline at Rasa is busy. I texted Ba to tell her I'm on my way home, and all she wrote back was 'good.' I'm the one who agreed to do the news segment. Ba didn't want to." She couldn't imagine what it said. "I can't even watch it anywhere. People on our accounts keep saying we lied and that our advice was harmful. How is this happening?"

Her knee shook, and Tulsi bit her lip to keep from babbling. She was terrified. Her mom wouldn't be able to handle whatever was happening. Aruna ba was likely protecting the store. "Can you help? I don't know if it's appropriate to ask, but I, we, might need it."

"You don't have to ask," Ash said. "I need to sort some things out here, but I'll be on my way there within a day or two. Once we know what we're dealing with, I'll ask my PR and legal teams to step in."

Legal? That sounded aggressive. "Thank you. Also, thanks for having me, and sorry it got cut short. I really enjoyed spending time with you."

"Hang in there," he said. "You don't have to thank me. It's what family does."

The car pulled up to the curb, and Tulsi jumped out, then grabbed her suitcase from the back seat.

"Your ticket is at check-in. You have about forty-five minutes until boarding. Breathe, get a bottle of water once you're inside. Do you have cash?" Ash opened his wallet.

Tulsi stilled. It was such a dad gesture. She'd seen it over and over again on television and with her friends. Without thinking too much, she let go of her suitcase and wrapped her arms around him. He hugged her back. Squeezed. Then let go.

"I have money," she said. "And I will get water after security."

"Text me when you land," he said. "I'm a phone call away if you need me."

"Please tell Lina and Bina that I enjoyed getting to know them and am sorry I had to leave like this."

"There will be more time," he said. "You will see them again."

She nodded.

A half hour later, she'd made it to the gate. Too anxious to sit, Tulsi hovered near the boarding area. She texted Lucas her arrival information. He let her know that both Aruna and Devi were back home, resting, and that he'd be outside of departures to pick her up when she landed. Her phone still clutched in her hand, she scanned Instagram and TikTok for any mentions of Rasa, Salem spice shop, or Sonia.

Fake! Fake! Fake!

+1 above, this is a giant con.

@SO'SheaWBXZ exposes another fraud.

Magical spice healers more like spice SCAMMERS

One after the other was directing their anger toward Rasa and her family. She searched again to find a video clip. A heavy weight settled in her stomach. Throughout the boarding process she silently willed people to get on faster, put their bags up, get their belts on. She prayed there would be no announcements about a delay.

She didn't breathe until the plane lifted off the tarmac. All she could think about was getting back and taking over so that her mom and ba wouldn't have to deal with any of this.

CHAPTER
THIRTY-FIVE

Lucas picked her up from Logan. As they drove up 93 toward Salem, he filled her in on what he knew. "The segment has only been on TV and hasn't been posted online yet. Gemma called the station and told them to not post it online, but they said you signed the release, and the story was theirs to do whatever they wanted with."

"You didn't see it?"

He shook his head. "We didn't know it was airing. Only found out when people came in to harass Aruna and Devi."

Tulsi checked the shop's email. There was nothing there from the channel. "How are they handling it?"

"Holding strong. Aruna insisted on staying open," he said. "She doesn't want to hide, believes that would mean that they did the things people are accusing Rasa of. Once my sous kicked out a few of the harassers, they mostly gathered outside after that. Betty has mobilized the rest of HSBA to lend a hand. Gemma sent out a message for everyone to only say Rasa is a spice shop. Nothing more."

"I found it, the interview." She'd searched again, and a video popped up from Sonia O'Shea's Twitter account. Breathless, she played it for both of them.

The video started as it did when they filmed it. Devi looked so serene, almost ethereal in her ice-blue salwar. She spoke softly and slowly about their work and why Ayurveda was an important practice that sat alongside modern medicine. The segment ended when Devi acknowledged the magic. Then it cut to something completely different. It was just Sonia in front of the camera, on a nondescript street somewhere in Boston.

Unfortunately, this feel-good story has a dark side. You heard directly from Devi Gupta's mouth that there was magic in these spices. Or as they claim on their website, "curative properties." Fascinated, I did some digging on my own. I could find no evidence of spice healers. It seems that this is yet another Salem business that is making outrageous claims. From their social media accounts, they offer ways to use spices to get rich, find love, and the most damaging of all, cure whatever ails you. For their profit. But you pay the cost. Not just with your wallet but with your life. Cinnamon oil can cause ulcers. The so-called spice healers don't post that on Instagram. Inhaling cinnamon powder can cause pulmonary embolism. Vanilla has ethanol in it. None of this is disclosed. They sell hope in a jar of saffron at the astronomical price of five hundred dollars, when you could buy the same for under ten dollars at Market Basket.

"Lies," Tulsi said. "This is all made up. Can they do that? We didn't post any of these things. Someone else did."

"You reported it, right?"

Tulsi rolled down the window to get a little air. "A while ago, yes. But then I stopped trying." She opened those accounts and reported them again. "It's too late." The truth was, she blamed herself. Once Rasa stopped being as busy, Tulsi had ignored the fake accounts, believed it had all passed. "I should have tried harder to find out who was posting about us. This is all my fault." She leaned against the headrest. "Aruna ba warned me, us. But I didn't listen. Take it seriously."

"Mental gymnastics?" Lucas's question startled her.

"I keep thinking that I could have stopped this."

"This isn't on you," he said. "I was there. You had prepped your mom; she stayed on script. It was supposed to be a good thing. This wasn't within your control."

She disagreed. "I didn't try hard enough to take those posts down." Then she started typing on her phone. "Skye. I need her advice on all of this. She would know how to navigate it."

"Breathe."

"This isn't fair," she said.

"No, it isn't." Lucas squeezed her hand, then let go. "We'll sort it out."

She glanced at his profile. "We?"

He nodded. "Yeah."

She took a big inhale, then let it out. She had to reduce the cortisol levels in her body. It worked a little as she slowed her heart rate. It was going to be okay. Rasa would make it through. She didn't let herself think about why that mattered when two months ago she was ready to let it all go.

"So how was it?" Lucas asked. "Your trip."

Less than seven hours ago, she'd been sitting in a pool chair. "It was nice. Parts of it." She told him how the twins were not fans but had started to warm up to her.

"I've been wondering about something," Lucas continued. "And it's been on my mind this whole time. You never mentioned it in any of your texts."

"What's that?"

"Do twins finish each other's sentences or do things in unison?" Lucas grinned before turning his eyes back to the road.

She let out a surprised laugh, a much-needed release. "Bina and Lina are close, but they don't even dress alike. They're very different. They do have each other's backs, though. Like they sense when one of them needs support."

"That's too bad," he said. "I kept thinking about *The Shining*."

She shuddered. "I never saw it. Too scary."

"We'll have to watch it." He squeezed her hand. "With all the lights on, in the daytime. And you can jump on me whenever you get scared."

"No, thank you. My perfect date movie is anything with Ryan Gosling. Except *The Notebook*."

"Who?"

She grinned. "I can't wait for an entire weekend of Ryan Gosling movies."

"I get it. You won't watch Stephen King movies, but I have to watch all the things you like," Lucas said.

"That's how friendship works." They were more, but for now it mattered that she and Lucas were friends.

A few minutes passed in silence, then Tulsi said, "Change is for the birds."

"New T-shirt?" Lucas asked.

"I was so bored of my day-to-day," Tulsi said. "Resented everything about my life. I wanted to live big, you know, see everything. Travel. Figure out who I am because what I had wasn't enough."

Tulsi turned away, pulled her hand out from his, and leaned her head against the edge of the window. The late-night air helped as she thought about the potential loss of all that she'd rejected.

CHAPTER THIRTY-SIX

"How was your flight?" Devi wiped the kitchen island countertop, more for something to do than anything else.

"You didn't have to wait up for me," Tulsi said. "Why don't you sit?"

"You're home." Aruna shuffled in and sat at the dining table instead of the counter.

"How are you, Ba?"

She said nothing. Tulsi went to sit with her. "You seem tired. It's late; go back to bed. We can sort through it all in the morning."

Devi brought over three mugs of hot water with mint. "Technically, it is morning."

"I worried about this," Aruna said. "This is why I insisted on a low profile. People don't understand us, what we do. I thought we would be safe here in a town that is open to different ideas. And we are responsible. We never promise cures or . . . magic."

"It's my fault, Ma." Devi cupped her mug. "I did the interview. I pressured you both to go along. I thought it would be good for us." She paused. "I think I wanted to impress Ashish. He was so successful. I was being a silly schoolgirl. I'm sorry for causing all of this."

"You didn't," Tulsi said. "I should have done more to get those social media accounts taken down."

"There is plenty of blame to go around," Aruna said. "It's happened. No need to look back; we will keep going. Stay out of the fray. Keep doing our work."

Tulsi disagreed with the approach but stayed quiet. She saw age and weariness on both of their faces. For now it was better to let them feel steady, not push them toward anything more.

"Beta, how was your trip?"

"It was fine." Tulsi didn't know how much to say or what their expectations were. Everything about it seemed too fraught, and now wasn't the time to go into it and add to what her mom and ba were going through. "It was good to spend time with Ash. His daughters are fun, and he's a really good dad to them. Their house is big, and the garden is pretty."

"Hema's doing," Aruna said. "She likes to show off."

Tulsi stayed silent.

"I'm so sorry you had to rush back, but I am very relieved you are home." Devi put her hand over Tulsi's.

Tulsi wondered if this was the end of it. Her mother's touch was a signal that things were settled, and it was time to move on from whatever had occurred. Tulsi pulled away to bring her mug to her lips. Devi pulled her hand toward her own. Now wasn't the time. They would have to deal with their current problems first. However, Ash and Hema were back in their lives, and none of that could be brushed aside.

"I think we should close for a few days," Devi said.

"We didn't do anything wrong," Aruna said. "We won't comment or talk to reporters. And we can handle any customers that come in to complain."

"This is different, Ba. I'm worried that it could get worse," Tulsi said. "We don't know what's going to happen."

"We keep going," Aruna argued. "Everything passes with time."

Exhausted in every cell of her being, Tulsi tried again. "Or we take the time to regroup, see what our options are."

"And admit defeat? No," Aruna said. "I have never given up. Not like my mother, who let the sickness take her instead of seeking help. She and I were always told we were worthless; she gave up. I won't. I have fought my whole life to honor who I am. Dharti gives us strength."

Tulsi leaned her head in her hands.

"I'm tired and am going to try to get a few hours of sleep," Devi said. "We all should."

Aruna stayed where she was. As a way to soften pulling away from Devi's touch, Tulsi took her mom's hand, squeezed, then let her go.

Her ba cupped a chipped ceramic mug in her hand. Was it only this morning that in another kitchen, in another city, Hema had done something similar? Except that cup had been shiny, delicate porcelain that they likely hadn't gotten at a flea market.

"Ba, I'm worried about you," Tulsi said. "It's been a lot these past few weeks."

"When I was a child, my mother would tell me these stories," Aruna said. "We had nothing, you know, only a room in someone's house. That was all. But the way she spoke about our ancestors and Dharti, it made me feel like I was someone. Not just a bastard daughter of an unmarried woman who'd been cast out by her family."

Tulsi ached for what her grandmother must have endured.

"I did everything to make sure Devi and you never felt less than," she said. "I didn't want you to hear any slurs or not know your value. It was important to me that you both knew you had power, that our ancient history matters. If we didn't conform to society, that was good. It meant we were special, not ostracized."

"We are," Tulsi assured her. "You know I've been fighting against taking over for Mom. But even now, it's not because I don't believe in what we do or who we are. But, Ba, we don't have to define our worth only through this one thing."

"When the world treats you like the dirt beneath someone's shoe, this is the only way I know that I am more," Aruna said.

Tulsi reached over and held her grandmother's hand. "You did your best, and I'm grateful."

Aruna looked directly at Tulsi. "But you will not ask this of your daughter."

"I'm barely dating," Tulsi hedged.

Her grandmother looked away. "I will be forgotten in a few generations," Aruna said. "All I ask is that you don't forget our history."

Tulsi wanted to tell her she would take the test, carry forward what Aruna had built. But she couldn't utter the words. "If I have children, they will know our history. I promise." She knew that, if nothing else, she would find a way to pass this on—Aruna's story—not just Dharti or spice healing, but her ba's struggles and accomplishments.

"I don't feel as attached to the goddess," Tulsi added. "But that I came from you, am a descendant of your strength and determination, that means everything to me. You make me believe I can do anything, because you did everything."

It was the first time she'd seen her grandmother's eyes damp. Quickly she blinked them clear. "Tell me about Hema."

Tulsi understood Aruna's need to change the topic. "I didn't spend a lot of time with her."

"Was she . . . did she accept you?" Aruna asked.

"In her way," Tulsi replied. "We didn't spend any time as just the two of us."

"And the girls, his daughters?" Aruna asked.

"They make a nice family," she said.

"Do you count yourself a part of it?"

Tulsi answered honestly. "Not yet."

Aruna rose from the table and rinsed out her mug. She said nothing. But on her way out of the kitchen, she patted Tulsi's shoulder.

CHAPTER
THIRTY-SEVEN

Tulsi got to Rasa well before it was scheduled to open. She needed to see the shop again. As she took it all in with her eyes, it seemed as if she'd been gone for months instead of less than a week.

Tulsi started with the wall of mini spice bottles. It was half-full, so Tulsi got more stock, but before adding them, she wiped off the glass shelves that had smears from fingers. The big jars were only a third full, and she replenished those. It took close to an hour to set everything to rights. The lessons she'd resented flowed through her as she handled each section. Whole spices and seeds should be dry roasted to bring out their fragrance and activate their healing properties. Black pepper, chilies, and ginger opened up a dormant appetite. Cumin and mustard seeds made rough vegetables easier to digest. Almond added to coconut milk could offer a quick burst of energy.

These weren't mere seasonings for flavor; they were necessary and beneficial in their own right. Each had its own history. Countries had fought over spices, from the nutmeg massacre to the salt wars. "Colonizers, all of them."

"Talking to yourself?"

She jumped at the sound of Lucas's voice. He was still sweaty from his run as he held out a mug of cha for her. She took it with both hands and breathed in the sweet floral aroma. "Thank you."

"Cleaning?"

"The stock was depleted." She wandered to the table by the glass storefront.

"They managed," Lucas said. "Today might be difficult."

She steadied herself. "I spent a lot of time researching PR crises in the middle of the night. Couldn't sleep. The least-scary version is that it'll pass in a few days or a week. Typically, people move on to the next thing to rage over."

"There's a story in the *Globe* this morning." He leaned against the doorjamb between the shop and the back office.

She leaned against the counter and clutched her mug. "Do I want to know?"

"A repeat of the same." Lucas pointed to her cup. "Finish your tea. I'll make you eggs."

Tulsi took a few more sips. "I'm not hungry, but thank you."

"You're going to get calls for comments," he said. "Aruna took the office phone off the hook yesterday, but I noticed you'd put the receiver back."

She nodded. "I'll unplug it. Ba is determined to open, and I want to support her."

"I'll be next door," he said.

She took him in. His hair was spiked with dried sweat. He was more handsome than the first time she saw him. Now, after getting to know him, he didn't just take her breath away; he'd become the air she needed. "You're perfect."

"Not that," he said. "No one can live up to it."

"Then tell me something that lets me know otherwise." She took hold of his hand.

"Too many to list out." He pulled her close.

"More like even *you* can't think of one thing." She gazed into his eyes.

"I hate sharing my bed. No matter how incredible the company." He toyed with her fingers. "I don't like most people." He was close enough that their bodies touched. "I don't get worked up over anything. I've been told I'm too laid-back. The worst thing about me is that if you change your mind about this, walk away from me, I'll let you go."

Just as she was about to kiss him, Tulsi paused. "Meaning?"

"I don't fight for anyone to stay in my life," he said.

"That's really sad, Lucas."

He brushed her lips with his, then stepped back. "See? Not perfect."

She took his arm and tugged him back. Kissed him the way she'd wanted to since he'd dropped her off last night. Remembering her cha in one hand, she wrapped the other over his shoulders. He squeezed her hip, pressed his body against hers, and Tulsi took what he gave her. Reveled in it. Found relief from the weight of what had occurred and what would come. In this moment, she stayed present. Just Lucas and her.

A tap on the window made him pull away and turn his body to shield hers.

"It's Mrs. Bishop." Tulsi went around him to let her in.

"I didn't mean to interrupt." Mrs. Bishop wore an orange-and-red caftan, and her bracelets jingled as she came in. "Guess I did mean to since you two were busy making out. I could have kept walking, but, well, it's a mess, and I want to check in on you."

"How are you?" Tulsi avoided her comment about making out.

"I'm going to shower and head in next door," Lucas said. "If you need me, call."

She thanked him for the cha and checked to make sure the front door was locked again. "My mom and grandmother are going to come in later. I told them I would handle the morning."

"The paper this morning," Mrs. Bishop said.

"Lucas told me," Tulsi said, stopping her. "It's going to be fine. I made notes on my walk over this morning about what to say, jotted down the legacy of spices, misunderstandings that can happen, and multiple meanings of magic, especially in the figurative sense."

"Good. That's all good."

Mrs. Bishop was still worried, and Tulsi needed to assure her. "We didn't do anything wrong. We are honest in our dealings. I know you're a client of Mom's—"

"Oh, stop it," she said. "I know you're on the up-and-up. I've been friends with Devi for over twenty-five years. I believe in these spices as much as she does."

Tulsi hugged her. "Thank you. It would break my mom's heart if she lost you."

"Listen," Mrs. Bishop said. "We need a plan. The *Globe* means local people are going to start wondering. Not the regulars, but the ones that don't know anything about anything."

"I can't control what people will say or believe," Tulsi replied. "I know that what we do here is good, and the idea that we would 'exploit' people's illness for money? Absurd."

"It's all such nonsense," said Mrs. Bishop. "Social media. Influencers. Everyone wants to take credit for other people's hard work while they just make videos to one-up each other."

"It's not all bad," Tulsi countered. "It's also a way to discover things. For example, I learned the right way to use a colander to strain pasta."

"I'm fine using it the way my mother showed me," Mrs. Bishop said. "I'm just . . . very midwestern."

"You left Minnesota when you came to Boston for college," Tulsi said.

"I was raised on that water, though," Mrs. Bishop argued.

Tulsi looked outside. A few people were congregating, waiting for Rasa to open.

Someone came close to the other side of the glass and snapped pictures of Tulsi.

"We should talk in the back," Tulsi said.

"I need to head to my place." Mrs. Bishop looked behind her. "But I'll go out from the alley."

Five minutes before opening, her grandmother came in. "There's a crowd outside."

"Not a friendly one," Tulsi added. "I thought you were going to let me handle things this morning."

"This is our shop. We will do this together," Aruna said.

A minute before they opened, Devi came in. "There are so many people out front. I'm glad I tied my hair up, and these big sunglasses helped me sneak past them."

"You should have stayed home," Tulsi said.

"You two are here." Devi put a hand on Aruna's shoulder. "Then so am I."

They were together. A unit. No, a family. It had always been the three of them. She'd forgotten, let her own restlessness take over and assume the worst about these two women who had raised her and loved her. "Okay. Let's do this."

It was brutal. By two in the afternoon, Tulsi lost count of how many people came in only to yell at them. Some came in to ogle, their phones scanning the shop and the people in it. Tulsi asked them to leave, put a sign up to say no photography, but it became an exercise in futility. Others made accusations about how their conditions were made worse from Hindu nonsense. One brought six bottles of ground cinnamon and sprinkled it all over the sidewalk in protest while smiling into the camera as she was filmed by others. The Gupta women explained, stood firm, backed each other, and still things did not subside.

"You waste of space, get out of my way." Mrs. Bishop jostled two people blocking the doors and came in. "They're handing out these garbage flyers."

Tulsi took one from her. "'Liar. Liar. Rasa should be set on fire.'" She crumpled it and tossed it in the small garbage bin under the register.

"Get a lawyer. Sue all of them for slander or libel." Mrs. Bishop's voice carried through the store. "Harassment. You have a lot of options."

Tulsi was surprised when two people who'd been loitering rushed out. "At least you got rid of two. Thank you."

"The police are standing around but say they can't do anything," Mrs. Bishop said. "Devi, I came in to say that the HSBA is ready to support you. Whatever you need, we are here for you. None of these people are welcome in our shops. Two men who had obviously been yelling at you from outside had the nerve to come in for a cheese tasting. Let's just say they got cussed out instead."

"You shouldn't turn away customers." Devi took Mrs. Bishop's hand. "We don't want this to affect you or others."

"They come for one," Mrs. Bishop said, "they'll have to deal with all. I'm personally boycotting the news on that channel."

"Me too," Aruna said.

"I keep waiting for them to disperse," Tulsi whispered. "But it seems like more people are joining them."

"That's what I came here to tell you," Mrs. Bishop said. "There are more videos of people saying that Rasa's magic made them sick. Some are even throwing up on camera after drinking black salt and water. It's getting worse."

Tulsi chewed on her lip. They should have closed. A few customers pretended to browse, but mostly they glared at the three of them behind the counter. Tulsi came around and approached them. "Can I help you?"

"No, I'm not here to get poisoned," a woman with short blonde hair and a dress made to look like the American flag snarked as she pointed her phone at Tulsi.

"If you're not buying anything, then please leave."

"I have a right to be here," the woman said. "Talk to the camera. Tell all of my followers how you use your foreign spices for mind control."

"If you don't leave," Tulsi said, "I'll call the police."

"My brother's a cop," she said. "They can't do anything to me."

The phone was close to Tulsi's face, and she knew it was important to stay calm and professional. Rasa couldn't afford another viral video. She moved away and toward the display table. If the woman was going to keep filming, she could divert her focus away from her mom, grandmother, and Mrs. Bishop.

As she pushed in the chair and straightened the table, a loud crash echoed in her ear. Tulsi instinctively ducked and fell to the floor. She heard a scream and footsteps. Gunshot? That couldn't be right. She glanced up and saw the woman who'd been recording had run out along with others.

"Lock the door," Mrs. Bishop called out.

Tulsi stood and shook her head to clear the ringing. Her knee burned and throbbed. She rubbed it over her blue cotton pants. Then she looked through the shattered window. The glass was fractured and caved in. Shards covered the table, the floor, and a few had landed in her hair.

"Oh no. Tulsi. Beta, are you all right?"

Devi frisked her, checked for injuries. Mrs. Bishop was on the phone with 911.

"What happened?" Tulsi asked.

"Someone threw something," Devi said.

She was relieved. At least it wasn't a gun. She hoped.

"A brick." Aruna pointed to the large red stone that had crashed through and landed on one of the chairs.

It must have been hurled with force to take out the glass like that. Her heart raced. "Is anyone hurt?"

"Only you," Devi said. "There are cuts on your forehead, and your knee is bleeding through your pants."

Tulsi leaned against her mother as she limped toward the back.

"The cops are on their way." Mrs. Bishop flipped the sign to CLOSED. "I called Sarah, who's spreading the word and finding out if anyone saw who did this."

Tulsi sat on the stool behind the register.

"Let me clean you up," Devi fussed.

"I'm fine. Just landed hard on my knee."

"I'll make a bag of ice." Aruna went to the back.

"I'll make a poultice with fresh ginger." Devi followed Aruna.

Lucas ran in. Then, a few minutes later, the cops came. They all gave statements, and the crowd finally dispersed. The officers told Tulsi where to pick up the police report for insurance. They advised them to consider closing the shop for a while because there wasn't much they could do. One of them slipped her a card for private security.

Lucas rested his hand on her shoulder. "Knee? How is it?"

She took his hand. Squeezed. "It's fine. Mom is on it, and so is Ba. I'm going to be bandaged up with a pungent salve with an ice bag over it."

"Or we can go to urgent care and have them look."

She stroked his hand.

"You two." Mrs. Bishop pointed at them. "You fit."

Lucas gave her a wink and walked away to assess the damaged glass.

"So when did this start?"

"With a fake Instagram account," she said.

"Be serious," Mrs. Bishop said. "I'm talking about you and that man who looks like he can lift a car with his bare hands. He's good people."

Tulsi stared at Lucas's back. "Beast to my beauty?"

Mrs. Bishop cackled. "That's what they say about Sarah and me."

Tulsi reached over and squeezed the woman's arm. "Thank you. For helping."

"You're not alone," Mrs. Bishop said.

"I thought it would pass quickly," Tulsi said. "Guess I was wrong."

"You're standing up for your family and this shop." Mrs. Bishop patted her non-bloody knee, then went to where Lucas was taking pictures of the damage.

Tulsi feared what could come next. The comments on social media were now calling for the women of Rasa to die. In horrible ways, including being set on fire, because apparently it was the appropriate punishment for living in Salem.

CHAPTER THIRTY-EIGHT

The next day the Gupta women stayed home. For the first time in its history, Rasa was closed on a day that it was supposed to be open. It wasn't because they were afraid, though Tulsi was. But the broken glass made it impossible. Too hazardous. Devi had brought home her client notebook to continue her work in their kitchen. Aruna spent most of the morning out back in the vegetable garden. From her seat at the dining table, Tulsi could hear her grandmother muttering through the open window.

Tulsi ended the call on her cell after another frustrating conversation with their insurance agent. The investigation was going to take a while, and then they would let her know how much of the damage would be covered. Tulsi rubbed her temples as she stared at numbers on her paper. The deductible alone was going to be steep. At least they'd had that busy period that gave her a bit of a financial cushion. And she had her travel fund. It wasn't going to be possible to leave now. Maybe not for a few years. Or ever.

"What would you like for lunch?" Devi called out from the kitchen.

"Leftover Chinese from last night is fine." Tulsi had splurged and got delivery just to avoid running into an angry Rasa detractor. She also didn't want to talk to any of the locals. There had been enough concern bordering on pity.

"I think we need something home-cooked," Devi said. "If there is ever a day for comfort food, today is it. Have you heard from Jack?"

Tulsi nodded. "He managed to board up the glass before the rain started last night." And had refused her payment. "He had spare plywood lying around and got a couple of his high school student apprentices to help."

"I'm glad." Devi folded and refolded the kitchen towel in her hands. "I need to make thank-you satchels for everyone. Dessert blend for kheer or peda." Then she paused. "Maybe that's not a good idea. They might not want our spices anymore."

"Mom." Tulsi comforted her. "They'll love your satchels. I promise. We will weather this. How about khichdi? The perfect comfort food. I can help you."

Devi gave a wry grin. "Because you want it to be edible."

"Well, you do have a tendency to forget salt. Actually, Ba makes the best." Tulsi called out to her grandmother and asked her inside.

"She's been out there all morning," Devi said. "Even with a hood and a raincoat, it's too damp and humid."

"It's been a light drizzle on and off." Aruna removed her boots and jacket. "Don't coddle me. Now what do you need?"

"Khichdi. Can you make it, Ba?"

"I forget salt one time!" Devi said.

Tulsi and Aruna glanced at each other.

"Even when you add it," Aruna said, "it's never enough. I'll also make fried chaas with ghee and cilantro. And plenty of salt and cumin powder."

"My favorite." The yogurt water helped balance the heat of the khichdi, which included cloves, cinnamon, and other masalas. The salty, tangy liquid was so full of flavor Tulsi could drink it by the jugful. "I'll wash the rice and lentils."

As they congregated in the kitchen, Tulsi thanked the universe for this moment to center.

The trill of the doorbell interrupted their agreeable silence. Tulsi left the fresh cilantro she'd been cleaning, wiped her hands, and went to answer it. Typically she would simply open it, but she stopped herself. Their home address hadn't been disclosed by the angry mob, but that could have changed.

"Who is it?" she called out.

"Ash."

She quickly undid the locks and flung the door open. Her surprise turned to shock. He stood on the front porch, his hair a glossy sheen from the drizzle, and he wasn't alone. Hema stood next to him, wearing a coral pantsuit and pearls. Behind them, Bina and Lina took in their surroundings and snapped a few cell phone pics. "You're here?"

"I told you I would be." He pointed to the rest of them. "We all want to help. Show our support."

Hema looked around at the front of the house. She probably hated the pink-and-purple exterior.

"Rasa is boarded up." Ash wiped his shoes on the doormat. "I popped in to ask Lucas what happened, and he told me about the brick and the protesters."

"You know him?" Tulsi opened the door wider to let them in.

"I saw him during your mom's interview," he said. "She'd texted me about him before."

As they all took their shoes off in the foyer, Tulsi said a little prayer. There was going to be a reunion and not the fun kind.

She led them into the living room, her focus on Hema as Aruna rounded the corner. The two came face-to-face, and Tulsi remembered the letter, the anger, and wondered whether three decades of being out of each other's lives would make for a more tempered first meeting.

Hema and Aruna stared at each other, said nothing as Ash introduced his daughters to Devi. Tulsi silently went to Aruna's side. Stood in solidarity. Their unyielding silence drowned out Devi's words of greeting. Her mother, as per her nature, was already offering water, asking about their flight.

It was Hema who broke the standoff. "You've aged."

"Have you looked in a mirror?" Aruna said. "You're older by seven months."

Hema straightened her back and fluffed her short silver bob. "I have an excellent skin regimen. I can recommend at least a moisturizer to soften the deep wrinkles on your forehead."

"Is that what they call Botox now?"

"We were about to make khichdi and chaas," Devi interrupted. "Have you eaten lunch? You're welcome to stay."

"That would be great," Ash said. "It's my favorite."

Devi ushered them to the sofas and chairs in the living area.

"Hema doesn't have a taste for it," Aruna said. "She preferred to throw away her money on fancy takeout."

"I wanted a little pleasure alongside the struggle." Hema brushed a nonexistent speck from the wrist of her suit jacket as she sat on the edge of the sofa cushion. "Aruna prefers martyrdom and praise for her tightfistedness."

"And you pretend you're more than you are," Aruna said.

Devi tried again. "Bina, Lina, is this your first time in this area?"

Bina nodded. She wore high-waisted jeans and a beige silk tee. Lina was in one of her flower-print maxi dresses. This one pink and gray.

"There are lots of colleges and universities you can tour while you're here," Devi offered.

"We're looking mostly in the Midwest. Close to Dad." Bina put her phone in her lap.

Ash must have given them a lecture, because the girls seemed to be on their best behavior.

"That's wonderful," Devi said. "I'm sure it makes him happy."

Ash sat forward. "They didn't want to follow in my footsteps and go to Stanford."

Silence. Every word that referenced their history was a conversation ender. Each of them had only known parts of the whole.

Devi bowed her neck and clasped her hands in her lap.

"Where did you go to college?" Bina asked Devi.

"I didn't," she whispered. "None of us did."

"Oh," Bina said.

"I told Dad I wanted to take a gap year," Lina said. "To focus on my designs, build my brand. He said no."

Ash ran his hand through his hair.

"Because college is important," Hema said.

"To lord it over people," Aruna said. "Education can take many forms."

"Tulsi didn't go to college, and Dad has been telling us how amazing she is," said Lina. "Maybe we can revisit the conversation, Dad."

Tulsi wanted to run over and hug her. It felt like she had Tulsi's back in the way that she had Bina's. "I took some virtual classes. Here and there."

"Lina, we have high expectations," Hema said. "University is not optional."

"That's right, Lina beta," Aruna said. "It's very important for your ba. She needs to be able to brag about you the way she did when Ashish was accepted into Stanford. It was her main talking point for a year."

"Is that why you snuck away in the middle of the night? You were bored of my conversations?" Hema asked.

"We left in the afternoon," Aruna said.

Bina interjected before Tulsi could jump in.

"You knew my dad when he was our age, right?" Bina asked Devi. She nodded.

"What was he like? Did he try to be funny? Was he cool?" Bina leaned against her dad.

Devi smiled. "Very. He had a lot of friends in high school. Played on the baseball team."

"Did he get in trouble?" Lina asked. "Because Ba always says he was the perfect son to everyone, but then again they also fight a lot."

"He was always nice, to me, to others," Devi said. "His biggest problem in school was homework. He hated doing it."

"Me too," Lina said. "We're in school all day, learning. We should get to go home and live our lives. Not have more work. At least he let us out of school for a bit by bringing us here. But we still have to stay on top of whatever we're missing."

"I only pretended to hate it to get you to help me," Ash said. "I didn't want to do it by myself."

Devi bowed her head again. Tulsi saw a faint blush on her mom's cheeks.

"What was my mom like?" Tulsi asked. "I can't imagine her getting in trouble."

"Quiet," he said. "I was a clown, liked to joke, but the hardest person to make laugh was Devi. She helped me improve my act."

"Maybe you can help him some more," Lina said. "He hasn't made a new joke since 2000."

Tulsi laughed. "My mom doesn't know any jokes."

Devi blushed. "People say I'm too literal."

"You have other qualities," Ash said.

Her mom avoided meeting Ash's eyes.

"Why are you here?" Aruna asked Hema.

"Because, unlike you," Hema countered, "we don't turn our back on family."

"Oh, that's right," Aruna said. "You'd prefer to betray them, steal from them."

"You would rewrite history." Hema's tone was sharp. "I am not a thief, and you did not stay long enough to hear the whole of it."

"You changed, Hema," Aruna said. "Especially when you decided to remarry. How long did your second marriage last?"

"Anil was a good man," Hema said. "I'm a widow now."

"Your clothes say otherwise." Though Aruna's voice softened.

"I don't need to wear pastel saris," Hema said. "It's not necessary in America."

"You always wanted to assimilate," Aruna said. "Turn your back on who we are."

"Here we go again with the history lectures," Hema said.

"Bina and Lina, would you like to help me in the kitchen?" Devi stood.

The girls looked at their dad. Ash urged the girls to go with Devi, and she ushered them out of the living room.

"Okay, let's finish this," Ash said.

Both Aruna and Hema turned to him. "This isn't for you to resolve."

Ash rubbed his temples. "Aruna masi, why did you leave us?"

Tulsi was surprised by the emotion in his voice. Her grandmother also noticed.

"House of Spice," Aruna said. "That's all I'll say."

Tulsi and Ash looked at each other. They were both taken aback. "I don't understand, Ba."

"It was my idea," Aruna said.

Ash ran his hands through his hair. "I don't remember."

"It wasn't yours," Hema said to Aruna. "It was ours. We used to talk about it all the time, starting our own business."

"At that time there was only one small market in Chicago for ethnic spices," Aruna explained. "That's how we met."

"Drooling over a small vial of saffron," Hema added.

"We saved and planned." Aruna clasped her hands in her lap. "We would start a small spice shop."

"Grocery store," Hema corrected.

"We were going to be partners," Aruna said. "A family business. Patel Sisters."

"Wait," Ash said, "you said House of Spice."

They both turned on him and told him to "be patient" and "we're not finished" at the same time. Ash silently asked Tulsi for help. All she could do was shrug.

"I was going to be the spice healer," Aruna continued. "*She* would be in charge of the business part. Then she decided to remarry instead."

"Not instead," Hema said. "Unlike you, I didn't want to be alone. Ashish was going to California."

"I thought *we* were family," Aruna said.

"I wanted more," Hema said. "You resented me for it. But you could have used the same matchmaking service."

"I had you two and Devi," Aruna said. "I was content."

"I wasn't," Hema said.

"You never were," Aruna said. "Your fatal flaw."

"What happened after you remarried?" Tulsi didn't want another volley of insults.

"Nothing changed when it came to our business plan," Hema said. "I even found a great location to rent. It was in our neighborhood, nothing fancy. Small, but a good start."

"The lease had already been drawn up," Aruna said. "I was trying to get the down payment together. Needed a few more weeks. Instead, you had your second husband steal it."

"I had him *help* us," Hema said. "He took the lease over so we would have a way to start sooner, grow faster. Your thinking was too small. People didn't need Ayurveda; they needed groceries and spices."

"That wasn't what we agreed on," Aruna retorted. "You cut me out. Changed the name."

"It was more upscale than Patel Sisters," Hema said.

"Always for show." Aruna stood. Hands on her hips. "To pretend you are better, more educated, higher class. You are not. And no amount of showing off will make it so."

"You're no innocent. You kept Tulsi from my son, my granddaughter from me." Hema stood and challenged Aruna.

Aruna flinched. "Yes."

Both went quiet.

"You left," Hema whispered. "Ten years of friendship and no note, no warning. I found out from our manager that you had quit, from your landlord that you'd moved. Then this. I didn't know you hated me this much."

"No," Aruna said. "I never hated you."

And that was the crux of it for Tulsi. It wasn't about spite or animosity, but pain. They'd done things that couldn't be undone. She wondered if there could ever be peace between them again. It was Aruna who turned away first. Left the room.

Hema asked Ash for his car keys. "I'll take Bina and Lina with me."

"I'll bring them with me later," he said.

Hema gave Tulsi a brief nod before leaving.

Tulsi sat back in her chair. "What did you say about holding things in? It all spills out at some point, right?"

He leaned over and touched her knee, the one that wasn't bandaged. "These words between them are long overdue. It may be hard to be a part of it, but this is healing."

Ash patted her hand, then headed to the kitchen. Tulsi stayed in her chair, brought her legs up, felt the scab twinge, and let one leg back down. She no longer knew what was within her control or what problem to solve first.

CHAPTER
THIRTY-NINE

Tulsi waited until after the Pearl closed to go see Lucas.

"How's the knee?" he asked as he let her in through the back.

"Bandaged and healing." She pulled up a stool.

"Food?"

She shook her head. "I ate. Khichdi that my mom and Bina made. Which turned out to be very good, mostly because Bina spiced it up. How did it go here today?"

"Steady," he said. "There were a bunch of people out front of Rasa, gawking mostly. Sent them away if they came in for anything."

"That's not good for business."

"I'm playing the long game," he said. "Don't want to get on Betty's wrong side."

She was too emotionally exhausted for banter. She should have stayed home, gone to bed. Except she wanted to see him. "Ash is here."

Lucas ran water in the sink and added soap to wipe it down. "He stopped by."

"Did you also meet his mother, Hema?"

"He came in alone."

"Not to my house," Tulsi said. "Everyone under one roof. I feel like that center part in a wheel; each one of them is a spoke connected to me. I'm the one that should be able to keep everyone together, in sync. Except I don't know how."

"Or you could let them do it."

"They won't," she said. "That's the problem. My mom is already glossing over the past, making lunch with Ash's daughters. My grandmothers are ten paces apart, ready to aim and fire. Ash. He's attempting conflict resolution like we're all coworkers. The problem is feelings. Everyone is angry, confused, hurt, and regretful. For different reasons."

"And you?"

She put her hands over her face. "I don't know. All I can see are the problems. Then there's Rasa. Someone threw a brick through the window, Lucas. The fake accounts. The accusations. I finally got a reply from Skye. At least she's going to help get the accounts down through her connections. What if the damage is already done? We weren't known widely, but we were well regarded. Now people will always think of this mess when it comes to Rasa. I can't wipe out the whole internet."

Lucas put his hand on her back. "Three options. One: wallow on my couch. Get it all out. I'll listen. Two: punch it out. I installed a boxing bag in the extra room. Three: sex."

She laughed. All great options. Well, maybe not the punching bag. But she needed to move. Even through her exhaustion, Tulsi needed air. "Four: How about a stroll? Then maybe three. The rain has passed, and I've been cooped up most of the day, and my knee felt better when I walked here."

"That works."

Once he locked up, they headed away from the alley toward Derby Street and the waterfront. It was a quiet night, and not a lot of people were out and about. They went past historic homes packed tightly on small side streets. The rain had cooled the air, and Tulsi was comfortable in her short sleeves. "I like that you don't fill the silence."

"I like that you do."

She looked up at him. "I don't know if I believe that."

He glanced down. "The way I see it, saves me a lot of effort when someone else does the heavy lifting."

"Talking is a chore?"

"About the weather or sports, no. When it gets more personal, yeah, it takes energy."

She put her arm through his as they walked. "I like all kinds of conversations, especially with strangers. You should have heard Hema and Aruna ba go at it. They were fierce and raw. I could hear it in their voices. I knew my grandmother could stand up for herself, but this was different. I could see how they would have been friends, if that makes sense. They had this rhythm even as they insulted each other. The secret, that my mom and Aruna ba kept me from them, that's what feels unforgivable. Ash says he's over it, but those are words. Sorry I'm repeating myself. And before you say 'don't apologize,' it's how I feel, so just deal with it."

He took her hand and squeezed. "Go ahead."

"I'm done," Tulsi said. "At least for now."

They walked in silence as they reached the edge of the harbor. He sat on a bench, his arm spread across the back. Tulsi was too in her head and stood at the edge of the pier. It was dark, but the streetlights cast a glow on the water as small waves lapped against the stone wall. All of this because Aruna ba and Hema wanted different things, and they assumed the other was on board. She didn't know if they'd actually talked about it or just went along until it was too late.

"Why have you never fought to keep anyone in your life?" She said it quietly.

He didn't answer.

She closed her eyes. It was for the best. Tulsi didn't want to upend whatever they had going right now. He was her place of comfort. With Lucas she could just be. He helped but didn't force her to take it. And he never told her what to do. He was steady. And she knew she loved him. Like missing pieces of a puzzle she hadn't started. Somewhere between that long-ago conversation about hard hats to now, her heart had made space for him. Forever.

"Can we talk about option three?" she asked.

"Always."

CHAPTER FORTY

A solid seven hours of sleep was what she'd needed. Less tired, Tulsi was ready to figure it all out. As the center of the wheel, it was on her to deal with all of it. Once Lucas left for his run, she walked back home. There were decisions to make and people to fix. No longer restless, she would see this through. Rasa was going to be closed for another day. She had no way to control what happened online. Hopefully Skye would be able to help there, but the train had already left the station. And that was going to be today's T-shirt.

She'd worked out her plan by the time she walked in the front door. First she showered and got ready for the day, then headed to the kitchen. Aruna ba was in the garden, and her mom had the kettle on. "This feels almost back to normal."

Devi sliced apples and drizzled honey over them. "Almost."

Tulsi could see the worry in her mom's eyes.

"We are going to reopen," Tulsi said. "Once the insurance company sends us a check, we'll get the glass fixed. By then people will have moved on to terrorize someone else."

"I don't want that for anyone," Devi said.

Tulsi began to unload the dishwasher. "I know. Unfortunately there is no blend or poultice that can heal that kind of anger."

When the whistle on the kettle went off, Devi turned off the stove and brought it over to pour into three mismatched ceramic mugs. They each had their own. Aruna ba's was plain and light blue. Devi's was a

Victorian teacup. Tulsi's was bowl shaped and trimmed with tiny yellow daisies. They'd been using these for years. If one broke, a new one was claimed for daily use. The routine she'd been so bored with now comforted Tulsi.

"Are we going to talk about you and Lucas?" Devi cut a lemon in half.

"Only if we talk about you and Ash." Tulsi was ready to wade through the minefield. She couldn't do anything about the public stuff at the moment, but she could start to fix her family. Ash had said fighting was a way to healing. She had the strength now to go all in.

"You first," Devi said.

She pointed at her mother. "If you avoid your turn, I will follow you around all day."

Devi crossed her heart.

"You like him," Devi said as she squeezed fresh lemon juice into a small bowl and forked out the seeds.

"I do." More than, but Lucas would be the first to know that. "He's a good listener and has seen and done a lot. Sometimes he says something, and it changes my view of a topic."

"I like that for you," Devi said. "I don't think he has anyone to take care of him."

"Then it's a good thing he's here," Tulsi said. "He now has you, Ba, and the HSBA."

"And you," Devi said. "You . . . know all of the business with us having to live alone isn't true, right?"

She nodded. "I'm embarrassed that I spent so much of my life believing it."

"That's my fault," Devi said. "Not yours."

For once there were no tears in her mom's voice or eyes. "I'm tired of faults. Ba's, Hema's, yours, mine. Things happened. There were layers to it, still are. I can understand the choices all of us made."

"Does that mean you forgive me?"

Tulsi touched her mom's hand. "If you had a do-over, would you make a different choice?"

Devi nodded. "I was afraid of the unknown. I see what that did to you. In my next life, I hope I'm not so fragile."

Tulsi clutched her mom's hand. "I love you." That would have to be enough for now. She needed to sort through a lot before she could forgive. It was a lifetime of avoidance, it shaped who Tulsi was, and she didn't want to gloss over the past anymore.

"I love you," Devi said.

She pulled back. "Your turn. Tell me about Ash. The whole story. I mean, you can leave out some details, but you were friends, and then I was made."

Devi took a fortifying breath. "He came home from California to visit. But secretly, it was to take me to my prom. Another cliché for your T-shirt collection. We'd plotted a way to make it work because our mothers wouldn't have approved of him taking me to his prom the year before. He was going to go to see his high school friends, and I was going to hang out with mine. Your ba wasn't too happy, reminded me of my curfew. She'd only let me go because I had agreed to leave Chicago and end my friendship with Ashish. I remember so many little details. My dress was the color of pink roses. It was secondhand, but I had cleaned it and fixed the hem. I felt so pretty. It was worth it to see the look on Ashish's face when we met up at the dance.

"Ma was hurt and so very angry," Devi said. "I had to be there for her. She'd taken care of me; it was my turn to do the same. I couldn't abandon her, and I wanted to take my rightful place as a healer. I love working with spices, always have. I wished Ba hadn't been so determined to leave, but I . . . never told her that."

"Or Ash," Tulsi said.

"I didn't want anything to spoil what I knew would be the only night we would ever spend together. It was magical. I have relived that night over and over again so many times. The memories sustained me."

"And now?"

"He's still a good man," she said. "Lunch with him and his daughters yesterday was nice. A different kind of family unit. He isn't angry with me, but I'm not sure he will ever forgive me for keeping you a secret."

"It takes time," Tulsi said. "If you have feelings for him, then don't avoid the tough conversations. Ash has told me multiple times that he prefers getting it all out in the open. Meet him there. Not just apologizing but tell him what you were thinking and why." She knew it would be tough, and even after the work, forgiveness may not come, but she wanted Devi to try, for Ash's sake and Tulsi's.

"He's the only man I've ever loved," Devi said. "That might be hard to believe, but I never imagined anyone else. Still can't."

"Then tell him that too."

"Don't be silly. We're old. I have an adult daughter. He has Bina and Lina. We're settled into our lives."

Tulsi noticed that Devi didn't refer to Tulsi being his daughter. Maybe they were both working on accepting that as well. "Forty-eight is not old, Mom."

"Tell that to my bones," Devi said.

"That's why you take ashwagandha every day."

Devi rinsed out her mug. "What are your plans today?"

"No changing the subject." She kept her tone light. "What does your sixth sense say about you and Ash?"

Devi put her hand on her stomach. "That there is still something between us."

Tulsi hugged her mom. "That's a good start."

"Now I'm nervous and out of sorts. I need to keep my hands busy," Devi said. "I'm caught up on all the client blends. I should go to Rasa and see what I can organize."

"No, it's too risky. We don't know who's out there," Tulsi said. "They could have found the alley and the back entrance. Why don't you spend the day in the sunroom? It's a hazy day; you can paint clouds."

Devi smiled. "Like Bob Ross."

"Happy clouds." Tulsi fixed her grandmother's drink, then let herself out through the screen door in the back.

She found Aruna near the fence, picking lilva, Tulsi's favorite green bean. "Do you need help?"

Her grandmother grunted and took the mug Tulsi offered. "Devi? How is she this morning? I made tea with aniseed and honey to help both of us sleep. I'm not sure she's rested."

"She's tired," Tulsi said. "But hanging in. Her mood is lighter today. She's going to spend time with her paints. That always helps."

Aruna drank from her mug.

Tulsi picked a few of the flat beans from the vine and added them to the metal bowl on the ground. Aruna had also plucked three mini eggplants from the nearby plants. Later today she'd help her grandmother prepare them for dinner. "I remember you teaching me how to tear the veins from both sides of the shell, then pop out the bigger seeds and tear the skin into pieces to cook it all together with the eggplant."

"They were uneven because you didn't take the time or make an effort to do it the right way," Aruna said.

Tulsi laughed. "Didn't affect their taste, though."

She noticed a faint smile on Aruna's lips. It was nice to catch. Even amid the chaos.

"It must have been hard," Tulsi said. "To settle here, to build Rasa."

Aruna kept her attention on her task. "I hadn't expected that Devi had brought you along with us. Luckily I had saved for the down payment on that lease, which helped. For a few years I worked, doing anything and everything; so did your mother. Coffee shops, retail stores, cleaned houses. We saved every penny we could. Then that space opened up. The HSBA was still forming, but they helped with the loan and taught me about small-business tax credits, grants for women business owners. It helped. That's when I knew I'd made the right choice. The people here would accept us."

"And no Indian families around," Tulsi added.

"My trust in our own people was lost," Aruna said. "Between Hema, the way I'd seen my mother be treated, me, your mother. It was more acceptable to be unwed with a child here. I didn't have to lie about being a widow here. No one judged us. They invited us to their functions. Socialized with us. There was no stigma."

"Didn't you miss it? Our culture."

"Look around you," Aruna said. "This home, Rasa, our work. That is our culture."

She understood. "It's better to go where you're welcome than to be unwelcomed in your own home."

"Platitudes?"

Tulsi shrugged. "Trying to sort my thoughts." She picked a few more beans. "Did you . . . ?" Tulsi hesitated, then went ahead and asked, "Was there ever a thought to maybe not go through with having me?"

Aruna sipped from her mug. "No. Dharti would not approve. You were there for a reason. Next in line."

"Thank goddess."

"I suppose there is a part of Ashish in you," Aruna said. "Bad jokes. As a boy, he tried to make me laugh, played silly pranks. I went along with it, maybe indulged him too much."

"You liked him," Tulsi said.

Aruna pinched and picked off dead bulbs and leaves. "I adored him. He was light and sunny. Unlike me or Devi. I liked the noise that came with him whenever he was around."

"And Hema?"

"Don't speak of that rakshasi," Aruna said.

Welp, no softening on that front. "How about lunch? I thought we could go out, to a café. I feel cooped up, and I'm not used to not working."

"If you're ready, I can give you your final test," Aruna said.

Tulsi stilled. She'd forgotten. In the chaos of this past week, she hadn't thought about October 15, which was now a month away. "I have a few more weeks. My treat." She'd become her mother, avoiding and changing the subject, but for now, she needed time. First, she would clean up this mess; then she'd think about what was next. *Not Rasa.*

"We should be saving our money, not splurging."

Tulsi crossed her arms. "First, a salad or sandwich isn't going to break us. We have a decent cushion, and you know that. Second, when have I ever asked you to lunch?"

Aruna fiddled with the mug in her hands. "Is this Devi's idea?"

Tulsi shook her head. "Mine. And Mom isn't invited."

Aruna furrowed her brow. "You're up to something."

Tulsi was, but she couldn't fully disclose her plan without Aruna backing out of it. "Aren't I always? We had a nice chat just now, and I wanted to, I guess, I want to spend more time with you."

"If you tell me half," Aruna said, "I'll believe only half."

"Great. Noon." Tulsi walked backward toward the house. "We can walk over together. I'm thinking Gulu-Gulu. Come in before it gets too hot." She turned and rushed back into the house. She had some texts to send and arrangements to make.

CHAPTER
FORTY-ONE

Gulu-Gulu café was cozy and familiar. Tulsi knew most of the staff. She and Aruna were seated at a round table near the huge windows that overlooked Essex Street. Aruna sat facing the restaurant, while Tulsi could see out onto the busy street.

"Everything looks good." Tulsi scanned the menu even though she had it memorized. "I always say I'm going to get something different but then wind up with Shiitake Happens."

"You and mushrooms," Aruna said.

"What looks good to you?"

Aruna looked around, then stilled. "Ah, I now see your plan."

Tulsi turned and looked behind her. Hema walked toward them. Her sleek platinum bob dared not move with each stride. When Hema reached their table, Tulsi smelled a waft of flowery perfume. "Please, join us." Tulsi held out a chair.

"I thought it was only you who wanted to see me." Hema sat, her clutch purse in her lap.

"And I'm here. I didn't want either of you to say no." Tulsi gave Aruna a look. "You're here. She's here. Can't we just sit and talk?"

They both ignored each other and didn't respond to Tulsi. It was a good sign that Hema had pulled out a chair and sat.

"I can recommend so many things." Tulsi decided to carry the conversation by herself. "Ba likes the Hummuside on a tomato wrap. But if you're a fan of mushrooms, I recommend Pretty Fly for a Fungi."

She saw the weighing of a decision on both their faces and kept babbling about the menu, the staff, anything and everything to cover the deafening silence between the two of them. It wasn't until Tulsi saw Hema place a napkin on her lap that she stopped. Relieved.

"You have more than one ba," Hema said. "If it wasn't for Aruna, you would have known me from birth."

Tulsi ignored the comment. She didn't want a repeat of what happened in the living room but to hopefully introduce a truce. "How was your morning?"

"I supported my daughter's decisions," Aruna said. "Did you even consult with Ashish before you swooped in and stole the rental?"

"Did you have a chance to stroll around?" Tulsi tried again.

"You can't let anything go," Hema said to Aruna. "It was like that time with Nalini."

"She insulted you," Aruna said. "And always yelled at Ashish for walking too loudly just because she lived in the apartment below you."

"You didn't have to permanently ban her from our card games," Hema said.

"She wasn't a good friend," Aruna said.

"We had so few back then," Hema countered. "Because of you she never spoke to me and then moved away."

"Why have people like that in your life?" Aruna asked. "It's better to be alone."

"For you," Hema said.

Lucky for Tulsi, the server came for their order, and there were a few minutes of peace while each chose their items.

"What do you think of Salem so far?" Tulsi asked Hema after they were alone again.

"It's a quaint area," Hema said. "In an obvious way."

"It's living history," Aruna contradicted.

"Magic and witches," Hema said. "I would say it's escapism, a facade, perhaps."

"Did you memorize the dictionary? You never used to talk like that." Aruna fiddled with the butter knife next to her water glass.

"Salem was built on defiance, persecution, the harsh treatment of the Naumkeag people, the theft of their land," Tulsi said.

"If you only see the way that has been commercialized," Aruna added. "Then, of course, it's obvious. Besides, who are you to judge how people make a buck?"

Tulsi clenched her hands into a fist. She had to let them get through this. Even if it led to yelling and making a scene. Like popping a blister and letting all the poison out so the wound would heal. A reminder of what was, not what is.

"You always hated that I had ambition." Hema sipped her seltzer with lime.

"No, it was greed," Aruna said. "What I've built here is to serve the community, to provide care for those in need, to curate spices that are beneficial, not plastic bottles of onion powder to season chicken."

Hema toyed with the pearl choker around her neck. "There is nothing wrong with wanting more. We shared our meager savings to buy even the most basic items. We couldn't afford toys for our children. Used board games with missing pieces were all they had. Remember that one time you wept in the supermarket because Devi wanted cantaloupe you couldn't afford? Didn't that change you?"

"I took care of Devi the best I could." Aruna raised her voice. "I taught her values, not craven materialism. That's what builds character. Not the constant chase for money."

"What you see as greed has come from labor."

Luckily the food came, and everyone busied themselves.

After a few minutes, Tulsi found a window. "How did you feel when Aruna ba left without telling you?"

"I'm over it," Hema said.

"It doesn't seem like that," Tulsi said. "Ba. Sorry, Aruna ba, how did you feel about leaving?"

"I'm not here for therapy," Aruna said.

Tulsi put her fork down. "I'm trying to get you to see that it's not about the things that happened but that you hurt each other."

They were quiet. Forks and knives clanked. They reached for water, drank, and ate. Tulsi had failed. Then to her surprise, Hema spoke.

"I lost my best friend and her daughter, who I loved as my own," Hema said. "And my son and I lost thirty years of knowing you, Tulsi. I don't know how to feel. It's all mixed up, and I can't separate it."

"You tossed me aside," Aruna said. "My mother died; the man I conceived Devi with shipped me off to a place that I knew nothing about, not even the language. But then I met you. We became best friends who supported each other, raised each other's child. When you remarried, I felt replaced. The lease was the sign I needed to go before I was tossed out by you and your new family."

Their words were laced with tears.

"I never intended to go into business without you," Hema said. "I only wanted to shore up the money. My idea was groceries and Ayurveda side by side."

"I wouldn't have agreed," Aruna said. "Not back then. It would have diluted the healing part of my work. I will admit that it was wrong to keep Tulsi from you. I spent my whole life cutting people out. It's better for me to not rely on others. It cost you, Ashish, and Tulsi. For that I'm sorry."

Tulsi didn't recognize this version of her grandmother. She'd never said anything remotely this vulnerable. It was uncomfortable to hear. And while she'd blamed her mother for the secret, her grandmother, the one who had also raised her, was complicit.

She waited to see if Hema would accept the apology. That wasn't the case. Hema dabbed her eyes with her napkin, then set it down next to her half-full plate. She stood. "Tulsi, thank you for inviting me." She didn't spare Aruna even the briefest glance before leaving the restaurant.

"Ba?" She wanted to see how Aruna was dealing with what Tulsi had set in motion.

"She's the one that can't let things go," Aruna said. "And proved my point by walking away."

CHAPTER
FORTY-TWO

Within a few days, the two factions, as Tulsi began to refer to the two sides of her family, formed a new pattern. An odd one. Hema would take off in their rental car to explore a different place each day, from Boston to Newburyport. Bina and Lina spent their days attending some virtual classes they were missing and doing their schoolwork, but at the house instead of their hotel. Bina would then spend time with Devi, making lunch, dinner, or spice blends while Lina spent time sketching or on her phone. The older twin wanted to know all about the plants and properties of various herbs and spices. Lina decided to reimagine the satchel design for Rasa's spices, and once Devi showed her how to hand sew, she turned half the kitchen island into her workstation. Whenever Tulsi went through, she would hear the three of them talking and laughing.

Aruna and Ash would gather at Rasa midmorning. They met with the glass installer and painter, discussed enhancements to the way the large window could best convey the shop, and settled on leaving it mostly plain and clear, with Rasa's logo in one corner. Understated and elegant. They then started the redesign of the floor. Apparently Ash had studied shopper behavior and flow to encourage buying over browsing, and Aruna became a student. In the afternoons, Ash would come to the house. He'd set up an area in the living room where he would spend time on work for House of Spice, while Aruna read or kept herself busy. Once, in passing, Tulsi heard Aruna give Ash advice on how to deal with a supplier problem.

At Ash's insistence, at the end of the day, all of them, including Hema, would sit down for a meal. Together. They would take turns praising Bina for teaching Devi how to use spices in cooking.

Her two grandmothers, while not friendly, had stopped insulting each other. Ash and Devi used Bina and Lina as a buffer. Tulsi decided this was the best they would do for as long as they all stayed in Salem. No one brought up leaving.

Things had considerably improved with Rasa as well. The fake accounts had disappeared. Likely thanks to Skye's efforts. There wasn't much more to do except figure out the rest of her life. And Lucas.

I don't fight for anyone to stay in my life.

She spent mornings with him but not evenings or nights. She said it was because of a full house, but what she really needed was space and time. She loved him. But was that his way of saying he couldn't feel that way for her? Then she berated herself for thinking about Lucas and their undefined relationship, when in reality October 15 was three weeks away.

At a loose end, her restlessness had returned, and Tulsi was consumed with thoughts of "staying or going" over and over again. Late one evening, she left her room to get something for sleep. Her mom had made a mix with valerian, pepper, ginger, and licorice powder that she could take with water. If nothing else, she figured it might help calm her mind. The house was quiet, and Devi wasn't in her room. She wandered in the gray darkness of the postsunset sky until she saw a light from the sunroom.

Tulsi headed in that direction. Watching her mom paint was something she used to love when she was young. It would be nice to just sit in her stillness. She redirected herself and got two mugs of hot water with mint, then headed to the sunroom. At the threshold she froze. The water in the mugs sloshed as Tulsi reeled from the shock of the scene.

As the scalding heat singed her skin, Tulsi couldn't help but yelp. Which alerted Ash and Devi. Who had been . . . kissing.

Tulsi looked anywhere but at the two of them as Devi gasped in shock. Ash cleared his throat and then filled the awkward silence.

"Tulsi! Here, let me take those mugs from you." Ash reached over.

"I didn't mean to interrupt." She didn't know how she even formed words.

"No, you weren't," he said.

"Tulsi, was there something you needed?" Devi rushed to Tulsi's side. "Here, let me help clean up. Ashish was just leaving."

Tulsi put her arms out and grabbed the doorjamb on either side. "No one is going anywhere."

Ash grinned. "You're right, Tulsi. We need to explain."

"Not now, Ashish," Devi said. "Tulsi and I should talk. Just the two of us. Why don't we go to the kitchen?"

Tulsi stayed firm. "We're no longer playing by your rules, Mom. Why don't *you* tell *me* about your evening?"

"Devi." Ash took her arm and brought her to his side. "She's right. This is for all of us to discuss."

Devi shook her head. "Beta, it's not what it looks like."

Both Tulsi and Ash laughed.

"Ma, I can't unsee it."

"It was only this one time," Devi added.

"She is correct," Ash said. "Though I do hope there will be more than this once."

Tulsi looked between the two and saw her mom's cheeks redden ever so slightly. Her hair was mussed, and Tulsi stopped herself from noticing anything else. "Do we need to have the talk, Ma?" She tried to ease her mother's nerves by making light of something that could forever change their dynamic.

"There are birds," Ash said.

"Then there are bees," Tulsi continued.

"Stop it," Devi said. "I knew she was more like you than me, Ashish, but this is too much. You can't gang up on me."

Tulsi didn't know how to react. Was it only a little over a month ago that she'd hoped for exactly this? She hadn't known their connection then, but now it made even more sense. "Ma, all I'll say is if you're happy, then that's all that matters to me."

"We have a lot to resolve," Ash said. "But, Tulsi, that's all I want. For you and Devi."

"You're both moving too fast," Devi said.

Ash took her mom by the hand. "Thirty years have passed. We will have to discuss the definition of *fast*."

"Just, you know, no more PDA." Another item resolved. Her mom might settle in, and Ash would push her and support her in equal parts. Her hands really were idle now. Nothing left except October 15.

CHAPTER
FORTY-THREE

Tulsi left Ash and her mom alone. Instead of heading back to her room, she needed air. It was a crisp evening, and she grabbed her hoodie from the peg by the front door. Keys in her pocket, she let herself out. The streetlamps offered a somber glow as she headed toward the water and her bench. By the time she reached the pier, Tulsi knew what was next. She had to go. Even after all of this, or maybe because of it, she still had no idea what she wanted for her future. Just that she couldn't do it. It was finally time to accept that she didn't want to take her mother's place. There was so much beyond the edge of the ocean she stood upon.

The Buddha tattoo beckoned her. She was stronger now. Believed in herself. If she didn't test it, do it now, she didn't think she ever would.

"Hey."

Her head snapped up as Lucas approached the bench.

"What are you doing out here?" She glanced away, hoped he would leave.

He sat next to her. "Your mom messaged me. Something cryptic around sending Ash back to the hotel and being available to talk. Since you left your cell in the kitchen, she thought you were with me."

"And you came looking." And here was the reason she so badly wanted to stay. "I saw my mom kissing Ash."

"Whoa," he said. "That must have been a shock."

"It makes sense in a way," she said. "It's fine. Just weird to see."

"But you still needed air." Lucas relaxed, arms stretched out over the back of the bench. "What's really bothering you?"

"Us." There, she said it. It was the truth. "And this conversation is necessary."

"I care about you," Lucas said.

"I know," she said. "I've known for a while. The way you listen, offer support, feed me. You show me with every touch and action."

They sat for a while.

"You asked me why I don't fight for people," he said. "I've been thinking about that a lot. What I've come up with is that I don't know how. Marianna, my mother, she told me she was leaving. I didn't know if it meant to run an errand or on a trip. I didn't know it was forever. Once I realized she wasn't coming back, I shrugged it off. Accepted it. I was busing tables at Mable's once; she was in a corner booth. I walked past her, and she asked if we could talk. She told me she'd had her reasons. She'd felt trapped. That it wasn't until she'd made it out, made a life for herself, that she learned who she truly was. I listened as she told me that the life she'd built, as a psychologist, was more meaningful than being a mother and wife."

Tulsi wanted to hold him but steeled herself to stay still. Let him finish.

"I heard her out," Lucas said. "I thought, why should I stand in the way of her happiness?"

"But her choices were painful to you," Tulsi said. "She chose herself over you."

"We all do that in some ways," he said.

"Maybe, but not like that," Tulsi explained.

"Are you still angry with Devi?"

She shook her head. "It's not the same thing."

"You lost a father; I lost a mother," he said.

She sat up, turned toward him. "What she did changed you. Every relationship you had or didn't was based on the way she treated you.

Her act was selfish. And because of that, you avoid anyone else walking away from you. It's easier to say you let them go."

He ran a hand through his hair. "I don't know how else to be."

She understood that. She'd felt the same. Didn't know who she was and believed herself to be as weak as Devi, incapable of doing the hard things. "Lucas." The words were right there. She hated what she was about to say to him. Especially in this moment. "I have to leave."

He didn't respond.

"I need to figure things out, for me, my future." She forced herself to explain. "If I don't, if I stay, I'm scared I'll never do anything. I can't live this life that has been predestined." She let the tears swallow the rest.

"The other day, we got distracted when you saw this tattoo for the first time." He pointed to the Buddha. "I got it because I lost a friend," he said. "Fallen marine. Couldn't save him."

"I'm sorry."

"Buddhas of Bamiyan, in Afghanistan. He and I had gone to see them once. The Taliban destroyed the statues that were carved into the side of a cliff. When he died, it was one loss too many," he said. "I asked the artist to wrap peace in barbed wire because that's how I saw war. I have been scraped by so many sharp metal prongs. I thought, if Buddha could be marred by weapons, why would I expect anything other than nicks and scars. We're all here alone and temporarily. Makes it easy to not hold on to anyone."

"I was envious," Tulsi said. "I saw it, and I wanted to be like you even though I had no idea who you were. I just wanted to have something that represented a bigger life than the one I had been living."

For a few minutes neither said anything.

"You should go," he said. "Do things that mark you."

She knew he would say those words. And she quietly wept. Couldn't make herself look at him. Then she leaned against him for comfort, and he wrapped his arm around her. The warmth inside warred with the cold air. She was leaving this for the unknown when it would be so much easier to stay. "Maybe you should take the time to look at every symbol you have on you. There might be more to each experience. You say *alone*, but these symbols are connections and threads of people in your life as well as events."

"Yeah," he said.

She didn't speak all her fears or worries. Tulsi didn't ask him to tell her he'd wait for her to come back. Not that she knew how long she'd be gone. She had enough for three months, but she could stretch it out. And she didn't know who she would be beyond that, where she might find her place. Devi might move to Chicago. Aruna ba might follow. Rasa might not survive.

"October 15," she said. "It was my grandmother's deadline for me to pass her final test and become a full-fledged spice healer. I think it's a good day for a flight out of Logan."

He said nothing.

She wanted to ease things between them, but asking to stay friends seemed too clichéd. Even for her. She snuggled closer. "I don't know where. Any ideas?"

He put his arm around her. "Do you like winter or summer?"

"Fall," she said.

"Not an option unless you want to fly around New England."

She smiled. "Okay, summer."

"Adventure or sightseeing?"

"I like this." Tulsi let his strength cushion her. "Sightseeing."

"Southern Hemisphere, Chile, Brazil, Australia."

They all seemed so far away. "That's a good start. I'll have to make a list."

Together, Tulsi and Lucas sat there for hours, occasionally talking about somewhere he'd been, someplace she'd watched a video about. Well into the night, he dropped her off at her front door. Lightly brushed his lips against hers. She watched him walk away as she stood under the porch light. He'd taken her heart with him.

CHAPTER
FORTY-FOUR

For the first time in ages, she unrolled her yoga mat and went through a Surya Namaskar series. Her muscles were pliant as she moved, strong when they held her body in pose. After a shower, she foraged for food.

In the kitchen, Devi was wiping the sink. "Tulsi beta, there is a bowl of yogurt for you on the island, with toppings. I made sure to save you blueberries. There's shredded coconut, almonds, and various seeds."

"Thanks, Mom. I slept in." She doctored the bowl and added two big spoons of homemade sweetened granola.

"You needed the rest," Devi said.

"I got some," she said. "Lucas and I ended things."

"What?" Devi rushed to her side. "Are you okay? What happened?"

"I'm handling it, Ma. It was the right thing to do."

Devi clasped Tulsi's arm. "Not because of all this."

"No," Tulsi said. "For me. I have things I want to do, and it's time."

"Beta, the shop is getting fixed," she said. "And there are less and less people out there with signs. Ashish believes it's all going to pass."

Tulsi took her mom's hand. "Good. That makes this a little easier for me to say."

"You're scaring me." Devi sat next to Tulsi.

"You and Ash," Tulsi said. "It's going well, right?"

Devi blushed and leaped off the stool. "Yes. But I'm not going to talk about anything intimate. We can be open with each other, but all you need to know is he went back to the hotel last night."

"Is he still in love with you?" Tulsi asked.

"I hope so," Devi said. "Once things are steadier with Rasa, he wants to spend time with me. A vacation. Only the two of us."

Warmth enveloped her. She was happy for her mom, this second chance with Ash. "Make sure it's somewhere relaxing."

"You wouldn't mind?"

"Of course not," Tulsi said. "As long as it's what you want, not because of me or any pressure from Ash. If you want to go away with the long-lost father of your only child, who am I to stop you?"

Devi laughed. "I feel silly."

"It's about time," Tulsi said. "And if Ba gives you any trouble—"

Devi came close and laid her hand on Tulsi's arm. "I will handle it."

Tulsi believed her. It would take them time. She knew they might even slip occasionally and fall into old habits, but she would be vigilant and pull them out when that happened. "Ma, I'm not going to take Ba's test. I can't be a spice healer. I don't want to."

Devi's face fell. "I don't understand."

"I can't get over the fact that it's never been my choice," Tulsi said.

"Then what is?"

"That's what I need to figure out," she said. "I want to travel. See something besides Chicago and the Grand Canyon. Figure out what I enjoy."

"Alone? It's too dangerous."

Tulsi stayed firm. "I will be careful. But I will not be afraid to do this."

"I need some time," Devi said. "And your ba. This is going to hurt her. Especially now when things are so unsettled. Can you wait?"

"I am going to head to Rasa to tell her now." Tulsi rinsed her bowl and placed it in the dishwasher. "The glass is being replaced today. I need to check what's happening online, restock, make sure the shop is in a good place before I leave. It's going to be okay. I promise."

She refused to see how upset Devi was and left without looking.

As she neared the store, she didn't notice any protesters. They might come back once Rasa reopened, but she would handle it if they did. They would go back to their day-to-day, and hopefully the locals would return for personalized treatments from the spice masters. The alley was clear and quiet as she unlocked the back door and stepped into Rasa. The familiar scent of ginger, cloves, chilies, and other pungent spices mixed with wood and dust from the construction. She waved to Jack, who was already out front, breaking down the boarded-up window.

She found her grandmother in the office. Alone.

"Ba." She didn't know how to start. With her mom, she'd done it fast, then left her to accept it. Her grandmother would be different. "I wanted to talk to you about the test."

Aruna was at the desk, sifting through paper, and didn't look up. "Finally. We can do it this Monday."

She stood on the opposite side, her hands on the table. "No. I've decided." She took a few deep breaths. "I can't carry on Dharti's legacy."

She waited. Her grandmother stilled. Then stacked the papers in her hand. It took a few minutes before she finally looked up. "I see."

She needed to assure her grandmother that this wasn't because of recent events. "I've been thinking about this a long time. You knew I was putting it off for years. Whatever was passed down through you isn't in me. I'm sorry. I can't see myself in this shop for the rest of my life. Not because of anything you and Mom did. I am not content. And you know that if I can't find peace, I can't heal others."

"What will you do?"

It was small relief that Aruna ba didn't reject her words outright. "I'm going to travel and figure that out."

Ba leaned back in the rickety chair. "And you're never coming back."

Tulsi shrugged. The idea of that scared her, and she forced herself to face it. "I'm going to take this month by month. I have savings, so at some point I'll have to figure out a way to make more. But I'm not leaving you or Mom. Video calls, texts, pictures. You won't even notice." Except they would. She was disrupting all their routines.

"I built it for you," Aruna said sadly.

"I know." But even so, Tulsi knew she could not back down. And she wouldn't.

"If you need time," Aruna said, "I'll allow it. But this will be here. Waiting for you. I can't accept that you will not take your rightful place."

It was a cushion Tulsi didn't want. Then she saw Aruna ba's frailty. Her grandmother needed to believe Tulsi would carry Rasa and all that it stood for into the future. Instead of agreeing, she wrapped her arms around her grandmother. Not an awkward side hug, a real one, with both arms. It was a relief to feel her grandmother's arms surround Tulsi.

CHAPTER
FORTY-FIVE

Tulsi navigated her way around a tour group and spied Bina and Lina at an outdoor table with iced coffees and their phones. They seemed to be in deep conversation. A disagreement. Curious, she got closer.

"We should tell her," Bina said.

"There's no proof," Lina said.

Tulsi went to them. "What are you talking about?"

Lina shoved her phone under her napkin. "Nothing."

She pulled up a metal chair. "Secrets?"

"No, just some online stuff."

"Like what?" Tulsi teased. "I'm older than you, but I scroll and lurk. I can be cool."

"It's not about that." Lina lifted the napkin and pushed the phone face up toward Tulsi.

Tulsi saw an image from Rasa's fake Instagram account on her screen.

Her stomach dropped. It couldn't be. "Why do you have a picture of the fake account? Did you . . . was all of this you?" She couldn't wrap her mind around it. She tried to remember the timeline, how Ash found her. Was this all . . . ? "Please just tell me."

"Lina thinks she's figured out who's been behind this," Bina said.

"It's just a guess," Lina said. "Doesn't matter anyway. It's all been scrapped."

Tulsi let out the breath she'd been holding in. Oh, thank God. She couldn't handle one more toppling of her world. "I don't understand . . . how?"

Lina opened the gallery app and showed Tulsi screen grabs of posts she'd collected. She'd written times and dates on the posts.

"I don't know what this is," Tulsi said.

"It's your friend Skye," Bina said.

Tulsi leaned forward. Shook her head. "No, she's the one that helped me get them taken down. She gave me advice on how to deal with the fakes." Tulsi paused. "And told me to ignore it at first, enjoy the attention Rasa was getting. She asked me about the uptick in business too. I thought she was being supportive. I don't understand how she could do this or why."

Lina grabbed her phone and showed her photo after photo of the posts. "See? This first post on Rasa's Insta was right after this post from Savasana Skye's first visit. Then I started to look at dates and times of Rasa's posts, which were always around the same time as Skye's. Skye talks about almost the same thing as Rasa, just a variation."

"I checked that, though. I didn't see the similarities," Tulsi said.

"It's in the hashtags and the words," Lina explained. "Like, she uses a lot of the same tags. Here on Rasa's it's all about how black salt can bring you abundance. Then on hers she has a video of herself talking about wellness tips while traveling. She talks about carrying a pouch of black salt in your purse to ensure your travels bring you abundance. Over and over, it's like a crossover. She's testing things out on the fake Rasa account, seeing the kinds of questions they get, traction, and then replicating it on hers. Probably to compare what works, and then she tweaks hers to get more comments, shares, and followers."

Tulsi was confused and baffled by the complexity. "But she came here twice. She never once mentioned it. That first time, she said her friend had found the Rasa account and implied that I was being cagey about creating it."

"You're just as gullible as Bina," Lina said.

"Hey!" Bina countered.

Tulsi took Lina's phone and scrolled through all the posts. "I can't believe it's been her all along."

"When did the accounts disappear?" Lina asked. "Do you remember?"

"I had asked her to help get them taken down," Tulsi said. "After the brick."

Lina shrugged. "It's a theory. That's all."

Tulsi took out her phone and read through her message history with Skye, then she and Lina spent time looking through dates of fake Rasa posts and real Skye posts, and the pattern emerged. "I helped her. I gave her advice on the right blends."

"Which she used for her account but not the fake ones," Lina said.

Bina finally spoke. "Say the word, Tulsi, and Lina will blow up her YouTube channel with links to what she's done."

The idea of it appealed to her for a split second. Then she remembered that for all their smarts and research skill, they were teenagers. Tulsi didn't want them involved in this. It was slowly quieting down, and there was no need to bring it up again publicly. She'd deal with Skye on her own. "No. We're not going to do anything. The glass is still new, you guys. Besides, you have your brand to build, Lina. This isn't the right way."

"But we're sisters," Bina said. "This is what we do, have each other's backs."

Tulsi was grateful. "I really appreciate that, but I'll deal with it."

"Don't be nice," Lina ordered.

"I'll try." Tulsi made an exaggerated mean face, and the three of them dissolved in laughter.

She would deal with Skye, but for now, enjoying an iced tea with her half sisters was what her soul needed.

"What are the three of you up to?" Hema approached them.

"We're bonding," Bina said.

"Did you finish all of your schoolwork?" Hema said.

"Ugh," Lina said.

"I only have history left," Bina added.

Hema raised an eyebrow.

Bina and Lina stood. "We'll see you at dinner, Tuls."

She smiled at the nickname; it felt like an official welcome into their lives.

Tulsi was surprised when Hema took Lina's vacated chair. Tulsi didn't know what Hema wanted from her, so she stayed quiet, let her lead.

"This town has grown on me," Hema said.

"Does that mean you're never leaving?" Tulsi said it with a laugh so that Hema didn't think Tulsi was being rude.

"I don't know if Aruna and I can share the same city," Hema said.

"Have you spoken to her?" Tulsi asked. "Just the two of you?"

Hema glanced away, watched people as they strolled past them. "No."

"She did explain and apologize," Tulsi said.

"She did," Hema agreed.

"You explained but didn't apologize."

Hema toyed with a gold bangle on her wrist. Tulsi stood. They were both obstinate, and it was up to them to resolve. "She's at the shop if you want to finish where you left off at Gulu-Gulu."

"Tulsi." Hema stopped her. "Is that a condition? For you to think of me as your ba?"

Tulsi shook her head. "No. Only advice. I know we're family, and we can figure out what that looks like for both of us. It's just going to take some time."

"Just know that Rasa isn't your only option," Hema said. "You also have another family business you're now a part of."

House of Spice. She nodded and left Hema at the café. The idea of working at or for House of Spice was even more unappealing than Rasa. She wanted something that was hers. And she would figure it out. On her own.

CHAPTER
FORTY-SIX

That evening she came home with a box of pastries from the Pearl. She'd stopped in for steamed cardamom milk. Lucas wasn't at the counter, but she waved to him through the open door of the kitchen. Her house was full. And quiet. Bina and Lina were setting the table. Ash was opening containers from a Thai place around the corner. Aruna was stirring fresh lemonade in a pitcher.

"The first thing I'm sending you, Aruna, is linens," Hema called out. "These paper towels don't belong at a table setting."

"Make sure they're new," Aruna said. "I don't want your hand-me-downs."

"For your information, I don't even regift," Hema replied.

"Am I in an alternate reality?" Tulsi plopped the box on the counter.

"Nope," Lina said. "We think it's weird too."

"Like they're sniping at each other," Bina said. "But also getting along?"

"Tulsi, can we speak in private?" Ash asked.

"That's only when you're in trouble," Lina said. "What did you do?"

"Nothing." Ash led Tulsi to the sunroom.

"I didn't do it," she said. "Honest."

He laughed. "This isn't . . . listen, Devi told me you plan to leave."

"Oh." Tulsi crossed her arms. "I have to do this for myself. I know she doesn't like the idea of it, especially because, well, I have no itinerary or plan. Just savings that can stretch for three months. I'm resourceful, remember? I will take buses, stay in youth hostels."

"I know we are still finding our way with each other." He stared out toward the backyard. "I want to be your father. Not only biologically. I want to do all the things I would for Lina and Bina."

"They're yours," she said.

"So are you," he replied.

He plucked the corner of Tulsi's blank canvas on the easel. "I have to get back to Chicago tomorrow, take care of meetings I've delayed. Bina and Lina have missed enough school. I asked your mother for the three of you to come to Chicago. Spend Thanksgiving with us."

"I see." She couldn't waver. She needed to stay the course even if it meant missing out on family. "This is hard for me. Not you or all of this, but me. I am finally taking this step and need to see it through. I don't know where I'll be in November, and while that's scary, it's also exciting. It's like I'm the type of person that does something adventurous."

"I understand," he said. "I want you to go. Explore."

"Wait, what?" Tulsi said. "Did you tell my mom?"

"She is not happy about my support," he said. "She'll come around."

"Okay." If this was what it meant to have a father, she could get used to it. "Thank you."

"And I will watch out for your grandmother as well," he added.

"Good luck," Tulsi said.

"I don't like the idea of buses and youth hostels," he said. "And before you say no to needing anything from me, it's more for me. I need to feel like your father, even if you're not ready to call me Dad. Or ever will."

"What are you saying?" she asked.

"I can fund this adventure," he said. "So you can do what you want and be safe."

"Money isn't a thing for me," Tulsi said. "I have respect for it, but we're comfortable, and before it all went bananas, we were doing well. I don't want you to feel like you have to do this. I'm an adult."

"You are," he said. "But I have the means. You're smart enough to know that it will allow you to see and do more."

"Are there conditions?"

He shook his head. "Though if you wouldn't mind letting Devi know where you are occasionally, that would help me."

"Can I think about it?"

"Of course." He smiled. "I took a gap year, right before taking ownership of House of Spice. My stepfather planned to retire, so I gave myself a year. I hadn't been to India, yet here I was about to start an Indian grocery chain. I decided to spend a year there. North, south, east, west. Learn each region. Along the way, I spent time volunteering at temples, shelters, and any other places that would have me. A way to help me see my life in context of others', understand what I had and what I lacked. I came back knowing that House of Spice would be something that was more than a grocery store. It would be a place that felt like home for Indians, Bangladeshis, Pakistanis, and Afghanis, and a place for everyone to explore our cultures through food."

"It gave you purpose," she said. "Beyond a family business."

"Exactly," he said. "You can travel for the sake of it; there's nothing wrong with that. Or you can be intentional. Think about your experiences and see if they guide you to what you want."

"You're . . ." She didn't know how to say it. "I think it's good to have you in my life. I hope you can say the same someday."

"I can say it now." He clasped her hands. "You are mine. And I'm grateful. Even though we missed so much, we have time."

CHAPTER
FORTY-SEVEN

Rasa reopened on Tuesday. The HSBA members spent the day stopping by, expressing their support, and leaving with a satchel. There were no protesters now. The video had been buried under other segments on the news channel's website. And as far as Tulsi was concerned, it was over. She'd even sent a message to Skye asking her if she'd been the one behind all of it, and there was no reply.

So it shocked her to see Skye walk through the front door of the shop. She waved at Tulsi, then waited until Tulsi finished up with a customer before approaching.

"Hi," Skye said.

"Did you get my message?" Tulsi was no longer intimidated, even if Skye looked like an ad for pumpkin-spiced lattes.

"I wanted to see you in person."

Tulsi waited.

"I'm sorry," Skye said. "I never meant for it to go like that."

Tulsi let the truth wash over her. "I thought we were friends."

"Yeah," Skye said. "I liked you and this store. I was only trying to help, and you didn't know how much it would help, so I set up some accounts to promote you. That was all."

"Someone threw a brick through that window," Tulsi said.

"What I did was wrong," Skye said.

"I get that you wanted to help," Tulsi said. "But you were doing it all wrong. I pointed that out to you."

Skye fidgeted with the strap of her pink-and-white tote. "I also did my own research on the internet about spices."

"The internet?" Tulsi then moderated her voice as a customer by the gingerroot gave them a look. "That was your source. That's the worst place. It's all about things that cause or prevent cancer. We don't make those types of claims."

Skye nodded. "I'm sorry. I can't tell you how awful I feel. This wasn't my intention."

"I told you we didn't want to be on social media. You should have listened."

Skye took a tissue out from her tote. Blew her nose. "I really liked your shop and couldn't understand why you all didn't want to tell the world. It's so cool what you do. And the whole spice-healing thing, that's amazing. Then I thought, What if I tried to set you up and show you how it all worked? Then we could merge the accounts and be like dual experts."

"But you're not an expert," Tulsi said. "Do you even know what *savasana* means? That it's a Sanskrit word?"

"I don't know what to say except I'm sorry, over and over. It wasn't until the interview where the comments started to change," Skye said. "Then you told me about the brick and wanted my help, and I knew I had messed up."

"But you didn't help," Tulsi said. "I asked so many times."

"I thought it would be too obvious," Skye responded. "Like you might catch on."

Tulsi clutched the glass counter. "Then why did you finally delete them?"

"I wanted to stop all of it, for you, the bad stuff." Skye picked at her pristine manicure. "Then I got the idea that I could tell you I used my connections. To get the accounts offline."

Tulsi couldn't believe the audacity of it all. "This is real life. Our life. What you did hurt us; our shop will forever be tainted by what happened."

"That's Sonia O'Shea's fault," Skye said.

Tulsi shook her head. Exhausted. Skye didn't get it. Rasa would bear the consequences from those with long memories. They would be questioned about their authenticity. "This is part of my heritage, my culture. You tainted it, made it okay for people to dismiss it as a scam. None of that is true. Ayurveda is an ancient method of healing. It benefits everyone. You spun it into something it never was. You can say it was for us, your intentions and all that, but really, it was about you and your brand."

"What can I do?" Skye pleaded. "How can I make it right?"

"You can't." It wasn't up to Tulsi to give Skye an out. "We all have to live with it. Whatever you do from here on out, just leave us out of it. Not just Rasa but Ayurveda."

Tulsi stared down at the saffron vials. No one could lay claim. The flowers were native both in the Mediterranean and Asia. The types they sold came from Iran, France, and Spain in addition to India. Rasa did not exist to be the sole purveyor of saffron. Market Basket carried its own version. But Tulsi could protect the practice, honor it as part of her culture and history.

"Okay. I understand. I'll just say I'm sorry. One more time."

Tulsi nodded and watched Skye leave. Then she unfollowed Skye on every platform. That was the only likely closure she would ever get.

Later that evening she went through the back door of Pearl after it had closed. The staff was gone, kitchen clean. Lucas was at the prep station with paper, pen, and calculator.

"I made a decision," she said.

He looked up.

"India," Tulsi said. "I was talking to Ash, and he said he had explored all of it, so I thought I'd start there. English is spoken in most of the major cities, so I can get my bearings. And maybe I'll have some sort of attachment because of my history. It could help give me some answers about the future."

"That sounds nice."

"I was hoping for some advice," she said. "We're still friends, right?"

He dropped his pen, then moved closer to her. "Yes. We are."

A bit of tension eased. "I'm glad."

"Unfortunately, closest I got to India was Afghanistan," he said.

To create a little physical distance, she leaned against the wide fridge. "India is just one option. I want to talk things through. You're great at helping me think. Offer another perspective when I can't."

"I try."

He was nervous. There was something less loose about the way he spoke, the way he moved. He was hesitant. Unsure. She regretted that it was because of her decision. "Ash, my, uh . . ."

"I know who he is."

It was soft, the way he said it. As if to help her through this. "Yeah, you're right." She hated being so nervous around him. It wasn't the way things had been between them, and she didn't want to leave like this.

"Ash?"

"Right, he offered to pay," she said. "For my travels. He said he would do it for Bina and Lina, and I'm his daughter, too, so it would make him feel like he was my dad."

"What's your hesitation?"

She loved this man. He saw her. And forced her to be direct. It was going to shatter her to leave him. "That if he did help, financially, it would mean that I didn't do this by myself."

He moved closer to her, reached around, opened the fridge. She could smell him, a little oil, ginger, and something sweet she couldn't identify. Instead of giving him room, she stayed in her position. He grabbed a beer for him and handed her a seltzer.

"There's on your own and by yourself," he said.

"There's a difference?"

"What do you want out of this?" Lucas asked. "What are you trying to prove?"

With anyone but him, she would take that as a combative question. Lucas was trying to get her to see what her true barrier was. Instead of leaning on him, she settled for their toes touching as they stood facing each other. They were shoe clad, so it wasn't as if there was skin contact.

She opened the tab. "I want to step outside of my tiny world. Expand my footprint. Experience different cultures. Understand what's universal about humans and the specifics of how differently we all live."

"For yourself."

She nodded.

"Money isn't important to you, right?"

She shrugged. "I mean, it's nice, and it helps us live comfortably, but no, I don't have that need to have more than anyone else. Enough. That's the sum of my expectations." She finally understood what he meant. "If I accept Ash's offer, it doesn't change my goal or my want. Just eases the path, lets me see more, do more."

He took a sip from his beer. "It's a smart choice."

She almost reached over to wrap her arms around him. Then gave in. He held her for far longer than friends typically would. She stayed. Wished for the right words. That she didn't want to leave him, but she had to go. This was her chance to do what she'd fantasized about for more than a decade. Still, she clung to him. "I'm sorry. I know it's unfair to lean on you like this."

It was Lucas who released her. She wiped her cheeks, drank more seltzer to steady herself.

"Thank you," she said. "For . . . well . . . everything."

The words were like vomiting out thumbtacks. They cut her throat into pieces.

As she turned to go, he took hold of her hand. Then clasped both of hers in his. She could see the bob of his Adam's apple.

"Go for as long as you want." His voice was raspier, deeper. "See all that you want to see. Then come back. To me. Us."

She closed her eyes as tears fell on her cheeks.

"This is me fighting for you," he continued. "I'll wait. A year, five. Doesn't matter. If you decide to stay, put down roots somewhere, I'll join you. Do something else besides the Pearl."

She looked into his eyes.

"I love you," he said. "I know it's not fair to tell you. Makes it harder. Just know that when you're ready, if you want, I'll find a way to be with you."

She never believed she was someone who could inspire anyone to say the things Lucas had said, offer himself, his life, so that she could live hers the way she wanted.

"I love you too."

They stayed still. Everything settled back into place. No nerves. Yes, there was heartache, the thought of not seeing him every day, not knowing what the future held for them, yet they had each given the other a piece of their heart. That was permanence she welcomed.

"Remember how you let people be?" Her voice cracked as happy and sad tears merged. "That's what this is, right? We can love each other and can still be."

"Yes," he said. "We can figure it out."

"Besides, this way you won't have to share your bed every night." She loved the way his eyes crinkled.

"You got me. Though when we do," he said, "I'll make sure it's a king."

He swallowed her laugh with a kiss. She clung to him. They poured their hearts out to each other through touch, taste, breath.

Much later, while Lucas slept beside her, Tulsi finished her last task. She emailed Ash a loose itinerary.

CHAPTER FORTY-EIGHT

Leaving was the hardest part. It was her last morning in the kitchen with her mom and ba. This Monday, however, there were no lessons or trays of spices on the island. Her one carry-on, a large backpack, was by the door.

"You have everything," Devi said again.

"We went through the checklist." Tulsi kept her tone even. Her mom wasn't enthusiastic but wasn't stopping her.

"Ba, I know you didn't like any of the candidates to take over for me at Rasa," Tulsi said. "I can ask Ash if he's willing to help find more."

"I already have someone," Aruna said. "She's starting next week."

"Right before Halloween?" Tulsi asked. "It's chaos."

"Perfect training ground."

"Are you grinning?" Tulsi asked. "Why?"

"I finally get to boss Hema around," Aruna said. "Payback will be so sweet."

"Ma, you have to be kind," Devi said. "She's helping us."

"I'm paying her minimum wage," Aruna said.

"Congratulations?" Tulsi looked forward to hearing about their working together. "My only ask is to not put Ma in the middle."

"Ashish has warned them both," Devi said. "And I will also handle it."

Tulsi wrapped her arms around her mom again. "I'm going to miss you."

Devi dabbed her eyes. "I don't even know how I will handle not seeing you every day."

"You'll be busy," Tulsi assured her.

"Bina and Lina are coming for Halloween and staying to do college tours," Devi said. "They invited me to join them."

"That's great." The twins were going to have Devi wrapped around their fingers. Her mom was going to love it.

"Ba," Tulsi said. "I'm not going to forget any of my lessons."

"Good, because when you're back, the test will be here. So will Rasa," Aruna added.

Tulsi ignored the last part. "I've packed the *Charaka Samhita*. I've been making my way through it, thinking it would be great to see what native plants, spices, and herbs are available, and if there are opportunities to teach people how to use them for their benefit."

"See? It's all there," Aruna said.

"Like a traveling healer," Devi added. "That's wonderful."

"Not a healer," Tulsi corrected. "I don't even know what it looks like, but I know I want to keep learning while I explore."

"Are you sure you won't be back for winter holidays?"

"No. I'm going to Tokyo after India. Then I'll see what's next."

The doorbell rang, and Tulsi hugged her family goodbye. There were tears and pleas to make good choices, stay safe. More pleas on daily updates. An open invitation to come home whenever she didn't want to do it anymore.

Tulsi took one last look at the family she'd always loved but had wanted to leave. It didn't matter where her travels took her; they would be here. And that was the steadiness she needed as she ventured to do something she never believed possible, mostly because she didn't think she could take this leap.

She opened the door.

"Ready?" Lucas said.

CHAPTER
FORTY-NINE

One year later

Tulsi lugged her busted-up backpack through the alley behind Rasa. The dumpster still smelled the same, and she welcomed the familiarity. For a few breaths she stood there to take it all in.

No one knew. She'd wanted it that way. The year she'd been away had inspired, awed, challenged, and replenished her. She was tired now, but it was a good kind. Three days ago, under the stars at a campsite on Easter Island, Tulsi had been staring at the Milky Way. As she breathed the awesomeness of an infinite universe, every cell in her body told her it was time. She'd finally come into her sixth sense. Aruna ba would be proud.

She had changed, but the core of her was still here. Rasa and home no longer felt like an invisible cage. It was a place to return to. Her wanderlust had been satisfied, and while there were still more places on her list, she believed in herself enough to know she would make her way to them. For now, she knew what her next step was, and she couldn't wait to share it with her family, all of them.

Their group chat mentioned that the whole family was in town and planned to help with Halloween. Lina and Hema had teamed up to convince Aruna to decorate Rasa and participate in the parade. Bina had been a sponge and was working with Devi to create special spice blends, not magical, but based on her love of herbs and plants. Everyone was pitching in, and tonight they were meeting at Rasa to review their game plan. The big day was two weeks away. And the perfect time to surprise them.

She opened the door, dropped off her things, and went toward the voices.

"Beens, I found the dresses," Lina shrieked. "Our costume is finally coming together. Lucas is going to be impressed."

"I'm almost afraid to ask," Tulsi said from the doorway.

They all jumped from where they sat or stood and rushed her. Hugs, tears, and questions came all at once, and she did her best to reassure them that this wasn't a dream; she was really there. In person.

"Your hair," Devi said. "It's in a big bun."

"I haven't had it cut," Tulsi said. "It's easier to tie it up."

"We need to book you a full spa day," Hema said. "Newbury Street. I know the perfect one. We can all go."

"Let her get settled in first." Aruna took both of Tulsi's hands. "You came back."

"I did," she said. "I'm staying."

Her grandmother squeezed Tulsi's hands, then pulled her in for a hug. The first one she'd ever initiated. Tulsi leaned her head on her ba's shoulder. "Thank you for answering my questions all the time."

"You showed me new things, stuff I'd never heard of. I've been working with bardi bush after you told me about Australian Aboriginal uses," Aruna said.

"She's even more of a know-it-all," Hema chimed in.

They'd built back their friendship, but Tulsi knew it had to be different. Too much had passed between them, and while they had made their peace, bickering was how they made up for all those years of things they'd never said to each other. It also provided entertainment in their group chats. Especially when Lina poked at one or the other to get it going.

Tulsi raised her mother's left hand. "Nice job, Father."

"Thank you," Ash said.

They'd eloped, and Ash had found a house for them. Bina started her sophomore year at nearby Tufts, and Lina started her freshman year at Brown. With Devi's support, the two of them had convinced Ash to let her take a gap year. Bina had spent most of her time with Devi and Aruna, and much to Hema's irritation, the older twin wanted to become a spice healer. It was going to be interesting to see how her middle sister's ambitions would tangle with Aruna and Devi's conservative approach.

"Beta, are you tired? Hungry? Maybe we should go home. Tomorrow is going to be busy." Devi began to herd them out. "Let's go home, and you can catch us all up."

Ash took her backpack, and the seven of them headed to Aruna's house. They talked over each other, had side chats, and laughed. A lot.

CHAPTER FIFTY

Tulsi sat on her favorite bench with the travel mug of cha she'd made herself. The familiar smell of seawater had more context. It was different from Sydney Harbour. More pungent, less refreshing. To know these comparisons made her feel whole. What she missed now was different. Her needs, her plans, had evolved. They were more definitive, less hesitant.

She heard footsteps she hadn't in over a year, turned to make sure he saw her. He stopped, then slowly moved toward her. She stood, her smile wide. As he came close, she lunged and clutched at him, her legs wrapped around his waist. Tulsi didn't care that he was sweaty.

She refamiliarized herself with his taste, the way his rough hands stroked her back under her T-shirt.

Once he let go and her feet were back on the ground, she kept hold of his hand. Palm to palm. All that time without touching him—she planned to never let go.

"You pulled off a surprise attack," he said. "Don't tell any of my COs."

"Never." She leaned her head against his arm as they moved to their bench.

"When?"

"Last night," she said. "I needed to reenter the family and wanted time alone with you."

"How does it feel? To be back."

"A couple of nights ago," she said, "I was staring up at the Milky Way, and it all came together for me. I know what's next."

"If you're planning to leave again," he said, "no dice. Either I go with you or you stay."

She stroked his arm. "Since when do you talk like this?"

"Twelve months and one day, Tulsi."

His growl of frustration was very clear. Though she'd never asked him to stay committed, and he'd never asked her for the same. For her, while she'd met so many different people, her heart was Lucas's, and nothing had changed. That wasn't completely true. She was more assured about her feelings for him. They would make it to forever based on her love alone.

"I'm staying," she said. "But not going back to Rasa."

"You want to come work with me?" He kissed the side of her head.

"Absolutely not." She tucked her head under his chin. "I am going to start a teaching program. I learned so much about how people all over the world use food, not only as part of their culture but their overall health. And it's going to be about balance. You can have potato chips and start each morning with warm water laced with what works well for your dosha. It's a mashup, or maybe an evolution. Accessible Ayurveda. I'll get Lina to help me with the marketing stuff. I sketched out a plan and am going to take it to my father. House of Spice has a foundation arm that Hema ba started a long time ago. I'll apply for one of their grants."

"Ambitious," he said.

She worried for a moment that it was too much. Then remembered that she could handle anything. She'd come through every challenge while traveling, from twisted ankles to slicing her hand while nowhere near a medical facility. She hadn't shared those experiences with anyone but Lucas. He'd been the person she'd vented to when she was struggling. Her family, especially Devi, got the "everything is amazing" messages.

"Do you plan to move back in with your grandmother?"

"It makes the most sense," she said. "Though Hema lives there, too, and I'll be working from home until I figure out all the things. Maybe noise-canceling headphones should be my first business investment."

He toyed with her fingers. "There's something you need to know."

She heard tension in his voice. Sat up. "You sound serious."

"I am," he said. "There are a few things I haven't told you."

"Okay." She could handle it. Whatever it was.

"I met someone."

She let go of his hand. Maybe she couldn't deal with this. She stood and walked to the water.

"Come back."

"Say it all before I figure out how to throw you into this murky water."

He came to her. "I go in, I'm taking you with me."

"Lucas." She bit her thumb. Then she saw it. He was teasing her.

She played along. Hands on hips. "Who is she?"

Lucas put his arm around her and turned them to face the water. "Her name is Maple, and she's not a people person, so it might be tough to win her over."

"I see." She waited. Knew he had more.

"She made me move in with her," he said.

"I am not enjoying this conversation, by the way," she said.

He took her by the hand. "Come with me."

A few minutes later, they crossed Peabody Street. He turned toward a small house on a corner lot. White and nondescript. Lucas pulled out a key, unlocked the front door, and tugged her inside. A furry gray-and-white fluffball lunged at Lucas and growled at Tulsi.

She reached out to pet Maple, and the big dog jumped away. Growled a second time. Lucas admonished her. Pointed to a dog bed in the corner, and Maple went there begrudgingly.

"Impressive training skills," she said.

"I missed you," he said.

"You got a dog? I'm not sure I appreciate the comparison."

"More like someone who I can hang out with at the end of the day." He tugged her toward the back. "Maple also taught me to share a bed."

"I see." She stood at the doorway. The bed was huge. There were sheets and a duvet on it. "Fitted sheets? For me?"

"For me," he said. "I didn't know when you'd be back."

She wrapped her arms around him. "I know it was difficult. For me too. But I can't tell you how much it meant to me that you just let me be. Accepted what I was doing. There was so much unknown. I'm glad I found my way back to you."

"Back to each other." He turned her in his arms. Nudged her toward the bed.

"Don't you have to go to Pearl?"

"Twelve. Months." He gently pushed her on the bed. Lay on top of her.

"Wait." She came out of his hold and sat up. "I need to take my T-shirt off."

Then he saw it. Ink, right below the joint of her right shoulder. He reached up and traced the design. "What is it?"

"*Dharti* spelled out in Sanskrit script. I thought about what marks me, and I needed to see and experience as much of the world as I could to figure it out. I have roots, and they don't have to be bound to a place. This is a way to remind me of that."

He reached up and kissed her shoulder, then her neck. She let go in his arms. Knowing that she was where she wanted to be in that moment.

ACKNOWLEDGMENTS

As I continue to grow as a writer, I am more aware of the book in my head versus the one that eventually becomes a draft. Two people helped bring what was in my head and what was on paper together to make this novel immersive and poignant. I am grateful to Megha Parekh and Jenna Free for their editorial support and confidence in my ability to write this story.

I'd also like to thank my agent, Sarah Younger, who made me breathe, walk away, and focus as needed when I wrestled with multiple aspects of this story.

To my parents and sister, who use Ayurvedic practices in their daily lives. My dad makes me drink a pressed juice concoction for my allergies. My mom, who has a remedy for every ailment. My sister, who sends gut-cleaning recipes. To all who continue to balance their body, mind, and spirit.

To Bart Staub, an Ayurvedic practitioner who helped with my research and made the connections between doshas and diet.

To Nisha, Mona, and Mansi for the brainstorming, for the "No, you're not stuck," and for the tough love.

To friends who continue to be patient, supportive, and merciless if they perceive even the slightest bit of ego.

To Angela Tripido, who has shown me perseverance, determination, and strength in ways that continue to inspire me.

All stories are collective by nature and even though it's my name on the cover, books don't get into readers' hands without a team. I am grateful to have this one.

ABOUT THE AUTHOR

Photo © 2021 Andy Dean

Namrata Patel is the bestselling author of *Scent of a Garden* and *The Candid Life of Meena Dave*. She examines diaspora and dual-cultural identity among Indian-Americans in her writing and explores this dynamic while also touching on the families we're born with and those we choose. Namrata, who has been writing most of her adult life, has lived in India, New Jersey, Spokane, London, and New York City and currently resides in Boston. For more information, visit nampatel.com.